Niobium Node

Earth's Oldest Secret

Mike Khouri

Published in Canada
Niobium Node – Earth's Oldest Secret
ISBN # 978-1-7775014-0-2
Paperback
www.niobiumnode.com

Library and Archives Canada

ISBN/ISMN Published Heritage Branch
Library and Archives Canada / Government of Canada
bac.isbn.lac@canada.ca / Tel: 819-994-6872 or 1-866-578-7777

Canadian Intellectual Property Office
Industry Canada
Place du Portage, Tower 1
50 Victoria Street
Gatineau, Quebec K1A 0C9
Telephone: 1-866-997-1936
Fax: 819-953-2476
Email: ic.contact-contact.ic@canada.ca
Website: Canadian Intellectual Property Office

To my dearest G and K, and our guardian angels N, T, and M.

Your sacrifices will not go in vain, as the Chrismere code is now in the Burkington sequence. Enlightenment begins in Natalia's cradle, in the shadow of the tree of knowledge.

Table of Contents

Chapter 1: Divine Intervention

It was an unusually warm Thursday afternoon. The air was humid and thick with a sense of trepidation, or was it excitement? *Trepidation for what?* Gada wondered, wiping a bead of sweat from her brow. *Nothing exciting ever happens to me.* She was seated at the front of the class during the final period of the day at Vermont High School—close enough that she could smell Ms. Ester's musky perfume every time she pirouetted to face the whiteboard. Whenever she turned her back on the class to continue her lecture on the French revolution and the rise of modern societies, Gada could hear the other students' conversations around her increasing in pitch and volume, and saw one or two spitballs miss the back of Ms. Ester's head by a matter of inches. However, Gada was *different*, or at the very least, she had always felt different, although she couldn't quite put a finger on why she felt this way. History enthralled her, and she had somewhat of a soft spot for Ms. Ester, who seemed to be the target of an array of different bullying techniques from students and the faculty alike (likely because she always smelled a little of cat urine and couldn't seem to tame her scraggly gray mane). Consequently, Gada did her best to seem as present as possible, so that poor Ms. Ester wouldn't feel that her passionate delivery of facts had gone to waste.

"Without the French revolution, a lot of European countries might still have been monarchies today," Ms. Ester concluded, passively weaving between desks as her curly grey hair bounced up and down as if it had a mind of its own. "Who can tell me what King Louis the Fourteenth's nickname was and why it was such a far cry from the opinions that the citizens of

France later held about King Louis the Sixteenth, his grandson?"

The class was thrust into a deafening silence as her shrill voice bounced off of the room's walls. No one answered. Despite Ms. Ester's frail appearance, none of her students dared to mess with her directly or to be openly defiant. She had been given many nicknames by pupils who had undermined her in the past, from "The Gray Monster" to "The Banshee." Gada thought otherwise; she knew that Ms. Ester was supportive and fair when it came to academics. Plus, she appreciated that Ms. Ester never mixed her social life with her job. Did she have a husband? Perhaps children? Nobody knew because she never spoke about any of it. *I wouldn't mind being like her one day,* Gada thought, *even if I do end up getting called "The Banshee."*

"No one? Okay," Ms. Ester continued. "We'll get to that later then. In many ways, the French revolution was the largest step in societal evolution since cave dwellers first formed organized villages. Can any of you tell me what 'evolution' is?" Ms. Ester asked, her tone notably more stern. Half of the class immediately diverted their gaze to the classroom's walls, floor, or ceiling in an attempt to avoid making eye contact with her. She surveyed the room with her sharp sea-green eyes, like a hawk looking for a rodent (or an absent-minded student) to grab. Mike raised his hand, promptly ending her hunt.

"Go on," she affirmed.

"Well, we learned about evolution from Ms. Peregrine in biology class years ago. It describes how living things change over a long period of time," Mike said, nodding his head as if to assure himself that he was correct. He looked over at Gada, who in return winked at him, gave him a subtle thumbs-up, and swiped a loose curl back behind her ear before grinning cheekily at him. "Societal evolution is probably much the same? Small changes within a society that take place over thousands, if not millions, of years until the original society is almost unrecognizable."

I can't believe that I used to hate this kid, Gada smiled, quietly reminiscing about her friendship with the once chubby blond boy who had since turned into a rather dashing, ashen-haired young man. *Although, to be fair, he was nothing short of an absolute annoyance when I first met him in junior high: Always trying to show me up when it came to schoolwork.* Gada and Mike had bonded over a science project that they had been forced to complete together a year or so after the first meeting. *I realized he wasn't a total punishment to have around when he was semi-decent at algebraic expressions, although he still believes he can do them better than I do, which is untrue,* Gada grinned, looking over at Mike's masculine side profile. Lots of the other kids subtly dodged Gada, some even claimed to find her intimidating, but Mike had never gotten tired of her. *In fact, he still tries to convince me he's smarter than I am every now and then,* she thought, *but I suspect he has started making peace with the fact that he isn't.*

She flung her dark ponytail over her shoulder as Mike continued rambling on about micro- and macro-evolution. Despite being a bookworm and self-proclaimed nerd, there was nothing about Gada's appearance that suggested that she was geeky in the slightest. She was markedly tall, enough so that some unkind kids had once made a point of calling her "Giant Gada" for an entire year in primary school. The regular bullying and mocking from her peers hadn't hardened her heart though—she refused to let it. Her mother, a staunch Abenaki woman, taught her that the only real mark of beauty was kindness. The Abenaki bands of the northeastern United States were well known for their welcoming demeanor and friendliness, a tradition that she sometimes felt slightly burdened by.

"Fair enough, thank you, Michael. Does anyone else have something different to say about evolution?" Ms. Ester continued her line of questioning, interrupting Gada's train of thought. The students remained silent; a few even started stowing their books away in their backpacks in anticipation of the class's end. Gada made eye contact with a homely girl named Ashley just as she managed to shove her notebook into one of her bag's cramped compartments. Gada didn't know Ashley very well; they had economics together but distinctly remembered hearing her admit that she'd rather end every day with detention than with a class as boring as history. Gada couldn't imagine a world in which history wasn't interesting.

"Humankind evolved over millions of years," Ms. Ester reiterated. "Both biologically, as homo erectus became homo sapiens, and in the societal sense as the world started moving away from absolute monarchs and embraced democracy. Unlike religious beliefs, science does not allow for the theological theory of 'divine intervention,' not in our biological processes and not in the development of our societies." She looked up as if trying to recall something important before she continued. "Evolution is indeed a process that describes the changes that occur in living things over a long time, exactly the way Michael explained." Ms. Ester started again: "The evolution of the..."

P-taf.......P-taf, P-taf.......P-taf.......P-taf

Without warning, a thunderous vibration from the loud cracks resonated eerily through the hallway, abruptly breaking everyone's train of thought. A bone-chilling screech echoed in the classroom from a student seated in the back. Others froze still in their seats with their eyes wide open and locked on Ms. Ester. The teacher, visibly distressed, stared at the door of the classroom with a panicky scowl. She appeared muddled at what she had just heard.

Bweep...Bweep...Bweep...

Before Ms. Ester could utter a word, the school siren sounded with a startling blare, anchoring everyone's thoughts into a dark chasm of sheer terror. It was a penetrating sound no teacher or student ever wanted to hear.

Gada, startled, turned around to Mike and silently mouthed the words, "Oh -no!" Mike gawked back at Gada in panic, his jaw dropping and his face void of color. Unable to utter anything coherent back to Gada. Unexpectedly, Ms. Ester yelled out, "ACTIVE SHOOTER!" Knocking both Gada and Mike out of their stupor. The teacher's shriek startled the other students into a frenzy. "Someone, help me push the desks against the door, quickly!" Ms. Ester yelled out while her eyes were locked in a staring match with the door. "Cindy, bring me that fire extinguisher behind you, quickly!" Ms. Ester added as she pointed at the large red canister. She knew that it might come in handy if the shooter tried to pry their way into the classroom. She also knew it wouldn't stop an aggressor, but it might slow them down.

Bobby and Mike rushed to the front of the class, nearly in a mechanical demeanor, and began pushing Ms. Ester's heavy desk towards the door. Cindy swiftly handed the teacher the fire extinguisher and rushed back to her desk, skidding to a stop on her knees while huddling back down. The other students started dropping to the floor and crouching underneath their desks as their training kicked in, overcoming their immobility.

The training and numerous drill sessions the school invested in had paid off well so far. The students knew what they had to do and did so, ever so silently, as to not attract any shooter towards them. Not Gada; she wasn't the type to easily get startled. For some odd reason, her overwhelming curiosity needed to look outside the window, and her urge to analyze the situation overtook her immobilizing fear.

Ms. Ester cautiously peered through the small door window to see if she could spot anyone in the hallway. Startled, she suddenly jumped back, her palm instinctively covering her mouth, catching a glimpse of two security guards whipping by her constrained view. They were running towards the other end of the hallway with their guns drawn. She quickly turned around to the students and gestured with both hands out, "Everybody, stay down!" with a glaze of distress on her face, she firmly and quietly spoke out to them. They all quickly huddled against the floor, staring right back at her with their eyes eerily wide open.

"Gada, get down!" Ms. Ester resolutely articulated as she stared deeply annoyed at Gada standing in front of the window.

"Sorry, Ms. Ester," Gada quietly replied as she hunched down next to her desk, "I just wanted to see if anything was going on outside."

The siren suddenly stopped, and the school loudspeaker blared out with the principals' distinctive voice, piercing through the terrifying mindset that had come across them, "Attention, Attention, to all staff and students. This was a false alarm. There is no active shooter on the premises. If anyone saw who had set off the fire-crackers in the hallway, please report them immediately to the principal's office or the security officers. This immature behavior will not be tolerated in our school."

For a brief moment, a pause of silence lingered in the air. A surreal and dumbfounded look was etched on the faces of everyone in the classroom. The silence was gradually broken as the student's murmuring came back to life from the abyss they were thrown into just a few moments ago.

"OK, everyone, let's settle down," Ms. Ester calmly called out, shaking her head in antipathy, "Everyone, push your desks back into their places and take your seats. Let's settle down, please. We've had enough excitement for today."

Gada and Mike glanced at each other for a moment with an assuring nod and cynical smile. "I can't wait till this year is over," Mike whispered to Gada with his head nodding in disgust.

It took a few minutes, but everyone finally settled uneasily back into their seats. Ms. Ester regaining her composure, spoke calmly, "Class is almost over for this afternoon, but I think we shouldn't let anyone distract us from getting our education. Let's not let them win, and let's pretend this distraction never happened."

Ms. Ester closed her eyes for a moment, took a deep breath, and continued, "Just like Michael was telling us just before the drama that was thrust upon us, evolution is indeed a process that describes the changes that occur in living things over a long time." Ms. Ester calmly started again: "The evolution of our species was ..."

"Excuse me, Ms. Ester," Gada interrupted.

Ms. Ester gave her a sharp look, a flash of irritation darting through her icy blue-green eyes. "Gada, what could you possibly be excused for? Or did you just think that interrupting me is the best way of getting my attention? I assume you have yet *another* question for me..."

Gada gulped. She was well-known by all of the educators for her inquisitive nature, but she'd be lying if she said that she wasn't aware that her regular questions (which often led to lengthy sermons) irritated her fellow students. They wanted to get out of class as quickly as possible, and she wanted to learn as much as possible—the very definition of conflicting interests.

"Here we go again," someone sang from the back of the class. "Little Miss Know-It-All needs to know it all!" The comment earned a round of roaring laughter from the others; only Mike abstained and managed to keep a straight face.

Gada wished she hadn't opened her mouth. Anxiously fidgeting with a piece of paper, she started, "If it's true that science does not allow for the theological theory of divine intervention, then how do you explain why we went through billions of years of primitive evolution, and then suddenly, within the span of a few thousand years, we became intelligent human beings and experienced the birth pangs of a societal structure?" Her fellow students started sniggering again.

"Calm down class!" Ms. Ester remarked. "I will not have this kind of malicious behavior in my classroom! Give Gada a chance to finish."

Gada continued, "It would make more logical sense to me that there was some kind of external intervention. Even the Old

13

Testament has a more plausible hypothesis with its creation story!" she stated passionately. "Something must have happened! I'm not claiming to know what that 'something' was, but it had to have been something almost unimaginable." She loudly exhaled as she finished her sentence, causing her overgrown fringe to flop around wildly on her forehead. Mike smirked at her, a look of pride crept its way up onto his face, curling his mouth at the edges.

"An interesting perspective, Gada. Good question. The truth is science and religion disagree. The relationship between the two domains of knowledge and history is complex. Science has its own theory of civilization, and it isn't ready to give any credit to divine intervention. Centuries back, religious beliefs in divine intervention were even more uncommon than they are now. Prior to this, science was referred to as natural philosophy," Ms. Ester alleged as she paged through the textbook, trying to get more facts from it. Gada anxiously looked at her teacher. She expected a more satisfying answer. Ms. Ester continued, "You see, scientific hypotheses, unlike religious ones, are in principle provable. The history of humankind, according to science, is very different from religious beliefs. With the help of fossils, the remains of every living thing can be found in old rock formations, proving that prehistoric humans, animals, and plants were very different from those we see today."

That doesn't really answer my question, Gada thought, furrowing her brow. She decided to let it go, Ms. Ester was clearly having a hard time shedding light on the subject, and she didn't want to annoy her any further.

"I hope this helps your understanding of the topic, Gada. However, we don't have much time left and a lot to go through. See me after school tomorrow, and we can discuss it some more," she told her, still feverishly paging through the textbook.

Gada needed to know more despite not wanting to push the envelope. She was not convinced of the scientific explanation for human evolution and the development of societies yet. *I'll just have to do my own research*, she told herself. *How hard can it be to web-search some ancient civilizations?*

Ms. Ester resumed her lecture, ostensibly relieved that Gada had dropped the matter. "You see, science tells us that we weren't the only 'humans' that evolved, so we're not necessarily that special. We're just a statistical anomaly. Neanderthals were considered early 'humans' too; between 350,000 BCE and 30,000 BCE, they thrived throughout the continent of Eurasia. There is some evidence that Neanderthals interbred with modern humans. We all share a small portion of Neanderthal DNA," she said as her students sniggered at each other. "So you see, we were just lucky to have made it long enough to develop technology and civilization, as our species could have easily met the same fate. Their disappearance puzzles scientists..." the bell rang, abruptly cutting her off. "Alright class, that's a wrap. See you tomorrow!" she waved as groups of students started stampeding toward the door.

Gada wished she could stay a little longer to have a private conversation with the history teacher about evolution and the theory of divine intervention, but Mike was already gesturing for her to leave the class with him. *It's impossible to say no to him*, she grinned, grabbing her backpack and rushing toward the door.

Mike and Gada headed toward their lockers, walking shoulder-to-shoulder. "I would be lying if I told you I wasn't thrilled

15

with the question you asked. You think deeper than anyone," Mike said, blushing slightly.

"That was just one of the questions I have. I have many more that I need answers to. I didn't want to give Ms. Ester a harder time than I already had," she explained, smiling sheepishly at her companion. "Sometimes, I feel like I'm nothing but an irritation with all of my questions, but once something pops into my head, I just can't let it go. Do you know what I mean?"

Mike held her in a sort of half-hug. "Can't say I know the feeling, but I find the way you obsess over things very endearing. Is the deal still on?" He asked hopefully.

"Sure, I already told my mom I was going to be home late because we'd be working on a science project at your house after school," Gada enthused. "I'm sorry I've been canceling our plans so often lately. I've... just had a lot going on. I promise I won't bail on this one."

"Perfect!" Mike grinned. "I was starting to worry you might not like me anymore... You know, as a friend, I mean."

"Don't be silly," Gada chortled, ruffling Mike's hair. "You're my best buddy, and you're stuck with me forever."

"Forever, hmm? I certainly hope so," Mike mumbled, turning scarlet. "What do you think about the way Ms. Ester answered your question?" he prodded, desperately trying to change the subject.

"Answered? I wouldn't use that word to describe the conversation we had," she whispered back, looking around in an attempt to make sure that no one else heard her speaking badly of a teacher.

"I've wondered about the same thing you asked about in class today before too... But everyone seems entirely averse to talking about it. The history of human evolution is complex. Science states that we are the descendants of apes but won't even entertain the idea that something bigger had a hand in it," Mike confessed. "I'm not saying that any of the religious theories make sense to me either, but I definitely can't imagine going from ape to Artificial Intelligence without some kind of intervention."

"I agree. As much as I'd love to admit that Ms. Ester is correct, I still feel there's more to it," Gada concurred.

"We'll do some research. Maybe we can come up with a more concrete explanation than Ms. Ester was able to give," Mike suggested, swinging open his locker's creaky door to stow away a handful of textbooks.

"Maybe we can start today?" Gada asked, raising one of her bushy eyebrows. "I was thinking that if we started by examining ancient civilizations, we might be able to find out when exactly the jump into modernity happened. Once we know when it happened, we can try to suss out what the catalyst was."

"Determined to win a Nobel Prize before the week's over?" Mike chortled, wrapping one of his arms around her shoulders as they made their way toward the parking lot. "You know I love your inquisitive nature, but maybe some things are just impossible to understand? I don't think we should be too hard on ourselves if we can't find an answer to all of this," he vaguely gestured.

By now, the parking lot was mostly empty except for the scarce faculty members' cars and two stray cats that were loitering

17

about. Mike ran ahead, leaving Gada quietly making her way across the tarmac alone. When she looked up again, Mike was leaning against his pickup with his arms and legs crossed like some kind of James Dean lookalike.

Gada knew that he was trying to strike a pose without being too obvious about it, but her heart skipped a beat at the sight of him anyway. *I just can't seem to think straight when he's around these days,* she thought. *I have to force myself to focus! He's a friend, nothing more.* She was more than aware of the fact that her ever-growing fondness of him stood a fair chance of ruining their unique friendship, her only friendship. *My mom always says I shouldn't think about boys until I'm done with high school, and there's less than a year of it left;* she told herself as she approached him, desperately trying to steady her breathing and hide her trembling legs. *Not that I think he'll have much time for me after high school,* Gada admitted to herself. She knew that they would probably end up in different colleges, and by then, she would probably have gotten over the crush she harbored for him. Regardless, the thought of being apart from him somehow pained her.

"What are you smiling at?" she asked as she approached him, catching a glimpse of her own reflection in his sunglasses. "You look ridiculous leaning against the car like that. Get in before someone sees us." She tried to usher him into the driver's seat, but he was slow to comply and purposefully sluggish.

"Like what you see?" Mike questioned, flexing each of his pectoral muscles (or 'pecs' as he referred to them) in turn. He'd always been an overweight child, but something had happened to him over the previous spring break, and he had returned back to school about a foot taller and far more muscular.

Gada went deathly pale. "What are you talking about?" she insisted.

"I saw the way you were looking at me," Mike teased. "I was just wondering if you were enjoying the view..."

"In your dreams, Mike," she angrily stated, slapping his shoulder. "I was staring because I can't believe how weird-looking you are. Now, are we leaving sometime soon, or are you planning on keeping me here all day?"

"I was only playing with you," he said as he darted away from her to open the passenger side door for her to enter, "Mi-lady, entrée," he sang in his best French accent.

"Don't leave your day job, kid," Gada joked, sliding into the pickup's stained gray passenger side seat. "I don't think you have a future in impressions or impersonations."

"Harsh," he responded, revving the pickup truck's engine and speeding out of the parking lot. After a couple of minutes of awkward silence, they slowly turned into his driveway and were warmly welcomed by Mrs. Corey, Mike's mom, who was working in the garden. She was a short, chubby woman with a contagious smile. Gada couldn't remember a single instance in which she'd seen Mrs. Corey without a glass of red wine in one of her hands.

"Gada, it's so lovely to see you. Where have you been? We thought that you and Mike might have had a spat... And oh my, have you not been eating? Look how skinny you are!" she gasped, ushering her into the house. "I just baked an apple pie, and your timing is perfect. Mike, will you fetch the whipped cream from the fridge, please?" Gada smiled apologetically at Mike as he scurried toward the large kitchen's furthest corner.

He returned with a bright white can and unceremoniously plopped it down in front of his mom.

"I'll be upstairs in my room," Mike stated, turning on his heel and disappearing from view.

"What's wrong with him?" Mrs. Corey asked, shoveling a spoonful of pie into her mouth.

"I wish I knew," Gada sighed, picking at the contents of her own plate. "Things have been weird lately..."

"Between the two of you?" Mrs. Corey inquired, arching her eyebrows in surprise.

"No... just in a general kind of way. I don't really have the words to explain it," Gada replied defeatedly. "I guess I just feel like something big is supposed to happen to me, but I don't quite know what it is yet. I think Mike feels it too."

"Oh, that's just called growing up, honey!" Mrs. Corey said supportively, squeezing her shoulder as she started clearing their plates. "I still feel like I'm supposed to accomplish something great, and I've been a housewife for more than twenty years."

"Maybe you still will?" Gada suggested, nonchalantly wiping the remaining crumbs off of her chest.

"Hmm, that's sweet of you to say," Mrs. Corey giggled, piling dishes into the sink. "You know Gada, Mike hasn't been himself since you started canceling your plans with him at the last minute. I don't want to burden you with it, but he's so happy when you're around, and that makes me happy too," she sniffed. "I think Mike actually likes..."

She was cut off as Mike loudly shouted down the staircase. "Gada, come on! We don't have all day! Are we going to study or not?"

Mrs. Corey smiled at Gada as she stood up. "Thanks for the pie Mrs. Corey; it was delicious," Gada grinned. "I'd be around every day if I knew that there would be apple pie!"

"Come back tomorrow? I promise I'll save you another slice until then..." she called after Gada as she rushed out of the room and up the steep staircase.

Mike's room was spacious and neatly arranged; Mrs. Corey ensured all her boys were tidy and organized. His bed was meticulously made, a temptation that was simply too great to resist. Gada took a short running start and launched herself onto his duvet, sending half of his pillows flying.

"Gada..." Mike started, catching one of his pillows mid-air and returning it to its proper spot.

"What?" she questioned.

"Nothing," he grumbled, digging through his backpack to find the science homework that they needed to work on. "I think we should each choose three chapters to summarize, and then we'll merge all of our findings at the end..."

"How would you explain science's view on sidelining the theological theories of divine intervention?" Gada interrupted, entirely unable to stop the words from spewing out of her mouth.

"Ahh! Not again," Mike muttered, knowing very well that Gada was not the type to simply drop the matter. He attempted to

21

end the conversation by turning his back on her and scribbling away in his notebook.

"Technically, finding out how humans really came into existence is science," Gada cooed, shuffling across the bed's now-wrinkled surface until she was sitting directly behind him. She twirled one of his short blond locks around her index finger. "Please, Mike?" she pleaded. "I promise we'll get back to our normal science homework in an hour or two after we've done a little bit of research..."

Mike dramatically slumped over in his chair, then sat up to answer her. "Fine, I'll play along. We can research whatever you want, but I see no reason why science would agree with the theory of divine intervention. Science and religion have contradicted each other since time immemorial, and I don't think that will end any time soon. However, I also agree that humans likely didn't just mysteriously appear from thin air. I think there must've been some kind of intervention that resulted in the creation of present-day humans. I agree with your entire premise Gada, but I don't know if we should waste any time on it. If the world's best scientists can't give us concrete answers, what would make you think that we can stumble onto any?"

"Because we're willing to consider things that those scientists won't," she stubbornly asserted.

"Fine. I'll help you search for evidence of your hypothesized divine intervention, but we've got to put a solid two hours into this science project first. We've got to keep our priorities straight."

"Fine," Gada defeatedly sighed, withdrawing her own notebook and textbook from her backpack. She moped as she opened her textbook to one of the chapters at hand and started highlighting bits of information that she deemed important with a neon yellow pen. "What are you going to study next year?" she decided to nonchalantly ask, hoping to break the silence.

Mike looked up, seemingly startled by the question. "You've never asked me what I want to be before? Why the sudden interest?"

"Well, the year's almost over... And I was just wondering what you'd be doing next year and whether it would be anywhere close to what I'll be doing next year," she blushed. "You don't have to answer if you don't want to."

"No, I know exactly what I want to do, and it's not a state secret. I've applied to a number of different colleges' engineering and science programs: Oxford, Harvard, Stanford, Princeton, Columbia..." he trailed off, his eyes glistening. "Anyway, I'd rather not get ahead of myself. I haven't heard anything back from any of them. Do you think I'd be a good engineer if I got accepted into one of the engineering programs?" he asked, nervously tugging at a piece of thread that had come loose on his shirt.

"C'mon, of course you would! You'd be an amazing engineer," Gada enthused. "Any of those schools would be lucky to have you. I bet they're just getting ready to get their bids in."

"What about you? What are you doing next year? Or at least, what do you hope to be doing next year?" Mike asked, rhythmically tapping his pen on his desk's tabletop.

Gada sighed, knowing she had no answers to give; it was surreal but true. Although she and Mike had bonded over math and science, she wasn't sure whether she should consider a different field of study altogether. "What would you say if I told you I have no idea?" she asked.

"You can't be serious," Mike gasped, throwing his pen into the air with surprise. "A lot of colleges won't be accepting applications for much longer. You need to decide what you want to do as soon as possible if you're hoping to be able to apply in time for next year."

"I am serious," she cheekily grinned. "I'm not purposefully trying to be rebellious or to freak anyone out. I just haven't figured it out yet. I guess I was just asking because I wanted to know where you had applied, so that I could apply there too," she added. "High school friendships don't normally survive the college years, and I don't want to lose what we have..."

"Gada, I have something I'd like to say to you," Mike interrupted, a sense of urgency filling the air. "And I'd like to tell you before I help you to win a Nobel Prize or run off to an Ivy League university for four years."

"Go for it," Gada smiled, hopping up and down on his bed's bouncy surface in an attempt to distract herself from the awkwardness of the moment. "Hey, maybe we'll end up at the same university together, and there'll be no need for this 'running off' business," she said optimistically.

"I really like you, Gada," he sighed, averting his gaze.

"Aww, I really like you too, Mike!" Gada softly replied. "You're a great guy..."

"I know you like me, but I mean, I like you *a lot*," Mike went further. "Getting to know you has been amazing and a privilege." Mike stood up and turned to face Gada. He gently took her hand and pulled her up so that she was standing in front of him. He held his breath for a moment and then continued, "Gada, I want to be more than a friend to you. I want to mean more to you. I want to be a part of your life forever, like we said. I know the feeling might not be mutual, but I promise I won't make things awkward if it isn't. I am going to respect your decision, whatever it may be... But please, say something," Mike begged, squeezing her hand tighter and tighter with every syllable that he let slip through his rambling lips.

Gada opened her mouth to say something, but nothing came out. Then after a short pause, she finally replied, "I like you too Mike, and in the same way." Her heart beat feverishly in her chest like a wild bird beating against the bars of its cage. She slumped back down onto the bed and stared off into the distance before continuing, "I'd like to be more than friends... If that's what you'd like?"

"Really, the almighty Gada Deere likes me back?" Mike asked, making Gada giggle like a bashful 5-year-old girl. "Does this mean we're... You know? Boyfriend and girlfriend?" Mike asked clumsily. "I mean, we don't have to put a label on it if you don't want to. We could even keep it a secret..."

"Of course, it means I'm your girlfriend now, silly," Gada chuckled, rolling her eyes and pulling him down beside her so that they were sitting next to each other on what was once an immaculately made bed. "We don't have to keep it a secret. You can shout it to the world if you'd like. It's not like I'm ashamed of you or something. Just promise to do me a favor and wait until I've left before you tell your mom? I know she's going to be overjoyed, and I just don't have the energy to deal with it today."

"Pinky promise," Mike agreed, lifting his little finger as a grin slowly crept across his face. "To be honest, I'm still trying to come to grips with it. I thought you'd definitely turn me away."

"What made you think that?" Gada asked, resting her head against one of his broad shoulders.

"You're just a little out of my league, and I wasn't sure whether you wanted someone... Better? Stronger? Smarter? I don't know. I just didn't think you would want me. I've already taken my good crying pillow out of the cupboard in preparation for the weeping session I'd have tonight, and now... All for naught!"

"You're a real clown, Mike," Gada chuckled, pecking him on the cheek. She was interrupted by her cellphone's shrill ringtone. It was her mom. A shiver ran down her spine, she was late for dinner back home, and they hadn't worked on the assignment yet. She decided to answer.

"Gada Deere, where on Earth are you?" her mom's angry voice crackled through the speaker. "Dinner is getting cold!"

"Sorry mom! I swear, I'm on my way! We're getting into the car right now," she fibbed as she started hastily packing her books away with one hand. "I'll be there in a couple of minutes."

She hung up and nodded at Mike, who had heard the conversation. "Time to go," she said. "Sorry, I wish I could stay longer..."

"Don't worry about it," Mike nonchalantly scoffed, kissing her forehead. "I'll wrap up the science assignment and put both of our names on it. Now, let's get to the car! It's best not to keep your mom waiting."

Gada waved at Mrs. Corey in passing as they scrambled down the stairs and back toward the pickup truck. Mike dropped her off at home, but not before attempting a somewhat awkward kiss goodbye. Gada turned to leave just as he leaned in to bestow it, leading to him planting it firmly behind her right ear. They both pretended that it didn't happen. Gada hopped out of the truck, waved at him, and shouted, "See you tomorrow!" as she darted up the overgrown pathway leading to her front door.

"I'm home," Gada called out as she strode inside.

"You missed dinner!" Mrs. Deere called out from the kitchen. "Yours is in the microwave, but I suspect it's freezing cold already."

"I'm sorry Mom," she apologetically sighed, making her way toward the kitchen and consequently the microwave that contained her apparently arctic meal. The kitchen was old, and the counters were all lined with an orange resin laminate, which was faded and beginning to peel off. It was indicative of the state of the other parts of the house. There was always something needing repair. Last week, the pipe leading to the sink broke when everyone was away. Mike and Gada had fixed it with duct tape, but a plumber still hadn't been out to fix it.

"Why's it so cold in here?" Gada asked, rubbing her upper arms in an attempt to generate some warmth. "Did you guys forget to turn on the heater?" she asked, squinting at her mom, who was washing dishes, and her dad, who was seated at the kitchen counter, reading a newspaper.

"Nah, we didn't forget," her dad replied without looking up.

27

"Then why's it off? It's freezing at night. At this rate, I'm going to die of hypothermia!" Gada dramatically motioned as she grabbed her plate of cold pasta from the microwave.

He said nothing but looked uneasy as he sipped his coffee to prevent him from having to answer her question. Her mother looked at him, walked over, and lightly touched his shoulder. Gada knew that gesture—her mother was trying to be supportive.

What is happening? She wondered.

"We thought we could save some money by cutting down on the amount of electricity we use in the house. You can see we need the money to make some repairs and to do some maintenance..." her mother answered gently.

"But it's only going to get colder as the week wears on! That's what the weather forecast says! It was freezing this morning," Gada stubbornly argued.

"We'll deal with it one day at a time, darling," her mother replied, looking unsure.

Gada knew they were having issues with money. However, she didn't think it had gotten so bad they had to cut down on the electricity they used. She wished there was a way she could help out, maybe get a job or something, but she knew what her parents would say about that. The same thing they always said whenever she brought up the topic.

"Don't worry, I'll get everything fixed in no time," her dad lied, leaning in to touch his shoulder to hers. "We won't be cold for long. We just have to make it through this little rough patch."

"Fine," Gada sighed defeatedly, melting into a chair next to her father.

Her father was a staunch adherent to the culture and beliefs of the Abenaki people, and theirs stated that a man should always be able to provide for his family. Being unable to do so was obviously making her dad feel like a failure. The beat-down house and his inability to fix it up well (or to even dream of buying a new one) ate at him more than anything else. Gada saw her parents' struggles, how her father had to keep three jobs and her mother had to work two to maintain things at home, but her hands were tied to help.

They had inherited the house they lived in now from her great-grandfather, and her grandfather had refurbished it. Her great-grandfather had built the house as a refuge for natives who were being hunted by those who supported the eugenics programs that they so often fell victim to.

However, with time, the hunting stopped, and the natives left to start families of their own in homes of their own, leaving their benefactor behind with his wife and two-year-old son, her father. The house wasn't built to accommodate many people, but they had made it work. Her grandfather once told her that they sometimes had over fifty people living in the house at once. Gada sometimes closed her eyes to imagine what it must have been like. It was almost impossible to picture.

"How did your visit with Mike go?" her dad asked, cheekily changing the subject and drawing Gada back to reality.

"It wasn't a visit. We were doing homework. It went... Different than I thought it would. He asked me to be his girlfriend," she admitted, shoveling a forkful of pasta into her mouth in an effort to avoid the subject. She didn't hide

29

anything from her parents, but she wasn't sure how they'd react to the news either.

Her mother squealed as she excitedly clapped and jumped up and down. "I told you the boy had a crush on you. It was written all over his face every time he visited," her mom trilled as Gada rolled her eyes. "I want to hear all about it! What did he say? What did he do?"

Gada shared the tale of Mike's confession, leaving out some of the more embarrassing details. She enjoyed the moments that she shared with her parents. She knew the time she had left with them was limited; she would soon go off to college and begin her own life. She wanted to make every moment with them count. Her dad listened to her recounting the series of events too, pretending to give it his full attention while his nose drew ever closer to the newspaper's surface.

"I think it's time for some glasses, dad," Gada teased as she finished her story. "Nobody should have to touch their face to the paper in order to be able to read what has been written on it."

"Maybe after we get the sink fixed," he smiled warmly. "Until then, the newspaper will just have to make peace with me invading its personal space."

After dinner, Gada retired to her room and quietly laid on her bed. She had a whole slew of new questions and thoughts ringing on and on in her head. The day had been exceptionally long, and she was exceptionally tired. She thought of Mike and smiled; he'd be waiting outside in the driveway to ferry her to school again in a couple of hours. The thought of getting to see him every day for the rest of her life, as she imagined girlfriends and boyfriends did, was almost too much to bear.

As much as she needed the rest, she hoped the night would be over soon.

She closed her heavy eyes and started dozing off. *What is my purpose in life? The reason for our entire existence as mankind? Are we really just here to eat, sleep, work, and repeat?* she wondered as she felt her consciousness slowly slipping away. Her dreams were filled with Ms. Ester's voice, scenes from her classroom, and visions of Mike's grinning face.

Last known picture of Gada & Mike in high school. Circa 1999

Chapter 2: Do You Believe In God?

Mike had been accepted into Oxford. And Gada? Well, she was still trying to figure it all out a couple of months later. Her parents had no problem with her staying at home for a while until she "found herself." They suggested that she get a job, perhaps as a waitress or shop attendant, until she knew what she wanted to study. However, Gada knew that she'd be frustrated doing anything that didn't require her to harness her gray matter's full potential.

For a while after graduation, she thought she'd slowly allow herself to descend into madness as she tried to decide what to do with her life. Then on one balmy Tuesday morning, a newspaper left on her doorstep by the cul de sac's paperboy brought her the answer that she had been searching for. The National Guard was offering training for a number of interesting courses. It was a hybrid of the Reserve Officer Training Candidate (ROTC) and Accelerated Officer Cadet School (AOCS), providing continued support through scholarships and grants until the recipient completed an undergraduate degree (whatever degree that might be). She signed up immediately.

Enrolment was a faster process than she thought it'd be, and before she knew it, she found herself staring at a drill sergeant through strands of sweat-soaked hair. It was the late 1990s, the weather was scorching hot, and the weatherman on the local news station swore it was 80% humidity outside, although it felt more like 100%. Gada's training mainly involved technical work, but that didn't mean that she got to escape the scourge that was physical training. Two hours in the sun, being barked at by a man who resembled a football teams' Defensive Tackle, whenever your push-up was deemed sub-par by him, was nothing short of a personal hell for Gada, who preferred the cool confines of the military library. She didn't expect a warm and loving atmosphere when she joined the National Guard, but she definitely expected that it would be less stressful. Either way, Gada didn't regret it, not one bit.

Her training as a signal officer involved making tactical decisions, coordinating the employment of signal soldiers, and most importantly, gathering information and data for the military's use. *A bit like a spy. Call me 007!* she thought the day she filled out the application forms. Sadly, she didn't feel like much of a spy as she struggled to lift her body off of the ground to finish a set of 50 push-ups.

Despite feeling incompetent, her technique couldn't have been too bad because, within 14 months of being at Fort Gordan base, she was appointed to the rank of Second Lieutenant (which honestly wasn't all that amazing because it was the most junior grade of commissioned officer, but she was excited nonetheless).

Her fascination with military defense weapons and tactics grew as she delved deeper and deeper into her training. She recalled one of the first classes that kindled this passion. It was a lecture on two unique adversarial weapons. The first was the "Silkworm Missile." The Chinese Silkworm Missile, the Colonel had explained, was a brutish weapon whose lack of evasive technology was made up for in its ability to carry a lethal payload. The armor-piercing warhead bore a time-delayed initiator for maximum hull penetration prior to detonation. In contrast to the Russian SS-N-19 Shipwreck or the French MM-38 Exocet, the Silkworm lacks advanced stealth technology. However, it would inflict catastrophic damage to the enemy warship if it ever got through enemy defenses. Gada considered it ruthless, although perhaps 'messy' was a more accurate description.

The second and more elusive weapon was the Chinese "Autonomous Satellite Jammer." The "ASJ" is a small disc 7 inches in diameter, packed with high-tech capabilities, secretly attached to enemy space satellites while in orbit. Activated remotely, they are highly efficient low energy signal jammers that cannot be detected by stations on Earth, allowing comms to be temporarily disrupted without telegraphing hostile intent (ground stations will assume it was just a malfunction). In kill mode, the jammer can also be activated as a low-yield explosive, destroying the host satellite in cases where the user doesn't mind discovery or risking direct conflict. She wondered whether the tingling sensation she felt in her stomach whenever she thought about it was immoral—it was a tool of destruction after all. She decided to embrace it, certain that it was the weapon's engineering that excited her.

All in all, Gada was enjoying her time training as a signal officer. Regardless, she still missed her family and friends. Her parents called from time to time, some of her friends too, but the person she missed the most was Mike. Occasionally, he'd call on the base's phone, and they'd talk for hours (much to her fellow officers' annoyance), but he seemed to phone less and less the longer they were apart. Gada was unsure what to make of his silence but tried not to obsess over it. She and Mike had never officially "broken up" when he left for the UK, but she knew she could no longer confidently state that their "boyfriend and girlfriend" agreement stood—it felt like eons had passed since Mike had declared his love for her. They had both grown up since then, and she wasn't quite sure what their relationship status now was.

Fortunately, Gada made a new friend at the base who helped her to keep her mind off of all of it: Colonel Vivianne Cuomo, Gada's training officer. Their friendship was more ritualistic than anything else; she and the Colonel sat together during lunch in the cafeteria every day while Gada bombarded her with questions about military life and, sometimes, just about life in general.

Gada finally "found herself" one quiet Sunday afternoon on the base. She and the Colonel were having a meal together. "How did you know what you wanted to be?" Gada asked, picking at a pile of mashed potatoes in front of her.

"I never figured it out," the Colonel replied, shoveling a spoonful of peas into her mouth. "I just kind of... went with it."

"Really?"

"Yep. I started serving directly out of high school, climbed the ranks, and here I am: a Colonel in the Guard. I always thought I'd eventually leave to study something else, but I just never got around to it."

"Do you regret it? Not leaving the Guard?"

Colonel Cuomo's eyes glazed over for a minute as she stared off into the distance. She blinked twice, pulling herself back to reality, then said, "Nope, not at all. I love my job, and I'm doing this for my country."

Gada admired the Colonel's passion for the USA, but she wasn't sure that she felt the same. She truly did want to go to college and study *something*. More specifically, she wanted to go to the same university where Mike was, she wanted to study science, and she wanted to learn everything that there was to learn about mankind.

"I think I'm leaving the base at the end of the year," Gada said to the Colonel, almost whispering as if to keep a secret. "I'm going to apply to Oxford. I want to study Social Sciences. If I get in, I'm out of here."

"Good on you, kiddo," the Colonel grinned. "Just as long as you come and visit every now and then. The folks back at home won't believe I know someone who's going to Oxford."

"I haven't gotten in yet," Gada blushed. "But if I do, I'll visit you so often that you'll get sick of me."

***

Oxford did accept her. In fact, they would have likely rolled out a red carpet for Gada if she had requested it. *To think that a year ago I was on my hands and knees begging a drill sergeant for a break,* Gada thought, *although I'd give anything to have those sweltering summers back.* Her train of thought was interrupted when someone loudly called out, "Gada! An extra strong Americano for Gada!"

She pulled herself together and shoved her way through the gathered crowd to claim her cup of coffee from the tired-looking barista. "Thank you," she said, depositing a sizable tip in the barista's tip jar before slinking out of the coffee shop and out into the icy English air. She sat down on an empty park bench and looked around, inspecting the busy streets, the same streets she had observed while drinking her morning coffee for the past couple of years, and it truly had been a fair number of years. Naturally, it felt like just yesterday that she had landed at Heathrow. She remembered telling Mike that she'd be studying Social Sciences in university and recalled his shock at her chosen field of study and his elation that they'd be at the same university. They hadn't seen much of each other during her first couple of years at Oxford. Her class schedule simply didn't allow it. Before she knew it, he'd completed his undergraduate degree and returned to America, leaving her behind in England. Her studies had all but consumed her—she chased her undergraduate degree, then fought for her masters' degree, and now she needed to think of a way to defend her doctoral thesis. She knew it was based on a polarizing topic and was unsure how it would be received by her professors.

She took a long sip of her hot coffee, trying to push the overwhelming sense of anxiety that threatened to envelop her to the back of her mind. She had heard less and less from Mike since he had left, a fact that pained her terribly. Her mom phoned her weekly and always inevitably asked how he was doing, a question that she'd lately been forced to answer with an, "I don't know." She still received calls from her old high school friends and people that she met at the base, though some people called far more often than others. One of these people was Colonel Cuomo; she had been the first person to call Gada after her plane landed in England at the start of her first year. Gada remembered being called out of her room by one of the building's receptionists to take a call at reception. She instantly assumed the worst, that someone was ailing or dead, who else would phone her mere hours after her flight landed? Even her parents knew better. She had begrudgingly made her way to the reception desk, where she was handed a grubby yellow phone. "Hello?" she remembered squeaking into the speaker.

"Hey Kid," the Colonel had cheerfully greeted. "You must be dying of excitement!"

"Dying of nervousness is more like it. I have my class schedule, and I can already tell that it's going to be a busy year," Gada sighed.

The Colonel laughed. "You take care of yourself now, don't let the stress get to you! You've got this! If you ever need something, you know who to call. I know some people over there that can help you out, okay?"

"Yes ma'am!" Gada's hand had instinctively flown up to the side of her head, and she was instantly aware of the passersby that were staring at her, some of whom were giggling.

"Good, you got a passion, kid. Don't let anyone take that away from you just because they don't understand it."

"Yes ma'am," she had said in much a quieter tone.

"Stay safe, Officer."

Gada smiled; the memory of the Colonel's voice was enough to make her grin. Cuomo always had something interesting to say. Gada's love for Colonel Cuomo translated into a love for the Guard, which meant that she didn't have the heart to break ties with it entirely, not even upon landing in a foreign country. Throughout her studies, she continued serving and training in this unique program on a part-time basis in the RAF Barford St. John, an American communication base in the UK that was just a 30-minute drive from the University.

As she made her way from the park bench back toward her dormitory, she thought of the impending doctoral presentation that she'd have to give. "There's a call for you on the line," Barbie, the receptionist, sang at Gada as she walked into the dormitory's main building. She sighed and reluctantly took the phone from Barbie's well-manicured hand, raising it to her left ear.

"Have you been eating well?" her mom's somewhat shrill voice demanded.

"Oh, hi mom..." Gada answered, trying not to sound disappointed that it wasn't Mike's voice booming through the speaker.

"Honey? Are you there?"

"Yes, yes, mom. I missed that last bit; the connection is bad. What did you say?" she fibbed.

"Are you busy? Should we call later?" She heard her dad's booming voice in the background.

"I could spare a couple of minutes," she giggled. The dormitory building was eerily empty. She assumed the rest of the students had sensibly relocated to the library where they could prepare for their exams.

"Don't worry. It's nothing serious, and you sound busy, honey. Call us back when it's convenient for you," her mom reassured her. "We just wanted to hear how you're doing."

"I'm doing well. Same old, same old," Gada joked. "I promise I'll phone back at the end of the week... I'll have more free time then," she vowed. She hadn't told her parents that she'd need to defend her doctoral thesis in a couple of days, and she wasn't planning on telling them either—her mother was just as prone to bouts of anxiety as she was, and she didn't want either of her parents worrying about it. *I'm stressed out about it enough for the three of us,* Gada thought, chortling to herself. She hung up and gratefully slipped up the hallway and through her dorm room's door, immediately flinging herself down onto her bed.

As the final days of her doctorate program drew nearer, it seemed as though she was losing hold of the world around her, although she tried to reconcile herself with this feeling by telling herself that she had also gained a more in-depth understanding of how things worked. The more she learned, the more she wanted to know. Her curiosity grew, and she kept feeding it.

The year had been uneventful, filled with nothing but studying. That is, of course, if you're willing to gloss over the funeral of one of Gada's old Guard superiors. A few months earlier, Colonel Cuomo had called with less than cheery news. "Brigadier General Henry Treston was killed in action. I know he was one of the people who taught you while you were here... I thought you might want to come to his funeral," the Colonel had sniffed from the other side of the line, clearly trying to stifle her tears but also very clearly not succeeding.

***

Before Gada knew it, she was back on American soil. She hadn't even told her parents about her return. She wasn't planning on staying long enough to visit them anyway. Dressed to the nines in nothing but black, she and the Colonel soon found themselves standing around a gaping hole in the ground, trying to hear each other over the ambient wailing. "How's the base these days?" Gada asked, bending down to pluck a daisy that had sprouted between two of the graves.

The Colonel lit a cigar between her lips. She puffed at it, sending little clouds of smoke through the mourners' ranks.

"Same as always, I suppose. The Brigadier General... It shook everyone. Nobody likes being reminded of their own mortality," she sighed, unapologetically ashing her cigar onto the well-polished dress shoes of a strange man who had dared to stand too close to them.

The sermon was over, and the casket had been lowered into the ground by the time the Colonel had lit her second cigar. "Is

41

a cigar really the most suitable accessory for a funeral?" Gada teased as they solemnly made their way back to the parking lot.

"Oh, hush!" the Colonel laughed. "Leave me my little pleasures!"

A young man stopped them in their tracks just as they were preparing to get into the car, running toward them at warp speed with a flyer tightly clenched in one of his hands.

"Oh! Please no," the Colonel said, rolling her eyes. "I always have to deal with these people. Do I look like Satan or something? Gada, I think I am going to let you handle this yourself," she grumbled, entirely ignoring the young man as she slid into the car's driver seat.

"I am from The Fellowship of Our Lord, and I've come to tell you about God," he panted, desperately trying to shove the pamphlet into Gada's hands.

"I think I've heard about him before, and I'm not interested," Gada grinned, trying not to sound too offensive as she attempted to make her escape. The Colonel sat grinning inside of the locked vehicle. Gada couldn't get in no matter how many times she jerked at the car door's handle. Every attempt sparked a new round of roaring laughter from her friend inside. The young man saw it as an opportunity to convert someone who he believed to be a heathen. He went on and on about how God, being a divine and loving being, gave his only son to set the world free. It was the same story every time. Gada must have heard it a thousand times while growing up. However, the psychology element of her studies meant that she understood that people had their reasons for believing what they wanted to believe because it proved effective at keeping existential angst at bay during difficult times. She didn't have the heart to do anything but listen to the young man, nodding sympathetically when she felt it was appropriate. She didn't want to embarrass him by challenging his beliefs. In fact, she'd rather just have escaped into the safety of the car.

The entire ordeal reminded her of a visit to the school library in middle school, during which she found a magazine on her favorite table at the back of the room. Its cover read, "Do You Believe In God?" As a fourteen-year-old, she suddenly realized she hadn't really given it much thought. Her parents didn't believe in anything specific, and if you pushed them to talk about their beliefs, they would talk about the Abenaki's creation stories and myths. The Abrahamic God was an entirely foreign concept to Gada. However, the more she thought about it, the more she decided that there had to be some kind of higher power—although she was hesitant to believe that it was necessarily a God in the traditional sense.

The Colonel unlocked the car's doors just as the young man turned on his heel to leave, confident that he had converted Gada.

"How did it go?" the Colonel chuckled, putting the car in reverse as Gada closed the passenger door.

"The same old story. God gave his son..."

"And the world is set free! Blah blah blah..." the Colonel finished off for her. They both burst into laughter.

"I have a weird question for you, but you have to promise not to be offended," Gada sheepishly replied.

"I promise not to be a snowflake," the Colonel vowed, drawing a cross across her chest with one of her index fingers.

"Do you have a reason for not believing in the existence of God?" Gada finally asked.

"The world is harsh. Hatred consumes people's hearts, and you are not sure who means to harm you or who means to love you. People are raped and murdered every day, more people are sold into slavery now than they were hundreds of years ago, and 25,000 people die of hunger every single day. When you dare to be different, you become an outcast, a sinner. What kind of a God would sit back and watch children die of leukemia, or malaria, or aids?"

"You know what? You are right. Looking at it from that perspective, I can't help but agree that the world often seems entirely godless." She patted the Colonel's shoulder as they turned onto the main road.

"Wanna grab a drink? My flight leaves in..." she glanced at her wrist, "in an hour."

"Sure."

***

Gada returned to England and left America behind once more. She hadn't told anyone except her old Guard friends that she had been in the country, but now she wondered whether she had perhaps missed a chance to see Mike again. She had been too nervous to call him to tell him that she had been in the country. She didn't want to intrude on his new life as an engineer. Before returning home from the UK, he had vowed to wait for her, promising that they would start their life together in the USA once she wrapped up her Ph.D., but a part of her wondered whether any man was capable of staying faithful to a woman he hadn't seen in ages.

Before Gada knew it, she was back in class. All thoughts of Mike, the Colonel, and the Brigadier General melted away as she tried to absorb the contents of the complicated lecture being presented to them. Professor Nori's frail figure stood at the front of the class, swinging a comically long pointing stick around as she strategically slammed it against the blackboard at the back of the room. "As a civilization expands, they realize that resources are not limited to compounds and chemicals alone. Development and extraction of raw materials are highly dependent on the civilization's ability to locate and develop an efficient workforce to extract these treasures. The Kardashev Scale is the system that is normally used to express how advanced a civilization's technology is. It does so by calculating how much viable energy that civilization can make available to itself. Any questions?"

Gada was the first to raise her hand, as always. "Yes, professor. I have one. Where does Earth fall on the Kardashev Scale?" she asked, squinting as she jotted down a series of notes.

"We are Type zero, with emphasis on the 'zero' part!" the professor replied in her thick Italian accent. The class burst into laughter, so did Gada. "If we get our act together, stop fighting each other, learn how to use renewable energy, learn how to unify our efforts globally, and more importantly, how to use our limited resources wisely, we may have a chance to harness the gifts of this planet and survive to make it to a Type 1 civilization. That is if we don't manage to kill each other with nuclear weapons before then."

Gada enthusiastically raised her hand again and asked, "If theoretical science assumes that the universe is so structured, that we can divide civilizations into different hierarchies, even though we're not even able to achieve the simplest category as a species yet, then I must ask... Do you believe in God?" The class went deathly silent.

The professor walked closer to the students as she answered, "Different faiths have different names for God. Some call out for Allah, Shiva, Buddha, Yahweh, and Akal Murat, to name a few. As a scientist, your question should be, do you believe in the 'ultimate being?' Whoever or whatever that may be..." She paused for a moment before shuffling across the classroom, her gray curls flapping against her pale cheeks. "Do I believe in an 'ultimate being?' By logical deduction, the answer must be: Yes, such a being must exist." Professor Nori heard the chatter of her students, some outraged and some overjoyed, as she walked toward the door. "Class dismissed," she stated authoritatively, looking notably exhausted as she stepped over the threshold.

Gada was late for her next class. She wanted to stop at every rock, tree, and blade of grass on her way there to ask them whether an ultimate being existed but settled for a slow stroll during which she mulled over the concepts in her head. Both ideas were equally terrifying: If there was an ultimate being, what did he or she want with us? Alternatively, if there wasn't an ultimate being, did that mean human life was entirely meaningless?

The next day started with another lecture from Professor Nori, not that Gada complained. Professor Nori was one of her favorite people in England; she wasn't scared to talk about difficult topics—a trait that Gada admired and sometimes envied. Her mind was still swimming with questions about the previous day's lecture when the professor suddenly started, "Today we will be talking about an even more interesting topic: Type II civilizations and the theoretical existence of Millenia Beings within such civilizations. Fascinating, right?"

She was right; Gada was fascinated.

"So, the evolution of civilizations on the Kardashev scale is typically categorized into three segments, namely Type I, II and III consisting of their abilities to explore and harness energy and resources from planets, stars, and galaxies," the professor continued, drawing a quick sketch of the solar system in chalk behind her. "These three categories of capabilities and knowledge development are separated by Millennia to Megaannum in time. The process of evolution on Earth took millions of years. During those millions of years, on Earth alone, there were various types of ancient civilizations. Imagine how many other civilizations could be out there."

"But do you think that Type II civilizations and our ancient civilizations were connected in some way?" Gada asked as she was simultaneously raising her hand.

"It's possible," Professor Nori said, still pondering the question.

"But what would a Type II civilization even look like?" Gada probed, not even bothering to raise her hand anymore. The class had slowly devolved into a casual conversation between her and the professor.

"The beings of Type II civilizations will take advantage of their surroundings in the name of development. They'll likely be able to travel in light-years, making their exploitation of resources much more widespread than ours is. They would also use their knowledge to take advantage of the available labor and materials throughout their interstellar conquest, even making use of local labor, perhaps through slavery, to achieve their goals."

Gada had always loved the topic of evolution, but the Kardashev Scale and the theoretical existence of Type II civilizations were nearly enough to make her squeal with excitement.

***

Gada couldn't stop thinking about what Professor Nori talked about during class. The idea that there might be extraterrestrials was exciting in and of itself without the added excitement of their possible superior technological development. Naturally, being as curious as she was, Gada had to research the topic further.

When she got back to campus, she changed into something more comfortable, and went straight to the library to use its computers. Gada sat down in one of the library's darkest corners and made herself comfortable in front of a glowing computer screen. She opened the device's internet browser and patiently waited for it to load. She feverishly typed a couple of keywords into the search bar and nervously glanced around her, trying to gauge whether anyone could see what she was searching. The search engine produced a single article, a document titled "Type II Civilizations and Millenia Beings: What You Need To Know." It was filled with scientific jargon that even she, a sociology doctoral student, found difficult to understand. However, she got the gist of it—Type II civilizations needed to locate Interspatial Nodes to enable them to travel the incredible distances that they'd need to cross to gather resources. Still, they weren't even the biggest fish in the sea: While miles ahead of humans, they were fetuses when compared to civilizations capable of harnessing the bountiful wealth of entire galaxies, Type III civilizations.

Another scientific journal that she stumbled across in one of the dustiest nooks of the internet claimed that nodes would have to be developed throughout several solar systems to allow the interstellar craft to continue traveling faster than the speed of light. *Kind of like gas stations along highways,* Gada thought to herself, making a note of it.

Gada considered using a statistical modeling technique to compile all of the information she had gathered on Type II beings, but found herself drifting off to sleep in front of the library computer's luminescent screen before she had the opportunity to do a proper analysis.

***

Two days before she had to defend her doctoral thesis, Gada finally worked up the courage to phone Mike. She stood in the phone booth with the phone pressed to her ear as she listened to the beeping sounds, waiting patiently for the receiver to pick up. Her knees were shaking, and her palms were sweaty.

"Hey there, Mike," she sheepishly said as soon as she heard the receiver click on the other end of the line.

"Hey, Gada," he chuckled in reply, "Thanks for calling me after all these years. How long has it been? Two? Three years?"

Gada giggled as she leaned against the side of the booth. It was like talking to an old friend. "Eleven months, I've been counting. I wasn't sure what to say... You could have called too, you know. I thought that you'd perhaps found something... or someone else to keep you busy back there in the US. "

Mike nervously laughed, "I thought perhaps you didn't want to hear from me either... I remember that one applied math professor that asked you out on a date after every lecture. I thought perhaps you had settled down with him or something.

49

least seven times every week, but they always told me you were busy."

"You tried calling?" Gada gasped. "The receptionists never told me that I had missed any calls... Ooh! I'm going to murder Barbara!"

"Barbara?" Mike chortled. "Sounds like her fate is sealed."

"Yes, Barbara. She insists on being called Barbie. She runs reception, or apparently just sits behind the reception desk looking busy and not letting people know when they've missed calls," she grumbled, aggressively twisting the phone's cord around her index finger. "I'm so sorry, Mike. I just didn't want to bother you. I had no idea you were trying to contact me."

"So you're not married to that pervy professor yet?" he anxiously chuckled, his voice cracking slightly toward the end.

Gada giggled. "I'm your girlfriend, remember? Why on Earth would I run off with anyone else?"

"My girlfriend?" Mike asked tentatively.

"Of course, I am still your girlfriend, right?" Gada probed, her voice notably shaky.

"Gada Deere, I couldn't look at another woman while you still walk this planet even if I tried. You've captivated me completely. Mesmerized, even! In fact, I was planning on becoming a monk in the event that you really had forgotten all about me."

"You clown," Gada giggled flirtatiously. "It would be a waste of a very attractive man if the world had to lose you to monkhood, and I'm certainly still your girlfriend if you'll have me."

"It's settled then! We'll get married and have five children immediately!" Mike joked.

"Five!?" Gada gasped. "You, sir, are out of your mind. Absolutely looney!"

"You sound like you're in a good mood today. I love it. I assume your classes are going well then?" Mike asked, regaining control of his markedly deep voice.

"Oh Mike, we spoke about the most interesting topic in class today. I wish you could have been there," Gada enthused as she twirled a single dark curl around her finger, still leaning against the booth's side.

"What was it about?" Mike asked.

"You really want to know? You might not be able to keep up."

"What? I can keep up. Come on, tell me."

"Okay. So, we've been learning about different types of civilization in my interdisciplinary theoretical science class, and Professor Nori was teaching us about the Kardashev Scale all week. Today we finally discussed Type II civilizations, and it completely blew my mind."

"The Kardashev Scale?" Mike enquired. His education as an engineer hadn't involved any theoretical science. "How do civilization types belong to any areas of study other than sociology, archaeology, and history?"

"The Kardashev Scale is all about civilization advancements, or rather the scale at which energy can be harnessed and actively used by civilizations. Does that make sense?" Gada checked, trying not to sound condescending.

"Don't worry, you haven't lost me yet," Mike laughed. "I'm not a total dunce."

"Well, Type I civilizations basically draw their energy from planets, Type II civilizations draw their energy from stars, and Type III civilizations draw their energy from entire galaxies. Can you imagine that? We talked about the possible existence of beings within these civilizations," Gada enthusiastically explained.

"So, aliens?" Mike chuckled, clearly not taking Gada's lecture nearly as seriously as she had hoped he would.

"Humans are nothing in the grand scheme of things; I'm convinced of that. There are probably greater beings out there. Who knows how many more planets could be out there going through the same process of evolution that we have? Some of them might be more advanced than we are. Some of them might be more primitive than us."

"My head hurts just thinking about it," Mike grumbled. "I think I'll stick to engineering. At least there are no aliens involved in designing bridges, or else I'd be out of work."

"Not yet!" Gada chipped in. They both burst into laughter

"Okay, Mrs. Smarty Pants. I always knew you had a fascination with extraterrestrial beings," Mike teased. "Poor Mrs. Ester..."

"You're never going to let that go, are you?"

"Nope," Mike replied, still laughing.

"Why are you talking as though you aren't smarty pants yourself?"

"Me? I only dabble in the intellectual arts. You've taken up permanent residence in the kingdom of genius." Mike was modest. He had gotten a job in one of the best engineering facilities in the US. He always talked about how he couldn't keep up when he was as much of a science lover as she was. "But seriously, that's interesting. The idea that there might actually be more advanced beings out there is quite intriguing. Terrifying, but intriguing."

"Not just advanced beings, advanced beings capable of unlocking the various unknown elements of the world. Who knows the knowledge they have? Who knows all the things they can share with us? Imagine beings that can live up to millions of years old. Imagine an individual being of an advanced race mingling with humans in 5000 BC. Trying to understand such a being's technology, advanced materials, manufacturing tools, and infrastructure would be crippling to the primitive human mind!"

"It's crippling to my mind... Anyway, to do that, they would need vehicles that are capable of some seriously impressive space travel, right?" Mike asked.

"Oh, yes. An advanced civilization would probably have vehicles that are capable of interstellar travel. Imagine what kind of equipment they would use for that, the kind of equipment they probably use for anything! The university is currently carrying out research to determine whether advanced beings from different civilizations made contact with early human civilizations. What other sister civilizations have they contributed to? What did they want? Most importantly, what were they looking for?"

"Whoa!" Mike said, letting out a husky laugh that made Gada blush. "Those are a lot of questions."

"Sorry. Topics like this just get me excited."

"Don't apologize. You know I love it when you get like that. It's sexy."

Gada turned scarlet and gasped for air as she tried to internalize the comment. *Sexy? Me?* She wondered, shaking her head in disbelief.

"Still there?" Mike asked, his voice laced with worry.

"Yes."

"How's everything going over there? Your mom is worried about you. She wants to visit, but I told her that now isn't a good time with your upcoming doctoral defense. I told her you wouldn't be able to spend time with her if she hopped on a plane right now. Nevertheless, she wants to be certain that you arc doing well. Shc askcd mc to ask you. Shc thought you'd be more honest with me than you are with her."

"I am..." she sighed. "You know my mom... She's always looking for something to worry about. School has been getting tougher these days, but it's nothing I can't handle. I was in the military, and this is nothing compared to the combat training that they put me through."

"Combat training coming in handy these days?" he joked. He had never entirely forgiven her for taking a gap year, leaving him to brave England alone for the first year.

"Ask me that when you see me again, and I'll show you exactly how handy it was," Gada cheekily threatened.

"Yes, sir!" Mike hollered.

"So, my exams are near, and you might not hear from me for a while again..."

Mike sighed. "It's fine. I miss you, but I know your doctoral degree comes first. Just wrap it up now so that you can come home to me, okay?"

"I'm almost done with all this, and then I'll be home for good," she promised, wondering whether that was the truth.

"I love you," Mike said matter-of-factly, "very, very, very much."

"I love you too," Gada replied, squirming in an attempt to subdue the butterflies in her stomach. After all of these years, Mike still excited her.

***

The day she had been waiting for had finally come. A bead of sweat rolled down her forehead. She wiped at it with the back of her hand. For a minute, the stern faces of the academic committee staring back at her were perfectly motionless. They were all seated in front of a long table on the dais. Gada stood on the other side of the table, making her thesis presentation.

She could feel her heart beating in her throat, but focused on maintaining a calm demeanor. *No one believes a scientist that looks like they're about to have a panic attack*, she thought, catching herself fiddling with one of her blazer's buttons.

Her defense presentation topic was on the determination of societal growth through statistical modeling of random events in sequential progression. She explained that through statistical modeling, she had been able to isolate outlier events rather than removing them from the data set entirely.

Some of the professors on the panel looked confused; others started murmuring among themselves. The more they murmured, muttered, and whispered, the more Gada's legs trembled beneath her. Just when it started feeling like the room was spinning at 200 miles per hour, the committee asked to be excused to deliberate on their findings.

"Of course. Time your take..." Gada fumbled. "I mean, take your time! No rush, I'll be here when you get back."

One of the professors chuckled; the others solemnly left the room in single file like some kind of morbid funeral procession. Gada waited for them for three hours, pacing up and down while biting her nails. She imagined going back to the USA and working as a shop attendant as her parents had originally suggested. *Perhaps it would have been less stressful,* she thought.

Just as Gada was sure she'd start suffering from anxiety-induced psychosis, the door to the conference room creaked open, and the committee assistant called Gada into the meeting room. She stepped over the threshold, flashing a smile at each professor in turn. It seemed as though they were trying to avoid making eye contact with her.

This is it, she thought. *Don't cry, don't cry, don't cry,* she tried to convince herself. Even the worst-case scenario would only mean that she'd have to spend a few extra months reworking her thesis. *It's not like you're being led to slaughter,* she thought, *even if it does feel like I am.*

"Please sit down," one of the professors told Gada, motioning at an empty chair at the head of the table. "We've discussed your thesis in length, Ms. Deere. Some of us initially failed to appreciate your work, but we soon realized the enormous potential of its real-world applications. It is essentially designed to solve anomalies that seem to be random in occurrence, 'non-deterministic' to use the right terminology."

"Meep!" Gada involuntarily squealed with excitement, hopping up and down in her seat.

The professor cleared his throat before continuing, "We thought about how your formulas can accurately predict the outcome of a wider range of events than even you yourself may have anticipated. It did not take long for us to recognize its full potential. However, with this kind of power, Ms. Deere, comes an equally immense responsibility. You have to use this formula in a morally-just and ethically responsible way, for humankind's good. What we're concerned about is whether you will make use of your work to benefit all, or whether you will use it for personal gain? This committee is responsible for the work that students present and also decides whether that work will be added to academia's broader wealth of knowledge. It is our responsibility to identify work that has the potential to be harmful... Perhaps even entirely malevolent." Gada gasped, but the professor didn't miss a beat, "However, we find the brilliance in your thesis too important to suppress. Therefore..." He looked back at the rest of the panel, all of them nodded in unison. "...This committee not only accepts your thesis without any modification whatsoever but also, we have unanimously decided to nominate your thesis for three of the highest university awards given to doctoral nominations. Congratulations, Doctor Deere!" The room was filled with applause as all of the professors stood up from their chairs and cheered.

"What?" she whispered, tears streaming down her cheeks. A female professor on the panel who Gada didn't know all that well left the table and walked over to Gada. She wrapped her arms around her and squeezed her until it hurt. "You did it! You did it! England is going to lose one of the greatest minds of our time when you go back to the USA. It has been a pleasure... No! A blessing to be able to read your work."

Another round of applause erupted from the panel of professors, and Gada continued to sob in the woman's arms. *I did it,* she thought. *I really did it.*

Chapter 3: Courting the Secret Squirrel

It was a misty Wednesday night and Flight 194 was cautiously approaching the runway. Gada was preparing to put her studies and England behind her. She wondered what the future would hold and whether she'd ever see England and her beloved professors again. She nervously stared out of the airplane's window and bit at a loose piece of skin on her lip, wishing she had chosen an earlier flight.

"Passengers, please fasten your seatbelts. We are beginning our descent. The ambient temperature below is 46 degrees Fahrenheit. Our estimated time of arrival is 01:30 am, right on time!" The pilot's voice crackled over the intercom. It was 02:00 am by the time that he finally managed to set the plane down on the runway. "Sorry about that folks, seems like the weather didn't want us getting home," the captain's anxious voice reverberated through the cabin.

"What a flight, eh dearie?" The elderly lady seated next to Gada smiled, placing her spindly hand on Gada's shoulder.

"Well, we're home safely, and that's all that matters," Gada sympathetically grinned, already making her way past the old lady's stockinged legs to get to the overhead storage locker.

"Rushing home to your husband, hun?" The old woman continued, staring off into the distance as if searching for something at one end of the plane. "I remember when my John was alive…"

"Sorry, I have to get going," Gada politely interjected, trying hard not to sound rude. "My mom is waiting for me, I haven't seen her in quite a while."

"Yer mum?" She piped up again as Gada swung her handbag over her shoulder and started making her way down the cabin's aisle, raising her hand in a half-hearted wave in an attempt to apologize to her chatty neighbor for making a quick getaway.

"I wish my Susie would visit me more often! Oh, won't you stay and chat?" She screamed at Gada, who was now zipping through the queued passengers in an attempt to escape the woman's barrage of questions.

Gada breathed a sigh of relief as she emerged from the plane, counting herself lucky to have gotten away. The sense of relief that momentarily calmed her breathing and slowed her pulse didn't last long. She soon found herself walking down an empty airport hallway, pushing a heavy luggage trolley and letting her thoughts wander. *What a weirdo*, Gada grimaced as she thought of the strange woman she'd met on her flight. *It was like she wanted to stall me or something.*

"Gada!" her mom screeched as she turned a corner and left the airport's arrival wing. "Gada! Gada! Over here!"

"Hi, mom!" Gada squealed, leaving her luggage behind and rushing to her mother's side. They embraced each other, joyfully spinning in clumsy circles. "I've missed you so much!"

"I missed you more!" Her mom replied, squeezing her even tighter. "Your dad's going to be so happy to see you!"

"Mom... you're s-s-quishing me!" Gada spluttered, trying to squirm out of her embrace.

Ding dong. The airport's intercom chimed. "Please do not leave luggage unattended. Unattended luggage will be removed by airport security."

"Whoops! Big brother is watching!" Gada chortled, walking back to her luggage trolley. "Straight home?" she asked. "I really need a bath, it was a long flight and I sat next to this really odd person..."

"Where else would we go?" her mom asked, raising a single eyebrow as she took Gada's hand luggage from her.

"I don't know," Gada grinned. "You're just exactly the kind of mom who'd plan a party for something like this... and I'm just really, really tired."

"Me? Plan a party?" her mom frowned. "It's like you don't know me at all."

The car ride home was filled with an exclamation mark-shaped silence. Gada couldn't stand it for more than a couple of minutes and resorted to switching the stereo on. Her mom's favorite ABBA songs loudly blared through the speakers, rattling the car's windows. *Money, Money, Money,* started playing when she began to get worried that something might be amiss.

"You okay, mom?" Gada inquired, leaning forward in her seat to peer at her mother's expressionless face.

"Hmm? Me?" her mom coughed. "Why wouldn't I be okay?"

"I don't know, you just seem awfully quiet," Gada mumbled as the car pulled into the driveway.

She was still struggling to wrestle the largest suitcase out of the car's trunk when her mom rushed into the house. "Gee,

61

thanks for the help," Gada grumpily mumbled under her breath, the sweat on her brow glistening in the streetlight's eerie glow. The cul de sac was even quieter than the car ride home had initially been. The hedge leaves ominously rustled in the wind. A feeling of icy unease ran down Gada's spine, causing her to shiver. "Mom?" she called out as she finally managed to lift her heavy bag out of the car, loudly plopping it down on the ground wheels first. There was no answer.

"Mom!" she yelled, slowly inching toward the front door. "This isn't funny!"

She reached the threshold and pushed the door handle down, sticking her head through the crack between the frame and the door's wooden edge. The house was obsidian black on the inside. She couldn't see the outlines of the television room's outdated furniture, nevermind spot any potential danger. She steeled herself to face whatever lurked inside and slipped through the doorway, careful not to make a sound as she snuck over the creaky floorboards.

"Surprise!"

The room was illuminated with the bright artificial light of the energy efficient light bulbs her father insisted on installing in every room. Gada blinked furiously in an attempt to clear her vision, unsure of who or what she'd run into. A few blinks cleared the haziness from her vision and the smiling faces of her friends and family became recognizable. Her mother and father were proudly huddled against one wall, holding each other as they stared at her with glistening eyes. Her cousin, Sheri-Lee, was holding up a cardboard sign that read "Welcome home!" and her young niece, Tammy, was holding up a similar poster. Its writing was mostly illegible, but Gada knew it read "Aunty Gada."

Gada was still gawking at the gathered crowd when it started parting like the biblical red sea. A well-dressed figure stepped forward, fidgeting with something in his pocket. He looked up, his eyes twinkling mischievously. "Mike, is that you?" Gada gasped. "I've never seen you in anything other than jeans and a t-shirt!"

"It's a rental," Mike chuckled nervously, straightening his tie. "And this is a clip on...I can't really straighten it."

"Well, it looks nice. I couldn't tell," Gada grinned, stepping toward him. She wrapped her arms around him and buried her face in his neck. He smelled of almonds and pine trees, a smell he always attributed to his mother's laundry routine, but one she'd never smelled anywhere else in his house. "Thank you for waiting for me Mike, I was scared I might get to meet your wife and kids by the time I made my way home."

"I made a promise and I always keep my promises," Mike softly mumbled. "Actually, speaking of promises, I'd kind of like you to promise me something too, Gada."

"Ugh... Sure?" she replied. "Would you like to go somewhere else? Somewhere more private?"

"No, actually. I'd prefer to do it here," Mike smiled, slowly getting down on one knee. He reached into the pocket he was fidgeting with earlier and produced a small black velvet box. Gada squealed as he opened it, revealing a white gold ring with a sizeable diamond mounted proudly on top of it. "Gada, do you promise to stay with me forever? Will you marry me?"

"Mike! I don't know what to say," Gada said, turning two shades paler.

"Just say yes?" Mike suggested nervously, still wobbling on one knee.

"Of course it's a yes! A thousand times yes!" Gada exclaimed, pulling him to his feet. "And to think that a few months ago I wasn't sure whether you still wanted me..."

"I'll always want you, Gada," Mike whispered, gingerly kissing her. "You're home now, and you'll never have to doubt that ever again."

"It's nice to be home," Gada sighed, melting in his arms. She could hear the faint applause and cheering of her friends and family in the background and the mechanical click of cameras' shutters, but they all seemed worlds away.

"Congrats, dear!" Mrs. Corey chimed in. "I always knew you two would make it! I couldn't have asked for a better daughter-in-law!" She squeezed Gada's shoulder as she made her way back to the platter table at one end of the room to scrutinize the quality of the catering. Gada was momentarily pulled back to reality, but only momentarily.

The rest of the night passed in a red wine haze. She went to bed with Mike's anxious giggling still echoing through her head and squeezed her covers against her chest as she dreamed of her perfect future.

***

"Are you sure it's in this street?" Mike grumbled, turning his shining new charcoal gray SUV into a one-way labeled "Twenty-First." "I feel like we're lost. I don't know D.C. as well as I'd like."

"In the news today, investigators are baffled at the mysterious deaths of several scientists," the car's stereo suddenly blared, interrupting Mike's line of questioning. "Interpol is investigating eleven mysterious deaths that occurred in a number of different countries in a very short period of time. Interpol representatives in Paris declined to comment on the investigation and simply stated that the investigations are ongoing and that there has been cooperation between various police departments around the world in an attempt to solve the baffling crimes."

"Hear that? You've got nothing to complain about. Those eleven people had something to complain about. Plus, we're not lost, I'm sure it's this street," Gada asserted, intensely staring out of the window as she searched for the Poto-Pine Apartment Building. "I checked the directions a hundred times before we got in the car. I'm certain we're heading in the right direction. Oh, Mike! Isn't it exciting! A new city, a new life, your new job!"

"Hmm. I wonder why Interpol is involved. Anyway, I'm sure you'll find work soon too," Mike encouragingly added. He paused and then continued, "I just feel like we should have turned right at the last intersection."

"Mike!" she exclaimed. "I'm sure, okay? Just trust me."

"I swear you've gotten even more hard-headed since we got engaged if such a thing was even possible," Mike chuckled, trying to lighten the mood.

"Look, there it is!" she excitedly shouted, pointing toward a building to Mike's left. "I think we should be able to parallel park right in front of it, I see an empty spot!"

"Yes, sir!" Mike replied, lifting his hand from the leatherbound steering wheel to mockingly salute his fiancée. He turned the wheel and effortlessly guided the car into the vacant lot. "What now?" he asked, pulling up the handbrake.

"The agent said she'd meet us at the front door. It's on the third floor, apartment 3019," Gada answered, already wiggling out of the passenger side seat. The late autumn breeze caught her blouse's long loose sleeves and tugged it toward the Poto-Pine Apartment Building as if to guide her to the structure's entrance. *This must be one of those old hotels they turned into apartments*, she contemplated, staring up at its many glistening windows. *If we rent an apartment here, it'll be the fanciest place I've ever lived*, she thought, remembering the state of her childhood home, its leaky pipes, and its faded linoleum.

"Windy today," Mike remarked as they made their way to the building's imposing main entrance. He wrapped his right arm around her tiny waist and pulled her closer to him.

"I think we'll get snow early this year," Gada stated, striding forward with a single-minded determination. Her boots' heels loudly clacked against the building's ivory white tiles as they sauntered into the lobby, searching for the elevator. They finally found it next to a modestly-sized marble statue of the archangel Michael that adorned the most forlorn corner of the sprawling room.

"Sheesh, how creepy," she said, pointing at the sword wielding figure as the elevator's doors slid open. "Looks like it's ready to chop someone's head off."

"It's just a statue," Mike chortled, leading her into the waiting elevator and pushing the bronze button that would take them up to the third floor. "It's supposed to be artistic... I think."

"A Picasso painting is artistic. That statue is just... blegh," Gada frowned, leaning against the elevator's red velvet lined wall.

"Blegh?" Miked asked as its doors slid open, revealing the third floor. It looked exactly like the first with the exception of the odd statue they had encountered on their way up. Its white walls with teak wood detailing could only have been inspired by some misguided 1970's fashion statement and its stipple ceiling looked like it belonged in someone's grandma's house, but other than these glaring flaws, it was definitely one of the most lavish interiors in all of Washington, D.C.

"I just can't imagine seeing that statue in a store and thinking, 'Wow, that's what my apartment building has been missing all of these years.' You know what I mean?" Gada sniffed, stepping onto the red carpet that ran the length of the long hallway that ribboned out in front of them.

"I'm not sure that I do," Mike laughed, taking a couple of quick steps to catch up with her. "But I promise not to buy one for the apartment."

"Good," Gada said, turning her head to grin at him.

A tall dark-skinned woman dressed in a beige pantsuit stood in front of one of the apartments close to the end of the seemingly endless hallway. She waved at the couple as they drew closer. "You must be Mike and Gada. I'm Anne!" she beamed, waving enthusiastically at them. "I can't wait to show you this place. You're going to fall head over heels in love with it!"

"Hi! Yes, that's us!" Mike panted, clearly exhausted from the walk. Gada had come off slightly better, she'd never lost the physical endurance that she had fostered during her time in

67

the National Guard. "Thank you so much for meeting with us at such short notice. My fiancée couldn't wait to see the place," he muttered, still trying to catch his breath.

"Lucky lady!" Anne cooed, flashing her snow white teeth at Gada. "There are women who'd give their left arm to catch a man that could afford a place like this..."

"We'll be co-signing the lease," Gada interrupted. "And we'll be splitting the rent... once I find a job."

"Oh, of course," Anne backtracked. "This is the perfect place for two young professionals. It even has an extra room that could be turned into a home office or a nursery! Come on inside," she charmingly smiled, opening the apartment's authentic oak front door.

Gada was instantly taken aback by the amount of light streaming into the open plan living area. "Wow, it's bright in here," she remarked, lifting her hands to shield her eyes. The paper white walls seemed to be doing an excellent job of amplifying the room's brightness even further.

"The architects designed this building with natural light in mind. It's always sunny in Poto-Pine!" Anne laughed robotically. "This is the kitchen," she added, motioning toward the black marble countertops and six-plate gas stove in one corner of the room. "It has a breakfast nook, and as you can see, it flows seamlessly into the rest of the living space which means that you can entertain guests while cooking!"

"It's lovely," Gada started. Her phone vibrated in her pocket. "Sorry, I've got to take this. Nobody ever calls me, must be serious," she muttered.

"Do you mind if I walk around the apartment while she takes that?" Mike asked the agent, motioning toward Gada who had retreated into one corner of the room. She was clutching her clunky cellphone so tightly that her knuckles were turning white.

"Sure," Anne warmly replied, flirtatiously flipping her long braids over her shoulder. Mike took no notice. "I'll walk with you. I'm sure your fiancée will catch up with us when she's done," she defeatedly sighed as Mike started wandering toward the apartment's bedrooms without her, mumbling something about cupboards as he went.

Gada watched as they strolled toward a door situated at the far side of the room. "Good morning, Gada speaking," she quietly said into the cellphone's receiver.

"Good morning! I've got some good news for you, pipsqueak!"

"First Sergeant Daniels? Is that you?" Gada gasped, her dark brown eyes widening. "I haven't heard from you in years. How did you get my number?"

"Cuomo asked me to phone. She has been deployed…"

"Oh my gosh! Is she okay?" Gada interrupted, her skin suddenly felt cold and numb as if all of the heat had leaked out of her body and seeped out onto the immaculate wooden floor.

"She's fine. She always is. She just heard about a job opportunity and recommended you for it, wanted me to contact you to tell you to expect a call from Lieutenant Colonel Margaret Dubois," he explained in a tone that could only be described as the verbal equivalent of rolling one's eyes. "Seems you're the favorite even though you're no longer here, working your ass off for her every day. Ungrateful doesn't even begin to descri—"

"Daniels, that's no way to speak about one of your superiors," Gada scolded, furrowing her brow. "Now, stop complaining and tell me who this Dubois woman is and what kind of job we're talking about?"

"Of course you don't know who she is," he tut-tutted. "Why would you? You're a civilian."

"Daniels!"

"Fine," he grumbled. "She's a commanding officer at the Defense Intelligence Agency. I'm sure you know what that is? Our highest military intelligence office? Anyway, I don't know what kind of job it is, Cuomo didn't deign to share that with me."

"Thanks for letting me know, Daniels. Listen, I always thought you were one of the good ones. Don't let the job turn you into a cynical asshole," Gada joked, trying to diffuse the tension. "There are enough of those in the National Guard already."

Gada's phone's speaker violently vibrated as Daniels erupted into a fit of laughter on the other end of the line. "Well, you're not wrong," he conceded, still chuckling. "Have a good day, Gada... and hey, I really do hope you get the job and I hope it's a nice cushy office job with a big fat paycheck."

"Thank you, Daniels," she replied kindly. "It was nice speaking to you again."

Gada had to peep into a bedroom and the bathroom before she finally found Mike and the real estate agent. Mike was examining some built-in cupboards, opening and closing their doors and sticking his head into their confines in an attempt to try to spot any latent defects. "Having a good time?" Gada asked to announce her presence.

"Did you see the bath?" Mike enthusiastically sang, nearly hopping out of a cupboard mid-inspection. "You could fit four people in there. It's basically a jacuzzi!"

"As if you need another reason to take extravagantly long baths, Mike," Gada teased, cheekily pulling one corner of her mouth up in a strange kind of half-grin.

"I do not!" Mike blushed, turning a comedic shade of red. He avoided making eye contact with Anne who had been unable to stifle her laughter and had surrendered to a fit of giggles. "I just thought you'd like it too. I imagine it would be easy to bath kids in..."

"Kids?" Gada asked nonchalantly, barely paying the statement any mind as she flitted toward the room's open window. It looked out on a street filled with two distinct streams of commuting pedestrians. It wasn't an unpleasant view, part of a small local park was visible and Gada thought she might spend some time simply watching the old willow trees that grew in it swaying in the wind.

"Yeah... well, eventually we'll want kids and I want this place to be big enough for all of us," Mike explained, attempting to shield his nervousness by making a show of examining a rather squeaky cupboard hinge.

"Who told you I want kids, hmm?" Gada grimaced, turning her face away from the window to glare at Mike. "I really need to focus on my career right now. I just finished studying..."

"We'll discuss this later," Mike said authoritatively.

The sternness of his voice gave Gada goosebumps. *You're definitely not the geeky boy I got to know in high school,* she thought, examining the sharp angles of his attractive jaw and drinking in the broadness of his chest.

"Would you like to see the last room?" Anne interjected, clearly uncomfortable with being caught in the middle of such a personal conversation. "It would be the perfect office for two professionals." She led them into an adjacent room. Its walls were lined with bookshelves and a large crystal chandelier hung from the ceiling's center, casting dancing shadows against the walls.

"Oh!" Gada gasped, visibly impressed. "I could live here! Could we rent just this single room? Mike and I could sleep on the floor for all I care... Look how much space my books would have!"

"So, we're sleeping on the floor just as long as your books are comfortable?" Mike chuckled, running his hand over one of the shelves' glistening wooden frames.

"Of course," Gada grinned, batting her naturally long eyelashes at him.

"What do you think?" Anne pried, stepping in between Mike and Gada to draw attention to herself. "You know, we've had a lot of interest in this apartment, it might not stay on the market very long..."

"We'll take it!" Gada dramatically shouted, thrusting one of her fists into the air like a keen fan at the end of a victorious football game. "My books will have nothing less!"

"Nerd," Mike jokingly scoffed. "When can we sign the papers?" he asked Anne. She was clearly taken aback by the sudden offer.

"Can we sign them today?" Gada asked, daydreaming of the meticulous Dewey Decimal Classification System that she'd implement in her own personal library. *And I'll give Mike hell every time he doesn't return a book to its rightful place,* she plotted.

"Sure," the real estate agent gasped, nearly jumping with joy. "If you'd like, I can run back to the office and print out a contract quickly. You could wait here if you'd like? This unit doesn't currently have any occupants."

"Sounds like a plan," Mike smiled, sitting down on the floor with his back against one of Gada's already-beloved bookcases. "We could hang around a bit while we wait for you."

"Fantastic!" Anne squealed. "I'll be right back!" she darted out of the room, clutching at her skirt to deter it from flying up as she sprinted toward the front door. Gada didn't see her leave, but the sound of the apartment door slamming shut confirmed that she and Mike were alone.

"Are you sure about this place?" Gada asked, sighing as she lowered her petite frame to sit next to him.

He looked up at her. She could have sworn she saw a flame dancing in his eyes. "I'm sure," he confirmed, his voice was deep, steady, and soothing. "This is where I'm going to build a life for us, or where I'm going to start, at least."

"You don't have to build it alone, you know?" Gada squeaked, resting her head on his shoulder. "I'm here to help, not to be helped."

"I know you're not some damsel in distress," Mike admitted, "but that doesn't mean that I don't want to save you."

"Oh, Mike," she sighed, tilting her head upward to kiss the nape of his neck. "I'll always let you save me."

He pulled away from her for a second, staring feverishly at her lipstick-red mouth. "I'm sorry, I can't control myself around you," he admitted, pulling her closer, and crushing his lips against hers. He lowered her onto the floor until he was leaning over her.

"Mike... We're in someone else's apartment..."

"You heard the woman, she said this unit doesn't have any occupants. Plus, we're planning on renting it..." he whispered, his breath hot against her collarbone. "So, technically speaking, it's our apartment."

"Hmm... You make a very convincing argument, Mr. Corey," she replied, biting her lower lip as she fiddled with his belt buckle. He undid her jeans' button in one smooth motion and passionately plucked it off of her body, revealing her cartoon-themed underwear.

"Nerd," he reiterated, kissing her just below her navel.

"But I'm your nerd..." she blissfully sighed.

The apartment's door slammed open again at the most inopportune moment, just as Gada and Mike were reaching for their undergarments which were now scattered across the room's floor. They were both sweating profusely and breathing heavily, an expected side effect of a quick but passionate encounter. Gada sent up a silent prayer to whatever being was in control that Anne wouldn't notice as she scooped her ponytail back into a tight black hairband.

"Yoohoo!" Anne called, her brown leather stilettos clacking across the wooden floor as she approached.

"We're in here! We're just... umm... admiring the view!" Gada lied, still trying to squirm back into her skinny jeans. Mike had managed to scurry back into all of his clothes and was now watching as she struggled to get back into hers, smiling smugly. "You look like a cat that managed to steal an entire pitcher of cream," Gada half-hissed, half-whispered at him. "Dial it down before she manages to guess what we did while she was gone!"

"She won't know, relax," he said dismissively, grinning even wider.

The words had barely left his lips and Gada had just managed to slip her blouse back on when the well-dressed real estate agent burst into the room, wielding two files full of paperwork.

"I hope all of that isn't for us?" Gada nervously giggled, motioning toward the reams of paper therein. "I hate paperwork."

"Don't we all, honey" Anne replied, looking for somewhere to put her binders down. "We all have places to be, people to see, and things to do, but paperwork is a necessary evil and as inevitable as death itself. That's what my nana used to say down in Illinois, anyway. No point in running away from it."

"It's just that..." Gada was unable to finish her sentence before her bulky cell phone started vibrating in her coat's pocket again. "Sorry, I have to take this. It's probably Daniels, but you never know."

"We'll get started on the paperwork," Mike nodded, steering Anne toward the windowsill where he motioned for her to deposit her files. The windowsill's rim was just wide enough that she was able to balance all of her paperwork on it. "Tada! A makeshift desk made with nothing but naturally abundant materials," he laughed, but the real estate agent didn't join him. In fact, her whole demeanor had changed since she returned with the promised contracts.

She's probably just a little irritated that she had to go all the way back to the office, Gada thought, trying to rationalize the situation. *There's no way that she knows what happened.* Gada slipped out of the room and made her way back to the living area before whipping her phone out. "Gada speaking! Good afternoon!" she greeted in her normal sing-song style.

"Miss Deere? Gada Deere?" the raspy voice on the other side of the line asked. Gada could practically smell the cigarette smoke through the speaker, a habit that the caller's crackling voice betrayed.

"Yes, that's me. Who's this?" Gada insisted, realizing that it hadn't been Daniels calling again after all.

"Lieutenant Colonel Margaret Dubois of the DIA. Apologies, I was told you were expecting my call." Dubois started. "I can call back later if now isn't a good time?"

"No, no! It's a perfect time!" Gada reassured her, plopping herself onto a barstool at the breakfast nook. She fiddled with a small succulent plant's leaves. It had been placed at the center of the table for decorative reasons, but its cute plumpness made it almost impossible to resist reaching out to touch it.

"Fantastic!" Dubois enthused, her voice increasing in pitch again. "My department needs to hire a new agent, specifically one that is comfortable with statistical modeling because they'll be working on our supercomputer..."

"What? That's really a thing?" Gada interjected, nearly falling off of her perch as she recoiled in surprise.

"Sure is," Dubois bragged. "Do you want to come over and see it yourself?"

"Does a shark live in water?" Gada joked. "I would love nothing more!"

"That's what I want to hear!" Dubois cheered. "Come around to our offices tomorrow; we'll have a chat about the position and I'll show you the computer."

"I don't know what to say," Gada humbly replied, swivelling around on the barstool. "I'm so honored that you'd consider me as a candidate! What time should I be there tomorrow?"

"Be here at about 10 am, but no earlier. I don't come to the office before 10 am—mornings are horrible, aren't they? I can't stand them. Anyway, I consider anyone that Cuomo recommends to be a serious candidate," Dubois admitted. "Living by that rule hasn't failed me yet! Plus, I've heard you can't go wrong with an Oxford graduate. Cuomo said you were the best in your class."

"I just hope Cuomo hasn't raised your expectations too much. I'm willing to work my fingers to the bone, but I don't consider myself to be special." Gada hesitantly replied.

"Oh, don't be modest! It's not an attractive quality. See you tomorrow, although not before 10 am! A security escort will meet you at the front desk, so leave anything objectionable at home," Dubois assertively stated before abruptly ending the call, leaving Gada with more questions than answers. She stared at her phone's screen for a while, almost expecting a "Just kidding!" text to pop up.

Gada's internal catastrophizing was interrupted by the real estate agent's loud voice booming through the room. "We're just waiting for your signature, honey!"

"I'm coming!" Gada grumpily replied. She disliked being shouted at, even when it was just because the other person was in a different room. *Military life... I'll have to get used to being screamed at again. Guess there's no time like the present,* Gada contemplated, striding toward the small bookshelf-lined room to rent the apartment of her dreams. She scooped a fountain pen up off of the windowsill and signed her large curly signature at the bottom of the last page of the contract. *Things can't get better than this,* she thought.

Mike insisted on going with Gada to Joint Base Anacostia–Bolling to meet Dubois the next day. She was thankful that he'd inserted himself into her job interview plans, although she'd never admit it. She always felt calmer and more collected around him. His happy-go-lucky attitude was infectious, and if you weren't careful, he'd manage to convince you that the point of living life was to enjoy it. His mysterious serotonin-inducing powers were the least of Gada's worries. Her mind was far too occupied with thoughts of what she'd say to Dubois. She wanted to sound confident, but didn't want to brag. *Can you mention your doctoral degree without sounding like you're a pretentious braggart?* Gada wondered. *Probably not,* she concluded, *but I'm going to do it anyway. I worked way too hard for that thing to not mention it.*

The DIA's offices were located in an imposing red brick building with a white plaster entrance marked by a series of Roman marble columns at the heart of Joint Base Anacostia–Bolling. The building was a landmark to the landscape, surrounded by nothing but wide sidewalks and the occasional sapling. Gada noticed that the double doors leading into it were open as they cautiously approached it, revealing its bustling interior. People from all walks of life were dashing around on the first floor, each looking more hurried and nervous than the last. "Please, step to this side," an armed guard said as they approached it, stepping over the door's threshold to meet them. His one hand was clamped around a handheld metal detector, while the other was clutching a silent two-way radio. Mike and Gada complied and soon found themselves being herded through an x-ray machine just on the other side of the entryway, all under the careful watch of their new armed friend. "What is your business here today?" the guard asked sternly, squinting at Mike as he stumbled through the humming detection device.

"I'm here to meet Lieutenant Colonel Dubois," Gada answered in her best military voice, straightening her back and puffing out her chest in an attempt to cultivate a self-assured demeanor. "This is my escort, Mike. He's here to ensure my safety," she explained, motioning toward her fiancé. Mike waved back awkwardly in reply.

"A safety escort? And what exactly do you think might happen while you're here that you'll need a safety escort?" the guard frowned, shaking his head at the nervous pair.

"Better safe than sorry?" Gada coyly suggested, batting her eyelashes at him in the hope that he'd be convinced of her innocence.

"Fine. Wait here; he'll need additional clearance," the guard angrily muttered before stomping toward a hallway to one side of the machine, leaving the couple under the careful watch of an even more heavily armed guard that he had summoned from the building's threshold. After what felt like an eternity, he finally returned, clutching two identification cards in the hand that once wielded nothing but a two-way radio. "You'll need these to access the parts of the building where you're headed," he growled, shoving one into each of their hands. "Please, follow me."

"You'd think they'd have better security here," Mike sarcastically whispered as the three of them set out at a slow amble across the building's busy foyer.

"Shh! I need to focus on not getting lost in the crowd, I can't see the other end of the room with all of these people moving around in here," Gada pleaded, grasping at his hand as she struggled not to be consumed by the throng of DIA employees flooding the room.

"Relax. You're stressing yourself out over nothing," Mike reassured her, gently squeezing her hand.

"This is the reception desk," the guard stated as they made their way to the furthest point of the foyer. "Please leave your phones in one of the Faraday cages provided." A petite Asian woman with short spiky black hair stood motionless behind the reception desk's counter. She seemed to be searching for someone in the crowd, or perhaps she was simply daydreaming of better days in better places.

"Excuse me, ma'am," Gada said. "Will you keep an eye on our phones while we're away? I don't know what I'd do if mine went missing. All of my personal information is on it," she chuckled as she slipped their phones into two open cages meticulously lined up on the wooden countertop.

The receptionist shook her head as if to force herself to wake from a terrible nightmare. "Apologies," she said, fiddling with her name tag. "I lost myself for a second there. Sure, I'll keep them safe. I'm going to store them in a safe under the counter until you get back," she smiled, quickly whipping the Faraday cages out of view. "The cages will only disrupt your phones' ability to receive or transmit communications until they're removed from them. They'll be in perfect working condition upon their return to you."

"Perfect," Gada nodded, rhythmically tapping her long manicured fingernails on the counter's surface, a habit she had inherited from her mother and unconsciously fell into whenever she was nervous. "This man is escorting us, but I'm here to meet Dubois about the vacancy. She is expecting me. She phoned me yesterday—"

"Oh, you must be Miss Deere?" the receptionist asked, typing away at the keyboard in front of her. "Don't let Frank scare you. He's like this to all of the new visitors he has to escort," she said, squinting at the armed guard standing motionless behind Mike and Gada.

"Yes, that's me," Gada confirmed, nervously smiling. "Glad to know everyone gets a warm welcome like this."

"I'm not here to meet anyone! Just here for moral support!" Mike enthusiastically chipped in, poking his head in between Gada and the reception desk.

"Hmm. She did tell me she was expecting you. You can head straight up to her office. It's on the second floor. Frank will take you there and leave you at the door. Knock before going in. She hates being barged in on. Trust me; nobody knows that better than I do," the receptionist giggled, an odd twinkle suddenly glinting in her eyes. Gada recognized it as a what could only be an expression of mischievousness. *What mischief could a senior officer of the DIA get up to with a receptionist?* she wondered, trying to analyze the situation.

"You heard the lady," Mike boomed, hooking his arm into Gada's. "Let's go, Frank! Thank you, kind receptionist!" he jokingly exclaimed as he pulled Gada toward the guard who was already making his way toward one of the hallways that snaked off from the main foyer.

Frank halted almost immediately after scaling the only flight of stairs Gada had seen in the entire building and motioned toward an office on their left. Mike and Gada found themselves standing in front of a door with a golden plaque on it that read: "Lieutenant Colonel Dubois."

"This is the place," Gada anxiously chuckled, pulling Mike closer.

"I'll be waiting at the end of the hallway when you're ready to leave again," Frank said, turning on his heel and marching back in the direction of the staircase they had just ascended.

"Well, what are you waiting for? Go ahead and knock. Let's see what this Dubois woman is like," Mike encouragingly advised, pushing Gada toward the door.

"I just hope we're not interrupting," Gada mumbled as she hesitantly rapped her knuckles three times against the wooden doorframe. "She might not even be here yet. It's only 10:10 am."

"Come in!" a raspy voice commanded from inside of the office. "The door's unlocked. Just open it!"

"Sounds delightful," Mike frowned, turning the doorknob for Gada, who stood stock-still as if frozen in time. The creaking of the opening door forced her to snap out of it. She strode forward, trying to look as confident as humanly possible.

"What do you want?" a figure seated with her back toward them asked.

"Umm. I'm Gada Deere. I was told to meet Lieutenant Colonel Margaret Dubois here today." Gada enquired shyly, stopped in her tracks by the figure's apparent hostility.

"Gada, my dear!" the figure shouted, her mien changed within a matter of milliseconds. She swiveled around in her chair before leaping out of it and marching toward Mike and Gada. *What an incredibly muscular woman,* Gada observed as she drew closer. *She could probably put Mike in a headlock.* Dubois was not only remarkably muscular, she was also taller than most men are. She had short bright blond hair that she gelled flat and parted in the middle. Her piercing blue eyes seemed to drink up every inch of Gada before she continued. "I'm delighted you could make it today. We'd love it if you'd consider joining us here—"

"I'd love to become a part of the team," Gada promptly replied, pulling out a heavy wooden chair from behind Dubois's desk as she tried to feign an air of self-confidence. Mike mimicked her, and soon they were both sitting facing the most intimidating woman either of them had ever met.

"And who are you?" Dubois enquired, squinting at Mike.

"Oh, I'm just here to make sure Gada's safe. I'm Mike, her fiancé," he blushed, trying to sink away into the chair's dark brown leather padding.

"More like her lackey," Dubois laughed, taking a mint from a jar on her desk and popping it into her unusually large mouth. Everything about her seemed to be bigger than life. "You've tamed him well, Miss Deere. Good job."

"Umm... thank you?" Gada responded coyly, apologetically glancing at Mike, who was now thoroughly embarrassed. "So, you said something about needing a supercomputer operator for your department. Is that the position you're considering me for?" she asked, trying to steer the conversation away from her bright crimson fiancé.

"Why yes, it is, more or less, anyway. Cuomo told me you likely haven't used one before, but your field of study lends itself to the kind of quantum computing that my department needs. Our supercomputer can do pretty much anything from determining the likelihood of an imminent terrorist attack to helping us locate enemies of the state. Still, it needs someone competent to operate it. That's where you come in," Dubois explained, using one of her stubby fingers to push her thick-rimmed glasses back up the bridge of her nose.

"You'd need to teach me how to use it. I'm very comfortable with the theory behind quantum computing, but as Cuomo said, I haven't had any practical experience. I'm an eager learner though, and a fast one too," Gada confidently stated, leaning back in her chair and propping her thin forearms up on its armrests.

"Oh, no need to convince me, Miss Deere! You've already got the job. I just want to show you around a bit. Would you be comfortable starting at the beginning of the third week of the month? That's when the vacancy officially opens up. I'm still waiting for payroll authorization," Dubois carefully explained, clearly frustrated with the bureaucracy that she found herself in.

"That's perfect," Gada grinned, suddenly sitting upright in her chair. She appeared to grow four inches within a matter of seconds. "We've just leased an apartment on twenty-first. We're moving in at the beginning of next month, so that gives me a bit of time to unpack before I get started here. Mike won't be able to take a couple of days off from work, so I'll be tackling the task of getting the house ready myself."

"Oh, so this isn't your house-husband?" Dubois asked, raising a single eyebrow as she dismissively gestured at Mike.

"Who? Mike?" Gada asked confusedly. "No, not yet! He's an engineer. He works on a lot of important projects for some of the world's most influential mining companies. It really is quite a prestigious—"

"Best not to dilly dally," Dubois interrupted, getting up and pushing her chair halfway across the room as she did. "Come, I'd like to show you around the building before you leave. Not all of it, of course. Just the most important parts." She didn't wait for a reply. Instead, she quickly marched out of her office and proceeded down the hallway toward the staircase.

Mike and Gada looked at each other skeptically before pulling themselves away from their comfortable seats to follow her. They caught up to her about halfway down the hallway, the sound of their footsteps sprinting across the floor somewhat muffled by the elaborately patterned carpet.

"Where are we headed?" Gada inquired, matching her stride with Dubois'.

"To the supercomputer room. It's in the basement," Dubois answered bluntly. "This floor is for the offices of department heads and their most valued assistants. I doubt you'll be spending much time here as you'll likely be spending most of your day working on the supercomputer, although you'll have an office on this floor close to mine to store any files or paperwork you might have in. It won't be anything fancy, mind you, but you'll have your own desk and some privacy when you need it."

"I really don't mind," Gada replied. Mike silently followed, close on her heel.

"Here we are," Dubois said, stopping in her tracks and pointing toward a bookshelf just opposite the staircase leading toward the first floor.

"A bookshelf?" Mike asked, panting from the brisk walk he had to maintain to keep up with Gada and the Lieutenant Colonel.

"No, not a bookshelf," Dubois answered, rolling her eyes. She stepped forward and gave the bookshelf's wooden frame a decisive shove. It quietly slid to the side, clearly moving on some type of well-hidden track. A pair of sliding elevator doors appeared behind it as it rolled out of the way. Dubois pushed a glowing button mounted on the wall. Within a few seconds, the doors opened, revealing a modest elevator with a stunningly shiny metallic interior. "Guests first," Dubois smiled, flashing her cigarette-stained teeth at the anxiously waiting pair.

Gada was the first to comply. She nervously stepped forward onto the reflective metallic surface that made up the elevator's floor. Mike followed her, ostensibly waiting to see whether it was safe before taking the leap. Once they were both inside, Dubois stepped in too and closed the doors with another quick push of a glowing button located inside the steel box. Gada barely had a chance to gather her thoughts before the elevator started descending into the building's maw, traveling at a surprising speed. She held onto a railing on one of the elevator's walls, trying to steady herself.

"This is the fastest elevator in the world," Dubois bragged, examining her rugged reflection in the shiny wall. "This building's basement is located about a mile under the Earth's surface. The journey should only take us a couple of seconds."

She wasn't wrong. A moment later, the elevator pinged, and its reflective doors slid open. The "basement" resembled another formal floor of the DIA building, although it was notably darker due to its lack of windows. Gada, Mike, and Dubois stumbled out into the darkness. Gada's eyes took a moment to adjust to the change of lighting, but once they did, she saw a lavishly decorated hallway stretching out in front of her. It wasn't your typical hallway. It was empty except for a number of oil paintings hanging from its walls. Each had an exotic pot plant placed strategically below it. *Seems odd to decorate a top-secret floor*, Gada thought. *I doubt very many people ever get the opportunity to see this place.* The hallway would have been entirely pointless had it not been for the heavily secured iron door at the end of it.

"Is that the computing room?" Gada asked, rubbing at her eyes.

"Sure is," Dubois proudly beamed, swinging her arm forward like an orchestra conductor. "The door leading into the super-computing room is heavily secured. You need biometric access to get in, and it's completely impervious to blasts and most other types of tampering. I'll make sure your fingerprints are uploaded to the biometric system before you get started, Gada."

"Thank you, Lieutenant Colonel. I don't think I've ever been trusted with such an important task before," Gada admitted, jogging to keep up with Dubois, who was practically running toward the reinforced door. Its locks clicked open one by one as Dubois presented her thumb to the biometric scanner located to the left of the door. It swung open, revealing a number of servers mounted on the walls. The room was dark and larger than one would imagine. A computer screen and keyboard on a small desk eerily inhabited the center of the room. "Who are those people?" Gada inquired, motioning toward four figures scrambling around the multiple servers. The room was filled with the incessant sound of computer cooling fans.

"Those are your technicians. They're responsible for controlling data streams, power consumption, and they keep the servers' temperatures in check...and that's it. Our wonderful supercomputer," Dubois grinned, an expression of unfiltered excitement momentarily flashed across her ordinarily stern face as she motioned toward the screen in the center of the room. "That's where all of the magic happens. It's the only supercomputer in the building. We call it Sandy. Supercomputers don't usually get names, but one of its previous operators dubbed it that and, well, it just kind of stuck."

"I think Sandy is a lovely name," Gada giggled, twirling a loose lock of her dark brown hair around her index finger as she craned her neck to get a better look at the device. "Rolls off of the tongue in comparison to 'supercomputer.'"

"Sure does," Dubois said, fondly smiling at it. "We're very proud of her. Just wish we'd be given a grant to get a quantum computer like the CIA has, but that's a complaint for another day. Anyway, we'll see you on March 15 then?"

"Yes, ma'am," Gada replied, saluting the Lieutenant Colonel, a military habit she was unsure she'd ever be able to break free of entirely. She immediately wished she'd negotiated a later start date, but in the moment, she simply didn't have the courage to do it. *March 15 will have to do*, she thought, staring into Sandy's mirror-like black screen, *and March 20, Mike and I will finally say "I do."*

***

March 15 fell on a chilly Monday, it was 40 degrees Fahrenheit outside, but Gada could have sworn it was at least 100 degrees in their bedroom. Their new apartment was perfect in many ways, but the central heating system had already caused a few spats between her and Mike. Mike preferred a relatively toasty setting, while Gada's time in London had imbibed her with a love for cooler temperatures. She rolled out of their king-sized bed and scrambled to her feet. Mike had already left for work. He was gone before the sun came up most mornings. *Probably doing fieldwork again today*, Gada thought, staring at the indentation his muscular body had left in their mattress. *He said something about a site inspection yesterday.*

Gada started every morning with a lukewarm shower and a piping hot cup of coffee, but this morning was different. The shower's water felt like tiny pebbles pelting her skin, and the sound of the water splashing was grating rather than relaxing. Her cup of coffee smelled terrible and tasted even worse; the first sip of it caused her to gag. No amount of sugar seemed to be able to coat its innate bitterness. Eventually, she gave up, leaving her steaming half-full cup on the kitchen counter. Her coat seemed to fit too tightly as she grabbed it off of the coat rack and wrapped it around her body. Its material felt coarser than she remembered. *Must be nerves*, she thought as she locked the apartment's front door behind her. *Who wouldn't be nervous on their first day as a DIA employee... Hey, am I like a secret agent now? Focus, Gada!* she corrected herself. *There will be time for daydreaming yet, but that time is not now.*

Mike had left the SUV so that Gada could drive it to work. Fortunately, it wasn't parked more than half a block away from the Poto-Pine Apartment Building in a garage they paid far too much for every month. Gada's legs were heavy as she clumsily trudged toward it, leaning into the wind as it battered her wavy brown locks against her face. She imagined she knew how mountaineers felt when they reached Mount Everest's summit when she finally got to the garage and stumbled toward the end of it to reach SUV's driver-side door—whipping it open and leaping inside to escape the morning's frosty bite. For a moment, she regretted that she'd ever complained about the apartment being too warm. She certainly wouldn't say no to 100 degrees Fahrenheit in comparison to the ice-laced breeze that was currently angrily cutting through Twenty-First Street.

Gada didn't bother switching the car's stereo on. She spent the ride to Joint Base Anacostia–Bolling anxiously wondering what her first day would be like. A wave of queasiness washed over her, threatening to drag her under as she pulled up to the looming red brick building. She found her assigned parking space without too much trouble but was disheartened to realize it was a fair distance from the building's entrance. Her shaking hands made gripping the steering wheel difficult. *Breathe, Gada!* she reprimanded herself, parking and pulling up the handbrake. *In, out, in, out,* she recited, trying to keep her breathing steady and even. *You're bigger than your anxiety!*

She aggressively shoved the SUV's door open and leaned out. The world threatened to collapse in on itself and her vision blurred at the edges. Before she could stop herself, she was violently puking all over the parking lot's spotless black tar. She heaved until nothing came out except for a pitiful groan. *What was that?* She wondered, straightening her back and digging through her handbag to find something to wipe her mouth with. She came up empty-handed and reluctantly settled for using the back of her hand. She hurried away from the scene of the crime, hoping nobody would associate her with it.

Gada didn't bother chatting to the security guards as she made her way through their multiple scans. Instead, she opted to head straight up toward Lieutenant Colonel Dubois's office without saying anything but a couple of words to answer the guards' routine questions. The Dubois's office door was slightly ajar. *I hope I'm not too early,* she nervously thought. "Lieutenant Colonel?" she called. "Are you in?"

"I'm here!" a reply came from inside the office. "Don't be shy!"

Gada pushed the door open and stepped inside. Dubois was seated behind her desk, hunched over in front of her computer screen. She was dressed in a dark gray three-piece suit, and her hair was parted midway in its signature style. She looked up at Gada. Her blue eyes looked colder than they did before. "You're not pregnant, are you?" she asked bluntly.

"What? Why? No!" Gada replied, gawking as she tried to answer the unexpected question.

"It's just that I like to watch the building's security cameras when I get here early. Good to know how your employees start their days. That's what I believe anyway. I saw you hurling chunks next to your car: Are you pregnant or ill?"

My cycle is a little late this month... Gada realized, a sense of dread filling the pit of her stomach like a boulder made out of corporeal anxiety. Everything suddenly made sense: Her bitter coffee, her uncomfortable shower, their overly hot bedroom.

"No, it's nothing like that," she lied. "To be honest, I'm just a little nervous."

"Do you always vomit when you're nervous?" Dubois grimaced, pulling herself away from the screen long enough to frown at her new recruit. "This is a high-pressure environment, so if this is a common thing for you—"

"I promise, it's not," Gada swore, drawing a cross on her chest with her index finger in an attempt to show the solemnity of her vow. "I usually work well under pressure. I won't make a habit out of being sick in the parking lot."

"Good. I don't have the stomach for bodily excretions," Dubois admitted, getting up from behind her desk and making her way toward Gada, who was still shivering like a leaf. "There's no reason to be nervous. Nobody messes with my agents. I won't let them."

"Thank you, Lieutenant Colonel," Gada blushed, unconsciously resting her hand on her stomach.

Dubois's suspicion awoke an entirely new series of anxieties inside of Gada, driving her to spend her lunch hour commuting to and from the pharmacy to purchase a pregnancy test. She took it out of its box in the parking lot in front of the DIA's offices. She didn't want to risk trying to smuggle it into the building in its bulky packaging. Instead, she slipped it into her coat's pocket and stealthily slinked toward the restrooms near the reception desk, avoiding making eye contact with the receptionist as she passed.

Once inside an empty cubicle, she double-checked the sliding lock on the door and set about utilizing her test. *How am I supposed to not pee on my hand?* She wondered as she wriggled around on the toilet seat. She couldn't bear to look at the results' screen immediately after. *The box says to wait at least five minutes before checking the results to get an accurate reading*, she told herself. *No point in looking at it earlier and freaking myself out over nothing.* She set a timer on her phone for six minutes and tried to pass the time by playing a game of Tetris. *Amazing how far technology has come*, she told herself as "Level 53!" flashed across her cellphone's screen.

It wasn't long before her timer's shrill ringing filled the restroom and reverberated through the narrow cubicle. *No delaying it anymore*, she thought, reaching for the pregnancy test that she'd placed on top of the toilet paper dispenser.

Two lines.

I'm pregnant, she gulped. *I'm pregnant, getting married in five days, and I've just started working for the DIA. Dubois was wrong; I do have reason to be nervous.*

***

The morning of the wedding rolled around sooner than Gada felt prepared for. She hadn't told Mike about her positive test yet, but she knew he had his suspicions. Anyone with two brain cells would after she'd spent the last couple of mornings hunched over the toilet bowl. The evenings weren't much better. She wasn't nauseous after work, but she was absolutely exhausted. She struggled to stay awake to have dinner with Mike, something she felt rather guilty about because she knew that it had always been his favorite part of the day. She hoped he'd be excited about the little surprise growing inside of her, but she was scared to tell him nonetheless.

"Picked up a little weight, dear," the old lady who had made her dress remarked as she started lacing its corset up. Gada was standing on a wooden pedestal in the center of the vineyard-themed venue's bridal suit. She felt like she was caught in a gelatinous sea of white: Her vintage wedding dress hung limply from her body, the whitewashed walls seemed to be closing in on her, and the room's ivory furnishings served only to punctuate the momentousness of the occasion.

"Janet!" Gada's mom scalded, shoving the seamstress out of the way to take control of the silk laces. "Don't listen to her, honey. You look absolutely beautiful. Like a dream! Like a vision!"

"Thanks mom, but I have been stress eating at work," Gada admitted disheartedly. "I'm not shocked to hear I've gotten a bit bigger."

"You could do with a few extra pounds, if you ask me," her mom tut-tutted, giving the corset's laces one final tug. "You can't look sixteen forever."

"How's Mike doing? Have any of you seen him today?" Gada asked, trying to shift the focus away from her weight.

"I saw him on my way in," Janet added from the corner she'd been banished to. "Willowy-looking fellow. Looked a bit anxious, if you ask me."

"He looked fine to me," Gada's mom interjected. "I'm sure your dad would have called if he looked like he was going to run away or have a panic attack."

"I think I might have a panic attack," Gada mumbled.

"Oh, nonsense! You're going to be fine! Women have been getting married and surviving it for centuries," her mother said reassuringly. "You'll look back on this day, and it'll be one of your fondest memories."

"I certainly hope so," Gada frowned. Her mother fastened a chunky silver necklace's clasp around her neck and checked her earrings.

"Beautiful! Stunning!" her mother cooed as she did a final inspection of Gada's hair and make-up. "You're going to knock that boy's socks off."

Before Gada could catch her breath [or loosen her overly tight corset], she was being herded toward a pearl-colored vintage wedding limo parked in the bridal suit's driveway. Her mother helped her scoop her dress up and shoved it into the vehicle's backseat. The drive to the chapel was brief and filled with nothing but the sound of her mother and Janet, who had somehow wormed her way into the official bridal party, bickering. Gada tried to block it all out and focus on the task at hand. *I just have to make it down the aisle. If I can get to the altar, the hardest part is over*, she told herself.

The limo pulled up in front of an old stone chapel. Its walls were covered in moss and ivy, although a stained glass window was able to peek through here and there. Its large wooden double doors were closed so that the excited guests inside wouldn't see Gada until she was ready to be seen. Her dad was standing to one side of the stone building, twiddling his thumbs and pacing around. He looked up as he heard the car approaching on the narrow gravel path that wound its way to the chapel's entrance.

"See! Everything's fine!" her mother said, pointing at her father, who was now hobbling toward the limo as fast as he could. "Your dad wouldn't be waiting here if Mike had decided to leave you at the altar!"

"That's not what I'm worried about," Gada grumbled, tugging at the door handle as the vehicle came to a stop.

"Your dad has to open it from the outside. Be patient!" her mother warned, swatting her hand away. "If you keep tugging at it like that, you'll break it off! Lord knows how much it would cost to replace."

"Hmph," Gada grunted, furrowing her brow.

Her father dramatically whipped open the door next to her, smiling from ear to ear. "My baby! You look so beautiful, just like your mother!" he beamed. "Are you ready? Are you excited?"

"Stop badgering her! Can't you see she's nervous?" her mother scolded.

"I'm excited too," Gada interjected. "Sometimes being excited feels a lot like being scared."

"Ain't that the truth," her father laughed, hooking her arm into his and leading her toward the chapel's entrance. The double doors slowly creaked open as they approached. The air was filled with the shrill sound of an organ playing the wedding march somewhat off-key. The crowd lining the pews cheered as she stepped over the threshold. Mike, who was already standing in front of the altar with his arms behind his back, spun around in response to the commotion. He appeared to gasp for air as he met her gaze, his eyes filled with tears. *Tears of joy, I hope,* Gada gulped, carefully trying to make her way toward the altar. She clung to her father for support, careful not to fall over her own feet. *Don't trip, don't trip,* she thought. *Not in front of all of these people!*

"You look magical," Mike whispered as her dad handed her off to him before taking a seat in one of the pews closest to the altar. "Like an elven princess."

Gada blushed, unsure how to reply. *An elven princess?* She thought. *I wonder how much he's had to drink.*

"I mean it," he whispered, almost as if he had been able to hear her thoughts.

"We're gathered here today," the preacher behind the pulpit started, halting any possibility of a conversation between Mike and Gada before the ceremony commenced. His sermon passed in what could only be described as a verbal haze. "Do you take this man to be your husband?" the preacher asked, turning his eagle-like gaze to Gada.

"I do," she nodded, biting her lower lip.

"And do you take this woman to be your lawfully wedded wife?" he asked, glancing toward Mike.

"I do," Mike confirmed. He puffed out his chest, and his white linen shirt visibly strained under his thin black tie, threatening to distract Gada from the proceedings.

"Then, you may now kiss the bride!" the preacher solemnly announced, glaring at the nervous couple.

Mike leaned in, Gada followed, and before either of them could catch themselves, they were swept up in a passionate embrace culminating in a Hollywood-esque kiss in front of their closest friends and family.

The preacher cleared his throat. They didn't respond. "That's enough," he said more sternly, using one of his knobbly hands to force them apart.

97

"Sorry," Mike blushed, cheekily smiling at the preacher. "You said I could."

Gada giggled. Mike took her by the hand, turned his back on the sour-faced wedding officiant, and started leading her down the aisle. Gada couldn't imagine being happier than she was in that moment. "I love you," Mike whispered in her ear as they stepped out of the stone chapel and onto the luscious emerald green grass that grew in front of it. "I love you more," she replied, squeezing his hand as they made their way toward the renovated barn they'd opted to host their reception in. It was only about 200 yards away, but it took them a while to navigate the distance as Gada struggled to cross the lawn in her white stilettos.

Gada and Mike were halfway through their first dance when she suddenly worked up the courage to reveal her secret. Mike twirled her around and pulled her back into his arms. She looked up at him with glistening eyes. "I'm pregnant," she whimpered.

"I know, Mrs. Pukes-a-lot," he chuckled, spinning her around in an attempt to hide their conversation from the eager onlookers lining the dancefloor. "I was wondering when you were going to tell me."

"You knew?" she gasped, a single tear running down one of her prominent cheekbones. "Why didn't you say anything?"

"I reckoned you'd tell me when you were ready," he smiled, dipping her before pulling her back toward his broad chest. She could feel his heart racing. "I can't tell you how happy I am. A family of our own!"

"Shh! Don't tell anyone just yet," she grimaced, trying to focus on not trampling on his shiny black leather shoes. "I need some time to come to terms with it before I tell anyone else."

"Come to terms with it?" Mike frowned. "Aren't you excited too?" He notably slowed his pace as they crossed the dancefloor again. There were no more dips or twirls.

"I am," Gada said, biting at her lower lip. "I'm so excited, but I also know that everything's going to change now, and I need some time to deal with it."

"I understand," he said softly, squeezing her against his chest.

The night quickly devolved into an evening of debauchery. The wine flowed, Mike was running around with his groomsmen consuming a copious amount of celebratory cigars, and Gada was no longer certain where all of the stains on her previously perfectly white dress had come from. She found herself sitting at the main table, looking out on the dancefloor like a monarch surveying the reach of her lands. Her family was mingling with Mike's, and some of her new coworkers from the DIA had taken her up on her invitation to attend. She heard a few of them cautiously explaining the work they did at the DIA to other guests. Naturally, they were all bound by stringent non-disclosure agreements, which made discussing their work somewhat tricky. Gada found their vague descriptions of their occupations rather amusing but not nearly as funny as the breakdance that Cuomo was attempting at the center of the dancefloor.

Gada smiled. *Everything will be alright,* she thought, gently resting her hand on her stomach. *It has to be.* "I wonder what you'll be like," Gada discreetly whispered to her tiny little bump. "Will you be rambunctious but a little awkward like your daddy, or will you be like me?" She remembered a psychology class she took during her undergraduate degree and the paper she had written on nature versus nurture in childrearing and wondered whether any of it would be of any use to her once she was holding her own baby in her arms. "I can't wait to meet you."

Chapter 4: Chromosome 2

"Are you ready for your first assignment?" Lieutenant Colonel Dubois asked, comically swiveling around on her office chair. Gada could see that she was excited to share whatever the assignment was, but she couldn't fight the sense of dread that was slowly creeping into her thoughts.

"I am," she replied, trying to push the doubt from her mind.

"Oh! I've got a real doozy for you! I'd take it on myself if using that darn supercomputer didn't make my head hurt. So, if you've been following any mainstream news outlets, I'm sure you've heard that several scientists have died under mysterious circumstances. The newsrooms are reporting that eleven have lost their lives, but it's actually more like fifty-seven—"

"Fifty-seven?" Gada interjected, noticeably taken aback. "What did they die from?"

"Well, that's what you have to figure out, isn't it? Along with who did it, of course. The deaths are far too suspicious to be coincidental. Someone has to be behind them, and that someone is considered to be a threat to the USA, which is where we come in. We're going to find this scientist-killer and bring them to justice," Dubois passionately stated, slamming her fist on the desk to punctuate her sentiment.

"You must have some idea of what happened to them?" Gada frowned, fiddling with the DIA identification card that hung around her neck like some kind of talisman. "I'm just curious as to what ultimately befell the victims. I want to know what I'm getting into before I dive in headfirst. I'm sure you understand." She glanced down at her growing stomach and back up at Dubois.

"You can't expect me to remember what happened to all fifty-seven of them," Dubois sighed, raising one of her eyebrows to grimace skeptically at Gada. "Here, take the file." She pulled a large manila envelope out of one of the drawers in her desk and handed it to her. "I know one of them drowned while swimming at a hotel she was staying at. Naturally, nobody saw what happened. If I remember correctly, one accidentally hanged himself in his cupboard."

"Accidentally hanged himself?" Gada spoke breathlessly, taking the heavy envelope. It was cool to the touch and had "CLASSIFIED" sprawled across it in thick red lettering. "Sounds pretty morbid."

"Oh, it is, but I'm sure you'll love it. You'll have the supercomputer at your disposal too. It should make things easier," Dubois smiled encouragingly. "Now, you've got lots of work to do, and so do I. I'll see you during lunch. Are you having lunch with me again today? I hate taking it alone, and you know these bastards don't care much for me."

"Everybody here loves you; you know that. You're the Big Kahuna around here, but I promise I'll swing around again at noon," Gada said, trying to sound as sincere as possible. She did have a soft spot for Dubois, and clearly, Dubois considered her a confidante as well. *Relaxing with one's boss always comes with a bit of peril,* Gada contemplated. *At the very least, the other agents will think I'm a brown-noser, but what am I to do? She's clearly lonely, and I'm not a monster.*

Gada waddled out of the door with a final wave of the hand and headed over to her desk. The manila envelope was tightly clenched in her fist. Dubois had kicked a junior officer out of a corner office to give it to her. It wasn't much as far as corner offices went. It certainly wasn't designed with the CEO in mind, but it was more than enough to meet Gada's needs. She had already made it her own. Her desk was covered in framed photos of Mike and her parents. She'd hung a motivational quote on her wall, and she'd acquired a large fern to decorate the room's darkest corner. She had just sat down in the plush red chair behind her computer when there was an unexpected knock on the door. "Come in!" she yelled, craning her neck in an attempt to see who it was.

"Sorry, ma'am. Lieutenant Colonel Dubois sent me. I'm from maintenance," he said, "I need to replace the plaque on your door. Are you busy? Do you mind if I quickly get it done?" the handsome young man at the door asked in a thick Spanish accent.

"Sure! You're welcome to do it whenever you'd like. If you'd like to do it now, you're welcome to do it now," Gada gently smiled from behind her desk. "I hope you don't mind if I don't get up to greet you. My ankles are a little swollen and sore."

"Don't worry; I won't take it personally. My wife had the same problem before our daughter was born. She spent most of the last month in bed. It was difficult on all of us, but it was worth it in the end," the young man grinned, removing a hammer from his tool belt and aggressively using the back of it to pluck the existing plaque out of the door's wood.

"Sounds like your wife is one tough lady," Gada replied sympathetically. "Say, what's your name? I don't think I've met you before. I'm Gada Corey."

"I know who you are," the young man cheekily smiled, pointing to the new plaque that he was preparing to nail into the door. "Says so right here! I'm Mateo de Wahl, but you can just call me Mat. I know Mateo is a mouthful."

"Mateo is a lovely name. You shouldn't be ashamed of it. I'm sure your mom put a lot of effort into picking it out," Gada half-scolded, furrowing her brow to emphasize the seriousness of her sentiment. "I'd hate it if my little one grew up shy of his name."

"It's a boy?" Mateo asked as he proceeded to hammer a nail through one of the plaque's corners. "You must be excited."

"Well, the scans say so. I certainly hope he's a boy. Otherwise, she'll be a girl with a dinosaur-themed nursery. My husband has already painted it out. We are pretty excited, although I'm not particularly looking forward to the actual labor part," Gada grimaced, reclining in her chair to shift the weight off of her tired back.

"My wife said you forget about the labor the minute you get to hold your baby," Mateo nonchalantly replied, examining his work. "Maybe it'll be the same for you?"

"Maybe," Gada replied, opening the envelope she had received from Dubois to start studying its contents. "Why did the Lieutenant Colonel ask you to put a new plaque up? I thought the old was fine."

"It says 'Captain Gada Corey' instead of 'Second Lieutenant Gada Corey,'" he replied, hooking all of his tools back onto his belt. "You know, I've seen a few people come through here. I've been working in maintenance since I was eighteen, and you're the first person to work here that managed to skip the rank of First Lieutenant entirely. You must be something special."

"I don't know about that," Gada laughed nasally, trying to keep her composure as she started paging through some of the crime scene photographs that had been inside of the envelope. She made sure not to let her expression betray the gruesomeness of the evidence in front of her, but Mateo managed to notice the change in her demeanor anyway.

"Some of the things that come across your desk must be pretty hard to look at," he remarked, still hovering in the doorframe. Gada thought he looked concerned more than curious, so decided not to turn him away entirely.

"Yeah, some of it is horrific. I try not to let it bother me. Naturally, I can't discuss any of it in detail... non-disclosure agreements and all," she sympathetically replied.

"Naturally. Anyway, it was nice chatting with you, Captain Corey. Not many agents acknowledge me, let alone ask me for my name," Mateo grinned, patting the door frame as he prepared to leave.

"Hey, why don't you come have lunch with me at noon? I'm having it with Dubois in the smoking area on this floor. You're welcome to join us," Gada offered while her stare remained locked on the file she was scrolling through. "I'm really sorry to hear the other agents haven't been treating you kindly," sympathizing as she looked up, momentarily putting the envelope and its mysterious contents down.

"I'm flattered, Captain Corey. I'll definitely consider it," Mateo grinned, revealing a dazzling white smile. "Well, I've got to be going before I get written up for taking too long. I'll see you around."

Mateo closed the door on his way out, leaving Gada alone with her thoughts and the somewhat nightmarish envelope that Dubois had handed her. She hadn't had time to do more than a preliminary review of some of the materials inside, but what

105

she'd seen had been enough to convince her that whatever was behind these mysterious deaths couldn't be described as anything other than pure evil. She steeled herself as she opened the secured envelope again and poured its contents onto her table. Photos and police reports went flying. Some slipped off of the desk's edge while others wedged themselves between her precious photo frames. She sighed. *I should have known this wouldn't be easy.*

She flipped over the report that landed closest to her and started reading through it. "Male, age 65," it read. "Cause of death: Murder-suicide." *The report says he killed his wife and three young daughters before drowning himself in the bath.* She tried to imagine how the event unfolded. *Seems unrealistic*, she concluded.

The following report that she opened up wasn't any better. "Female, 34," it read. "Cause of death: Natural." *This one died... of a heart attack? That can't be right*, Gada thought. *It says here she didn't have a medical history of cardiac problems or any pre-existing conditions that would have put her at risk. Who the hell signed off on this death certificate?*

By the sixth coroner's report that she examined, a pattern started emerging. *They're all microbiologists*, she realized. *Hmmm... that's what connects all of them.*

That night, she and Mike spent the evening reading next to the modern stone fireplace in their television room. She was rereading an old fictional crime mystery novel she left by the coffee table, and he was reading a mining journal. It was blissful, but Gada had far too many questions swimming around her mind to appreciate it fully.

"Do you remember, just before we rented this place, the local news kept doing reports on scientists who died under mysterious conditions? They must have mentioned it during every broadcast," Gada asked, loudly turning one of her book's pages.

"I sure do. There were eleven of them. If I remember correctly, Interpol was looking into it, right?" Mike inquired, lazily popping a plump grape into his mouth. He reached for another from the fruit bowl on the coffee table. "Why do you ask? Seems like a strange time to bring it up."

"You know how bad I am at leaving work at work," Gada blushed, closing her book and placing it on the couch next to her. "Do you mind if I bounce something off of you? You have to promise to keep it secret, though. I'm not supposed to be discussing any of this with anyone outside of the DIA."

"Have I ever not kept one of your secrets?" Mike frowned, abandoning his grapes in favor of giving the conversation his full attention. "Now, out with it! I'm dying of curiosity."

"Fine, fine," Gada conceded, shifting her weight forward until she was sitting at the edge of her seat. "I've just been assigned to an investigation involving those deaths, and I'm feeling a little overwhelmed. Looking at all of them, it is apparent that it's impossible that they were all coincidental. Some of them were really bizarre too, Mike. There are coroners' reports that claim numerous people accidentally hung themselves or drowned themselves on purpose. More than one murder-suicide that involved claims that the scientist in question killed their entire family before taking their own life. It's just really fishy."

"Wow, that does sound suspicious," Mike agreed, a flash of worry panning across his face. He rubbed at the thick patch of stubble growing on his chin. "So, what do you need help with?"

"Well, I've managed to put two and two together, and the common denominator is that all of these scientists were microbiologists. I did a quick internet search on most of them, and some were involved in developing biological weapons or defenses against biological weapons. Still, there were simply not enough of them that fell into this category to mark it as another common denominator. What baffles me is this. I can't seem to figure out what connects them all other than their occupations, and for the life of me, I can't imagine why someone would want to kill any of them."

"I'm pretty up to date with the latest developments in the scientific world. I like to read research journals while I'm waiting to see clients. Do you remember any of their names? Might help me to remember whether I read anything about their research recently," Mike replied in a deadpan tone.

"Sure do," Gada smiled, quite proud of herself for having committed the names of the victims to memory. It humanized them to her. She started rattling off a list of surnames, and watched as Mike's eyes grew wider and wider the further she got down the list. "What is it, Mike? I can see you know something that I don't. Out with it!"

"I can't say for sure, but I do remember reading a recent article in a scientific journal that contained a fair number of those names. If I remember correctly, they were all conducting research on Chromosome 2," he answered. Gada could hear the concern in his voice.

"Chromosome 2?" she asked, raising one of her thick brown eyebrows. "I feel terrible for having to ask, but what's that?"

"Don't feel bad. Most people don't know what it is. I didn't either until I read about it. It's complicated, so I won't lie and say I understand it in its entirety. Still, I think I have a pretty good idea regarding its most basic principles," Mike started monologuing. Gada could feel her eyes glazing over.

"Mike, baby, I love you, but please don't get boring on me. Short, sweet, and to the point? You know I find biology tedious," Gada giggled, picking a grape out of the fruit bowl and catapulting it playfully at her husband's head.

"It's nicknamed *The Creation Gene* by a small circle of scientists. I guess it's some kind of allegory to one of MichaelAngelo's famous paintings," he whispered, as he looked over his shoulder as if strangers were listening in close by. "Well, in most people, Chromosome 2 is fused, meaning that they have a total of forty-six chromosomes. In rare cases, Chromosome 2 is unfused, leaving the individual with forty-eight chromosomes. A recent study of the human genome revealed that our ancient ancestors didn't have fused Chromosome 2's in their DNA, proving that they came into existence because of the end-to-end fusion of two ancestral human chromosomes. Scientists aren't really sure what that means yet. However, the universities are planning to incorporate information on it into their genetics courses by describing that this DNA adaptation may have come into existence through the process of genetic evolution," Mike rambled on, excitedly spewing a volley of facts that he'd clearly gone through some effort to memorize.

"Mike," Gada interrupted. "I get that it's a weird genetic change that biologists might swoon over in their spare time, but why is it significant?"

"I can't say with any amount of certainty that it is," Mike concluded, picking up his magazine again as he gradually brought up his tone back up to normal. "But it might be another common denominator. I'm almost certain that all of the scientists who you named had participated in the study."

"Thanks, Mike," Gada said, getting up to wrap her arms around him. "Sometimes, I think you might be smarter than I am."

"Really?" Mike asked, grinning up at her.

"Yeah, but it normally only lasts a minute or two," Gada loudly laughed, ruffling his hair.

The next morning, she skipped breakfast, heading up to her office with a determination and hope of advancing the case. She quickly greeted Dubois and then headed straight to the basement. Riding the world's fastest elevator down to it never got tiring, but the dark hallway at the end of the elevator ride never became any less creepy either. The supercomputer at the other side of the biometrically accessed door seemed to be waiting for her by the time she got to it. The technicians all nervously greeted her, but she didn't have it in her to offer them much more than a smile and a coy "hello." The supercomputer's screen emitted an eerie glow in the otherwise dominating darkness. She entered her username and password. The words "Welcome Captain Corey" flashed across its screen in bright green text. *Dubois is really on the ball,* she thought. *Plaque and computer login updated with my new title already. She clearly made sure that a number of different departments prioritized this change. I wonder why?*

"Are you going to be long?" a voice squeaked, startling Gada. She looked up, momentarily blinded by the screen's bright light. As her eyes started adjusting to the darkness again, she saw a figure standing just inside of the doorway. It appeared to be female and was a full head or two shorter than Gada was (and at least three heads shorter than Dubois).

"Umm, hi. Yeah, I might be a while. Sorry, I don't think we've formally met. I'm Captain Gada Corey from the Department of Analytics. I work with Dubois..." Gada started, anxiously locking the computer's screen. She was unsure what to expect from the unexpected visitor. *As far as I know, only a handful of people are allowed down here, and I could have sworn I met all of them already.*

The figure took a couple of steps closer to Gada, revealing herself to be the Asian-American receptionist who staffed the front desk. "Apologies, I didn't mean to scare you. I'm Jane from reception; I think we've met before. Maggie sent me down here to find out whether you'd like some coffee. I'm going on a Starbucks run. She said you'd probably need it if you were going to spend the day down here."

"Maggie?" Gada asked, furrowing her brow as she tried to recall who that might be.

"Lieutenant Colonel Margaret Dubois? Your boss? My girlfriend? I'm sure you know her," Jane chuckled, running her hand over her spiky black hair. "I'm sorry if I'm overstepping a boundary. I just thought I'd extend a hand of friendship, considering Maggie sees you as a close chum. I like to think any friend of hers is a friend of mine."

"Your girlfriend?" Gada asked. Her expression betrayed her surprises despite her best efforts to hide it.

"Yes, my girlfriend. I hope that's not a problem for you?" Jane replied, looking somewhat disappointed.

Darn, now she probably thinks I'm a closet homophobe, Gada scolded herself. "No, not at all! I'm married to an engineer, so I'm not in the position to judge anyone's taste," she joked, trying to lighten the mood. "Actually, I'm honored to get to formally introduce myself to you. Dubois has been the most amazing mentor to me so far, and it's a blessing to have her as a superior. I've been in the military before, and I know it's rare to find someone that really has your back."

"Very true," Jane said, relieved. "I'm just glad you don't have a problem with it. I know a lot of people in this building do. I've been called the worst things before. Anyway, I don't want to waste any of your time. I know you have a lot on your plate. Maggie told me a bit about it. I don't know if I would cope with having to work on something so dark and morbid. Can I bring you that coffee? I imagine you need it."

"Thanks, Jane, that's very kind of you. I'm okay, though; I had a big cup before coming down here. I'll get the jitters if I have too much of it," Gada sympathetically smiled, brushing a strand of hair behind her ear.

"Well, I better get going then," Jane answered, starting to make her way toward the supercomputer room's door. "Maybe I'll see you during lunch now that the cat's out of the bag?"

"That would be nice," Gada agreed.

Before long, she was alone with the supercomputer's glowing screen again. *I need to determine three things;* she reminded herself. *Only three things: motive, means, and opportunity. The means were different for each crime, the opportunity too, which means that the motive must have been the same for each murder. I can only assume they were killed for their research, considering that their research is the only thing that truly connects all of them to one another.*

Gada decided to try to draw up a list of suspects using the supercomputer. *I'll insert some criteria. Firstly, the suspect needs to have a grudge against the scientific community, preferably with the study of Chromosome 2. Secondly, they must have been in the same area that the victims were in at the time of their deaths to orchestrate the murders. Finally, they may need to have a history of violent crimes. Nobody goes on a killing spree without some kind of history.* She used her skills in statistical modeling to set the parameters and started the search. She sat and stared at the hourglass the supercomputer displayed while it was searching its connected databases for more than an hour before eventually deciding to close her eyes. She folded her arms on the desk in front of her and rested her head on them. When she lifted it again, two hours had passed, and the supercomputer still hadn't managed to complete its search. "Darn this piece of garbage," Gada growled, getting ready to storm out of the room to report the machine's ineptitude to Dubois. Just as she gathered her coat to leave, the screen finally changed, revealing the supercomputer's search results. "Thirty-three thousand results found!" she screeched to herself. "Ugh! How am I supposed to make sense of that many results? There's not enough time in the world to cross-reference that many people." She angrily switched off the uncooperative machine and stormed out of the biometric door, fleeing up toward Dubois's office. The door was closed when she finally got there. *Gosh, I hope she hasn't gone home already. I really don't want to wait. We need to find a solution for all of this immediately,* she thought. With a sense of renewed determination, she knocked and waited for a reply.

"Jane, is that you? If you bring me any more coffee, I might die of an overdose," Dubois roared from inside of her office, ending the sentence with a chesty chuckle.

"Colonel, It's me. Can I come in?" Gada nervously replied, sticking her head into the Lieutenant Colonel's office to reveal her face. "Can you spare ten minutes to chat about the case I'm working on?"

"You've got forty-five minutes, but after that I'm going home," she laughed, "but you're welcome to come in if you don't think you'll keep me here longer than that."

"Oh, I'm sure I won't," Gada amusedly replied, stepping onto Dubois's carpeted floor. "I've just finished running some equations on the supercomputer. I was hoping to come up with a list of suspects, but—"

"But it gave you a list that was ten miles long?" Dubois asked, tilting her head to the side as she examined the contours of Gada's anxious facial expression. "That is what happened, isn't it?"

"How'd you know?" Gada gasped, immediately wondering whether she'd done something wrong to encourage the supercomputer to give her an incorrect output. "Has it done that before?"

"Once or twice," Dubois admitted, disappointedly shaking her head. "It's not quite as effective as we'd like it to be in certain cases. We're not entirely sure why it sometimes acts up or seems incapable of narrowing down a list. It's likely just a software glitch. It isn't the best device of its kind on the market, so it's really not surprising that its performance isn't always up to scratch." She paused for a moment, contemplatively staring at Gada before continuing. "I'll ask if we can use the quantum computer at The Company."

"The Company?" Gada asked, raising one of her eyebrows as if to punctuate her question. "Where's that?"

"It feels like I've known you forever, Gada. Sometimes I forget that you're new," Dubois chortled, getting up out of her chair to stare out of the window behind her desk. "We refer to the CIA's headquarters in Langley as The Company, makes it easier to talk about confidential things in public without breaching any of our non-disclosure agreements. It's only about nine miles away. You could go there as soon as they agree to allow us to use it. Its' software and hardware are far more sophisticated, and you should be able to narrow down your search results a lot better than you were able to with our supercomputer."

"That would be amazing!" Gada beamed. "It would make the entire investigation a lot easier. I've come to a surprising conclusion that should help me to draw up a concise list of results if its search restrictions are applied properly: All of the scientists were doing some research on the origins of Chromosome 2."

"Don't get too excited," Dubois said gently, the corners of her eyes softening with sympathy for her enthusiastic young recruit. "The Company is notoriously stingy with their quantum computer, but I'll lodge the best argument that I possibly can for it. That's all I can promise. Your discovery of the Chromosome 2 connection should serve as an incentive for it, though. I'm sure they'll be just as concerned to learn about that commonality as I am. If that's not enough, I actually have more upsetting news to share with you—"

"What is it, Colonel?" Gada asked, plopping herself down in one of the leather chairs in front of Dubois's desk.

"There have been three more deaths related to your case. That makes sixty deaths in total," Dubois sighed, lowering her head as she closed her eyes for a moment. The window that she was staring into reflected her sadness back at Gada.

"What... what happened?" Gada inquired solemnly, sensing the seriousness of the information being shared.

"Gada, keep this to yourself for now, but I actually went to school with one of the victims. It's very sad. The group that fell victim to the killings was made up of an environmental biologist, a conservationist, and an ecologist. They were on a climate research project in the South Pole's UN-13 climate observation station," Dubois started explaining, turning around to face Gada head-on. The wrinkles on her forehead looked deeper than ever before.

"Climate researchers?" Gada asked, looking noticeably confused. "Are you sure their deaths are related to the killings? Up until now, all of the other victims have been involved in genetic research. If the killer is going after climate scientists now, that means that the modus operandi of the killings has changed."

"I'm certain," Dubois confirmed, her eyes full of sorrow. "Their deaths occurred under the same kind of mysterious circumstances... and as always, they were gruesome."

"I'm so sorry, Colonel," Gada sympathized, lowering her head out of respect for the Lieutenant Colonel. "I promise I'm going to do everything in my power to bring this killer to justice."

"I know you will," Dubois said, walking over to Gada to rest her hand on her shoulder. "I wouldn't have assigned the case to you if I thought that there would be any other outcome."

***

"It has been more than a week," Gada complained, biting into the bacon and cheese sandwich she had designated as her lunch for the day. She, Dubois, Jane, and Mateo were sitting around a rickety table to one side of the DIA's designated smoking room. The "room" was not much more than a square glass cage in the furthest room at the end of the hallway, seemingly designed to separate the delinquency of smoking from the rest of the building.

"I've actually heard back from The Company," Dubois admitted, taking a long drag of her cigarette. "I just haven't had the heart to tell you. They phoned me yesterday. They denied our request, said they're not going to make one of their most expensive pieces of equipment available to us based on a new recruit's hunch."

"You're kidding me!" Gada exclaimed, abandoning the last piece of her sandwich entirely.

"Can I have that?" Jane asked, pointing to the remaining half. "I'm on a diet, so I'm not bringing lunch to work, but I'm starving. Terrible diet, I don't recommend it."

"I told you, you don't need to go on a diet," Dubois scolded her, placing her hand on Jane's knee.

"Sure, go ahead," Gada laughed, handing it to her. "I don't know much about diets, but I agree with Maggie that you don't need to be on one, but back to the matter at hand. What can we do to change The Company's opinion to our request? I really need access to the quantum computer if I want to stand a chance of solving this thing. The supercomputer simply doesn't have the computing power I need for the equations I'm inputting."

"I know," Dubois sighed, "but I always get that feeling that seems to portray a discriminatory bias from some of my counterparts. They received a request from a known homosexual to allow a BIPOC recruit to use their fancy-schmancy computer, and almost immediately said no. We'd both get much further if we were two old white men."

"Thank God you're not, Maggie" Jane chuckled, ripping at the sandwich with her molars. "That would have definitely changed the dynamic of our relationship."

"Oh hush!" Dubois laughed, depositing her cigarette butt into an ashtray on the center of the table. "I'm serious, though. The military seems like one big Old Boys Club. We're neither boys nor old, and you're the wrong race. You know, if an alien being looked down onto earth and saw the human race, they would definitely not differentiate us from each other. Unfortunately, we humans do, and everything is going to be just that little bit harder for us than it is for most of the other agents, but that doesn't mean we're going to give up. Does it?"

"Certainly not," Gada replied, an air of determination illuminating her silhouette. "If anything, I'm more determined than ever that I have to crack this thing. For the victims and for your team." "It's not my team; it's our team!" Dubois asserted back as she placed her hand on Gada's shoulder.

***

"I hate it here," Gada complained, poking at her taut round stomach. The baby kicked her finger from inside her womb. It was a game they sometimes played and one that brought great comfort to Gada in times of stress. *At least I know you're okay in there,* she thought.

"You hate it here? You mean, here at home?" Mike asked. They were lying on their king-sized bed on a small mountain of fluffy blankets. Mike was resting his head on Gada's chest, listening to the rhythmic beating of her heart. In one corner of the room, the television dully blared out a news report that no one was listening to.

"Kind of," Gada admitted, playing with Mike's thick hair. "Does that make me a terrible person? It's just that I miss work. I can't make a difference sitting here at home. Who knows what the scientist-killer is plotting next, and there's no one actively working to stop him because I was the only person assigned to the case."

"Gada, you're due to have this baby at any moment. You're already planning on taking less than a week's worth of maternity leave. You're pregnant, super pregnant. You need to rest, at least until the baby arrives. Can you promise me that you'll at least try to put the killings out of your mind until you go back to work?" Mike asked, tilting his head up to look at Gada's expressionless face. He could see the cogs in her head turning. "What are you thinking?" he asked, a concerned frown decorating his usually handsome face.

"I just don't know how I'm going to go about this investigation even when I do get to go back to work. The CIA is still refusing to let me use their quantum computer, and the supercomputer simply can't narrow down the search enough. I mean, it's impossible to seriously consider 33,000 possible suspects," Gada sulked. She appeared to be close to tears.

"Well, you're pretty good at programming. Can't you write something that would help the supercomputer to eliminate a few of the suspects it's currently giving you?" Mike suggested, sitting upright and hopping off of the bed's edge in one nimble motion. "Would you like something from the kitchen? I'm going to get myself some orange juice—"

"Mike, you're a genius!" Gada excitedly exclaimed. She did a lively celebratory dance from her perch made of pillows and blankets, nearly rolling out of bed in the process.

"Careful!" Mike warned. "You promised me you'd relax, remember?"

"Sorry, but you may have just helped me crack the case!" Gada beamed, smiling from ear to ear. "Have I ever told you how much I miss you while I'm at work? You're the only thing that makes being stuck at home bearable."

"Bearable?" Mike frowned, pausing on his way out of the room.

"Fine! Enjoyable!" Gada giggled, wriggling about on the bed again. "I in love with you, Mikey."

"I love you too."

Chapter 5: Stand Not on the Tracks of Change

"Okay, honey. You've got to push for me now," an elderly nurse clad in blue scrubs said encouragingly, patting Gada's stirruped knee. "The baby is crowning; you're almost there!"

"What do you think I'm doing? Baking fricking cookies?" Gada growled through gritted teeth, squeezing Mike's hand so tightly that his knees were threatening to buckle underneath him.

"Waaaaah! Waaaaaaaaaah!" a screeching cry suddenly split through the room. The doctor on the other side of the stirrups lifted up a blood-coated squirming bundle still attached to the umbilical cord. It was loudly protesting and kicking its fat little legs around.

"It's a healthy baby boy!" the doctor confirmed, clamping and snipping the umbilical cord. He handed the baby to the elderly nurse, who quickly scurried into one corner of the room with him.

"Is everything okay? Where's she taking him?" Gada worriedly asked, trying to sit upright to get a better view of what was going on. Her feet were firmly strapped into position, and no matter how much she wriggled, she was unable to see what was happening to her newborn. "Mike, what are they doing to him?" she pleaded.

"Relax, Mrs. Corey. The nurse is just cleaning him up for you and assigning him an APGAR score. She'll return him to you for skin-to-skin bonding in a second. How are you feeling?" he asked, strapping a sphygmomanometer to Gada's arm to measure her blood pressure.

"After passing a bowling ball, I'm okay, I guess. I just want to see my baby," Gada insisted, looking up at Mike in an attempt to gauge how he was feeling. He looked a little paler than usual. *I guess that's to be expected,* she thought.

"Well, there's no tearing, and you appear to be in good health," the doctor confirmed, smiling at the new parents in the most charming way. "If you pass the afterbirth soon, you and your bouncing baby boy can go home tomorrow. Does that sound agreeable to you?"

"It sounds perfect," Gada sighed, an overbearing tiredness suddenly washing over her. She closed her eyes for what felt like only a moment. When she opened them again, the elderly nurse and Mike were standing over her. Mike was cradling their new bundle of joy in his arms.

"He needs to be fed," the kindly old nurse said. "The first feeding is the most important. Do you think you're up to it?"

"Of course," Gada replied, rubbing the sleep from her eyes. Mike placed the tiny baby on her chest. He latched on almost immediately.

"What are you going to call him?" the nurse asked, her eyes twinkling.

"We're not sure," Gada started, looking down at their baby's perfect little features. He had Gada's long, curly eyelashes, dark skin, and dark eyes, but there was definitely a little bit of Mike in him too. "Look, Mike! He has your chin!" she excitedly exclaimed, gently poking the tiny dimple at the bottom of his face.

"I don't know what you're talking about," Mike laughed, gently stroking Gada's messy hair. "Looks like he has about three chins to me. On the subject of his name, I was thinking maybe we could consider 'Kevin.' It's my dad's middle name, and I think it suits the little guy."

"He does look like a Kevin," the elderly nurse agreed, merrily bobbing her head up and down to show her approval.

"Kevin... are you the handsome beloved birth in Gaelic Folklore?" Gada whispered with a smile. The baby opened his eyes as she said it and looked up at her from the comfort of her bosom. "I think he likes it too," she chuckled. "Kevin it is then. Kevin Corey. It definitely rolls off of the tongue."

***

"I've got good news and bad news for you," Dubois announced, marching up and down the length of her office. She paused to straighten a photograph of the president that hung on the wall behind her desk. It was Gada's first day back at work, and she wasn't sure what to expect.

"Good news about The Company, I hope?" Gada nervously chortled, taking a mint out of the glass jar on Dubois's desk and popping it into her mouth. *Hopefully, she managed to make some headway while I was away on maternity leave,* she thought.

"Sadly, no. That's actually what the bad news is. They're still stubbornly refusing to grant us access to their precious quantum computer. At this point, I've practically exhausted all of my contacts there. I've called up every favor a CIA agent has ever owed me, but no one has been able to help me so far," Dubois admitted defeatedly, pausing at her office's window to open it. The sound of birds chirping in the tree outside seeped

123

into the room along with the scent of the jasmine flowers that vined up one side of the red brick building.

"Don't worry, Colonel; I concocted a plan while I was away to deal with the eventuality of the CIA turning us down completely. Mike helped me to come up with it. I'm planning to write a computer program that will assist the supercomputer in narrowing down its search," Gada explained, bundling the mint up in one of her cheeks as she spoke.

"Really? You could do that?" Dubois said, raising both of her eyebrows in surprise. She made her way back to the chair behind her desk and flung herself onto it. She leaned over the table, supporting her weight with her muscular trunk-like arms, and stared intently at Gada with her shockingly blue eyes.

"Well, I didn't learn how to program for nothing. At the very least, I could give it a shot," Gada grinned sheepishly, fiddling with a paperclip that she had found at the edge of Dubois's desk. "So, what's the good news?"

"I've got your second assignment for you," Dubois smiled, tapping her fingers against the desk's hard wooden surface.

"What? But I haven't managed to solve my first assignment yet!" Gada hiccoughed, nearly falling off of her chair as the shock of the news hit her.

"That's not exactly how it works here, kiddo," Dubois chortled, rummaging through one of her desk's drawers. She withdrew another manila envelope from it and shoved it in Gada's direction.

"Oh, no. Not another envelope," Gada complained, dramatically reaching for it nonetheless. It wasn't quite as full or heavy as the previous one that Dubois had given her. "What's all of this about?"

"It's another fun one that no one else on this floor is brainy enough to solve," Dubois frowned, contemplatively staring at the envelope in Gada's hand before continuing. "Syria is rapidly advancing its technology, like super rapidly. Like, inhumanly rapidly. It's absolutely insane. We have evidence that they have managed to draw up plans for hyperspace missiles and advanced guidance systems."

"Seems unfair to prosecute someone for developing fancier missiles than we have," Gada chipped in, cautiously opening the envelope to do a preliminary examination of its contents.

"It's not the technology that we're worried about," Dubois said, lowering her voice until it was barely a whisper. She almost appeared concerned that someone might be listening in on their conversation. "There's a clear gap between the technology being developed and what Syria currently uses with no evidence of theoretical work or research experiments done to lead up to the discovery of the technology they're currently designing."

"Perhaps, it could simply be a normal case of espionage," Gada suggested, scanning the main report inside of the envelope to gather information on the case's main facts.

"In Pakistan, Indonesia, Ecuador, and Zimbabwe too?" Dubois asked sarcastically. "If you read through all of the documents in there, you'll see that Syria isn't the only country that's technology has rapidly surpassed ours with no apparent research ever having been put into it. We just need to know what's going on and whether it poses a threat to national security. Do you think you could take a look at it and report back to me on your findings?"

"Yes, ma'am," Gada confidently replied, saluting the Lieutenant Colonel. "I didn't understand the full extent of the problem before I questioned you about it. My apologies."

"No need to apologize, Captain Corey. Just do your best to get to the bottom of it before we find ourselves in the middle of another missile crisis," Dubois said, getting out of her seat to open her office door for Gada. "Oh, and welcome back! We've missed you during lunch."

Gada silently made her way back to her office, paging through the documents that had been inside of the envelope as she went. She opened the door with her plaque on it. *Just as I remember it,* she sighed. *It's good to be back.* She reclined in her plush office chair and started analyzing the facts of the case.

She quickly identified individual paradigm shifts. *Yeah, that's what I'll call them,* she thought, rather impressed with herself. *"Paradigm shifts." It has a certain ring to it and perfectly describes the jumps in technological advancement that these countries are experiencing.* Closer examination of the documents revealed something even more shocking. All of the countries involved were working independently of each other to develop an advanced hypersonic missile. "Strange," Gada said out loud. *The technology shift occurred differently in each country,* she realized. *Syria developed the ideal propulsion system, Zimbabwe created the needed guidance system, Pakistan revolutionized the metallurgical strength of their materials, Indonesia worked on a groundbreaking structural design for the missile, and Ecuador was making impressive strides in the development of the thermal heat resistance of the missile's design elements.*

Still clutching the assignment's documents in one hand, Gada leaped out of her chair and charged back down the hallway to Dubois's office. She knocked, there was no response. *Where could she possibly have gone,* Gada grumpily thought. *She was here just fifteen minutes ago.*

"Looking for someone?" a junior officer who happened to be passing by asked, stopping mid-stride to gawk at Gada.

I must be quite a sight if I look as frazzled as I feel, Gada concluded, straightening out her pencil skirt. "Uhm, yes. I'm looking for Lieutenant Colonel Dubois. Have you seen her?"

"She went home early today, something about a migraine. Maybe I can help? I'm supposed to be assisting anyone who needs help in the Data Analytics Department as part of my training, and it definitely looks like you need someone to lean on right now," the young officer said, warmly smiling at her.

"I'm not sure I'm supposed to be sharing information about my assignment with anyone else in the department. It's highly classified," Gada stated, furrowing her brow as she tried to weigh the risks of using the enthusiastic noob as her sounding board.

"Oh, I have top-secret clearance," he grinned. "You don't have to worry about getting in trouble for sharing anything with me if that's what you're concerned about."

"It's exactly what I'm concerned about; it's also on a need-to-know basis," Gada admitted, still unsure what to make of her new acquaintance. "But I guess I could ask you something that I need an opinion on without revealing too much about the assignment. OK, here it goes...What's the likelihood of Syria, Zimbabwe, Ecuador, Pakistan, and Indonesia all working closely together to design a new piece of technology? Do you think their relationships with each other are strong enough that they'd be able to have that kind of exchange of information and cooperation between them?"

"Eh, I doubt it. Syria has a decent intelligence agency, but Ecuador, Zimbabwe, Pakistan, and Indonesia certainly don't. I can't imagine that they'd be able to foster the level of cooperation needed for something like that," he replied, sounding incredibly confident of himself.

"Thank you. In that case, I've got to run. It has been nice chatting with you. Before I go, what's your name? I'd like to recommend you as an excellent candidate to your supervisor," Gada explained, readying herself to continue her dash down the hallway.

"James Standon," he replied. "My rank is not important."

"If you say so, Standon. Thanks again for the help," Gada grinned, reinvigorated by the thrill of the investigation. She made her way down into the basement and headed straight for the supercomputer at the end of its long dark hallway. She threw herself into the chair behind it and switched it on. She spent the rest of the working day running data through the supercomputer and extracting information about smaller paradigm shifts that had occurred in the five affected countries. Leading up to the more significant paradigm shift represented by the development of the advanced missile they were all working on.

She sat back and revelled in the quality of her work after typing the last sentence of her report. *I need some educated input,* she thought, picking up the landline phone on the desk. She dialed Nori's number, still her favorite professor. The dial tone felt louder than ever before. *I wonder if she still remembers me. England feels so long ago and so far away.*

"Hi! Nori here! Who's speaking?" a cheerful voice suddenly burst through the other end of the line.

"Nori! It's me! Gada Corey! Well, I used to be Gada Deere. I'm not sure if you still remember me, but—" Gada started, nervously swiveling around in the office chair behind the supercomputer. She was conscious of the technicians watching her but tried to remind herself that the phone call was official DIA business and nothing to be ashamed of.

"Of course I remember you! What a silly statement. How have you been, Gada? I haven't heard from you in ages. It has been too long! I told you to keep in touch," Nori half-scolded her.

"I'm doing well, Nori. I've got a job at...I mean, in the military. I'm married now; I ended up marrying Mike. We have a little baby named Kevin. He's the love of my life. I hope life has treated you kindly too?" Gada asked, genuinely interested in Nori's response.

"Same old, same old. Still lecturing at the university, still have too many cats," Nori snorted. "What's up? Is this a social call, or—"

"You've got me," Gada anxiously chuckled. "I really need help with something, Nori. Something serious, but you have to promise not to speak a word of this to anyone."

"Ooh. Sounds serious. I promise that I'll keep it between us," Nori agreed.

Gada described the paradigm shifts in each country, emphasizing that it was impossible that they were working together or sharing information with each other, and then concluded by asking, "What do you think? As a scientist and sociologist? Is it possible that these shifts occurred organically?"

"In my professional opinion, no. No, it isn't. Are you sure they aren't working together? Your description of the scenario almost makes it sound like someone is handing them information, and they're just developing technology with what's given to them. Is that possible?"

"Not as far as I know," Gada replied, disappointed that Nori didn't have any clear answers for her.

"Do you remember that lecture I gave on Type Two civilizations during your final year in university?" Nori asked, trailing off toward the end of the question.

"Sure, but what does that have to do with anything?" Gada inquired, her voice thick with confusion.

"Maybe nothing, maybe everything. If a Type Two civilization did exist, their meddling with a civilization like ours would likely lead to paradigm shifts just like you've described. Naturally, that's all just theoretical. I'm not saying that is what is going on. It's just interesting to consider the similarities between what's currently happening and what sociologists have been predicting would happen if we came into contact with such a civilization," Nori explained, sounding notably concerned. "You're not involved in any of this, are you Gada? I'd hate to think you were investigating something that might be potentially dangerous."

"I am," Gada admitted, lowering her voice.

"Gada, listen to some words from an old friend that cares for your safety. 'Stand not on the tracks of change, for the train of progress has no brakes!'" Nori hesitated for a moment, then continued, "Please be careful, Gada."

"I promise, I'm being careful.", Gada retorted kindly.

"Knowing you, I suspect that's the best I can ask for," Nori chuckled. "It has been a pleasure talking to you again, Gada. Don't be a stranger, okay?"

"Okay," Gada conceded, bursting into a fit of laughter at the ridiculousness of the situation. "I have a feeling I'm going to be asking you for a lot of help over the next couple of months anyway."

After hanging up, Gada sat behind the computer contemplating the profoundness of Nori's idiom while reading through her report long after the call had ended. She decided to add a footnote about Type Two civilizations and crossed her fingers that she wouldn't be entirely discredited because of it. *I promised myself all of my statistical modeling would always be honest*, she thought, *and I wouldn't be honest if I didn't mention what Nori had said.*

Gada presented her report to Dubois the very next morning, storming into her office with a file filled with calculations and findings relating to the case at exactly 10:01 am. "You're not going to believe this," she panted, lunging at the closest available chair.

"What happened to knocking? I thought Jane warned you about barging in on me on the first day," Dubois frowned, leaning back in her chair. "I'm still busy reading the morning paper. It's kind of important when you're the head of the DIA's analytics department to keep abreast with national news, wouldn't you say? I hope whatever you have for me is urgent or groundbreaking."

"It's a bit of both, Colonel," Gada announced, sliding her report over the desk's smooth surface toward Dubois. "My

131

findings are... unusual, to say the least. To summarize: The five countries involved that we discussed yesterday have not been communicating. I had a hunch that they weren't thanks to James Standon, a fantastic guy, by the way, but I managed to confirm it by intercepting outgoing communications from each country. They definitely haven't been collaborating."

"Who the heck is James Standon?" Dubois interrupted, scooping the report up. She started reading the first page of it as she waited for a reply.

"A junior officer I met in front of your office yesterday. I bounced some ideas off of him, didn't mention anything classified or sensitive though," Gada explained, anxious to depart from the topic of James and to discuss her findings instead.

"There's no one by that name who works here," Dubois replied in a deadpan tone, her expressionless gaze burned straight through Gada. "You must be mistaken. Anyway, if I'm understanding you correctly, the findings of your report are that the technology described therein popped up as if by magic?"

"Kind of," Gada sheepishly answered, staring at the pattern on her pantsuit in an attempt to avoid having to make eye contact with the Lieutenant Colonel. "I can tell you're disappointed, but hear me out. The fact that the technology is unexplainable is indicative of something bigger. There's something brewing on a global scale: The scientist-killer, the advanced missiles being designed in less developed world countries without proper military research funding—It's all connected somehow. I just have to figure out how."

"Look, Corey. I trust you, and I know you're not an idiot, but I'm going to need more than this. We can't report hearsay or hunches to the POTUS. We need hard facts," Dubois started, paging through the report like a student paging through a textbook looking for a specific answer.

"I know you do, which is why I need access to the quantum computer," Gada passionately declared, standing up out of her chair. She started pacing around Dubois's desk, circling her like a vulture. "I'm really close. I can solve this, Maggie, but not with the supercomputer. There's no program in the world that I can design to give it the capabilities that I'm going to need for this project."

"I suspected that might be the case. There have been new developments in the scientist-killer assignment too... I received notification of it this morning. Three more scientists have been found dead in the South Pole, exactly where the previous three's corpses were found. So, you now have sixty-three deaths to investigate," Dubois admitted solemnly. "I know I've put a lot on your plate, but I also know you're the best person for the job."

"I'm flattered. Truly, I am, but I'm still going to need the quantum computer, Maggie. No amount of belief will circumvent that. Do you think we could possibly put a little more pressure on the CIA? The sooner I get access, the better. If we solve this, we could prevent a whole host of future murders and perhaps thwart a larger and more diabolic plan," Gada pleaded, stopping to hover next to Dubois's left shoulder. "Please, Maggie."

"I've been trying, Gada," Dubois grumbled. "I'll call them again. Have a seat. Who knows how long I'll be on hold this time." She dialed the CIA's number on her office's secured landline phone as Gada slowly sauntered back to her chair on the other side of the desk. They sat staring at each other as the

133

grating waiting tune blasted through Dubois's phone's speaker. It came to an end surprisingly quickly.

"Langley. Who can I put you through to?" the voice on the other end of the line asked, abruptly ending the irritating melody.

"Your quantum computing department," Dubois stated assertively. "It's Lieutenant Colonel Dubois from the DIA's analytics department. I doubt they'll be surprised that I'm calling again."

"I'll patch you through immediately, Colonel," the voice confirmed. "Please hold."

"Oh great, more waiting," Dubois mumbled as the waiting tune started playing again. The word had barely left her lips when the music came to a sudden end again.

"Agent Johnathan Greene speaking, how can I help you?" a deep male voice boomed through the phone's speaker, causing some of the baubles on Dubois's desk to vibrate as its baritone tone rattled across the desk.

"Greene, it's me again," Dubois said authoritatively, squeezing a bright yellow stress ball that she usually kept next to her computer screen. "I'm sure you've heard about the new murders at the South Pole."

"Of course I have," Agent Greene replied somberly. "The three victims were CIA scientists sent to investigate the original murders. We're all very upset about it. They were our colleagues—"

"Greene!" Dubois roared, slamming her large fist against the desk's wooden surface."Why didn't you tell me you were investigating those deaths as well? Do you know how many resources we've expended on launching our own investigation? This is precisely the kind of competitive inter-departmental bullshit that is keeping us from making a breakthrough. Someone, or even an enemy nation, is globally targeting scientists involved uniquely with the two main fields of microbiology, and we're caught in the middle of a dick measuring contest. This is ridiculous! I demand that you grant my analytics expert access to your quantum computer immediately, or I'll make sure that your superiors hear that you've been impeding an investigation that could have potentially saved the lives of three of your colleagues!"

"We're sorry, Colonel. We didn't know it would go this far," Agent Greene started, sounding genuinely remorseful.

"I don't care what you thought, Greene," Dubois hissed into the phone's receiver, coating it in a thin layer of spittle in the process. "Here's how it's going to go down: My analytics expert, Captain Corey, will report to Langley first thing tomorrow. She's to be met by your best quantum computing expert. She's going to use your quantum computer for two things. Firstly, she's going to investigate the suspicious deaths and use it to narrow down the search criteria she's using to find a possible suspect. The data she needs to create linkages is enormous. Her mathematical modeling requires bank transactions, cell phone data and locations, travel tickets, rented vehicles, police reports in the area, common denominators relating to triggers, information on loans, potential enemies, recent quarrels, spouse issues, insurance policies... you get the gist. Secondly, she's going to employ it to investigate the manufacturing of advanced missiles in some of the countries on our watchlist. She needs to expand on her report on the emerging technology's origins. The cases might be related if we're dealing with a hostile nation trying to hinder the advancement of our technology by offing our scientists while simultaneously advancing their own. It's a matter of national security."

"I understand, Colonel," Agent Greene conceded, his voice was heavy laden with sadness and regret. Gada couldn't help but pity him. "I'll make sure that Agent Duncan, our best quantum computing expert, meets her at the reception desk tomorrow. Send over her security clearance certificate in the meantime. I'll fast-track it on our side."

"Thank you, Agent Greene. I'll do that. To think that all of this could have been avoided if you had offered us assistance the first time that we requested it," Dubois growled before loudly slamming the phone down onto its stand.

"Thanks, Maggie. I really appreciate how hard you've been advocating for my projects these past couple of months, and I promise I won't let you down," Gada squeaked from her chair, unsure how to approach her superior, who was still angrily panting on the other side of the desk.

"I'm sorry you had to hear that. I hate involving my employees in interdepartmental conflicts, but it seems somewhat unavoidable when it comes to those pompous blockheads. Nonetheless, I apologize that you had to bear witness to me going off like that. It has been a long time coming, and Agent Greene has been nothing but obstinate since he took over the quantum computing department," Dubois explained, removing a handkerchief from her jacket's pocket to dab at the beads of sweat that had appeared on her brow. "Now, if you'll excuse me, I think I'm going to take Jane out to lunch today. That woman does so much for me."

Gada's anxiety about the following day's visit to Langley only increased as the working day neared its end. She found herself hyperventilating in the elevator ride up to their apartment on the Poto-Pine Apartment Building's third floor but consciously decided to hide her distress from Mike. *He has enough to worry about,* she thought. *I don't need to burden him with my unwarranted nervousness too.* She put on a happy face as she strolled through their front door. The smell of gravy and roasting meat hit her as soon as she opened the door. "What's going on here?" she smiled, skipping toward the kitchen. Mike was standing behind the stove, stirring something that was rapidly boiling in a large pot.

"Hey, honey! You're home late! I thought I'd get started with dinner while I waited for you to get home. That way, you can kick your shoes off and relax a little. Kevin has already been bathed and nodded off to sleep, although I'm not optimistic enough to say that he's out for the night. I imagine you've had a long day," Mike grinned, sprinkling a pinchful of thyme into his bubbling concoction.

"Not longer than usual," Gada replied, fishing a spoon out of one of the kitchen cupboards before waltzing over to Mike to sample his cooking. "I should be the one helping you to relax. How did that mine proposal go today?"

"Very well," Mike said proudly, puffing his chest out. "We won the bid. It's another multibillion-dollar contract for the company. The guys wanted to go out for a beer to celebrate, but I told them I'd rather come home to celebrate with my beautiful wife and adorable son."

"Aah, Mike. You should have gone! I wouldn't have blamed you!" Gada exclaimed, putting her spoon down to fling her arms around his neck. "That's quite the accomplishment. I can't believe you're the awkward kid I used to explain quadratic equations to during recess." She pecked him on the cheek before releasing him from her vice grip.

"I would have gone with them if I thought I would have enjoyed a night out more than I enjoy a night in. This is the best way I could possibly imagine celebrating, just being here with you," Mike gently replied, looking deeply into Gada's eyes.

"I think your potatoes are burning, Mr. Hopeless Romantic," Gada teased, gazing past him at the smoke that was slowly seeping out of the gaps around the oven door.

"My potatoes!" he gasped, spinning around to run to their rescue. He ripped them out of the oven just in time to save them from being completely incinerated. He was scraping the burnt bits off of them when he turned to face Gada again. "How's that scientist-killer investigation going?"

"It has gotten more complicated. I'm no closer to solving it than I was before I had Kevin. It's very frustrating," Gada admitted, stealing one of the piping hot (very crisp) potatoes that Mike was trying to save. She popped it into her mouth and immediately hopped up and down in regret as it scalded her tongue. "I got assigned to another project that might be connected to it. This new case is pertaining to unexplainable military technology advancements in lesser developed countries. I did some data analysis on it today, and it's impossible that these countries have been working together. What makes it extra creepy is they're all designing the exact same missile, despite it being clear that they haven't been sharing or stealing information from each other."

"That is really strange," Mike replied contemplatively, giving up on his scorched potatoes and swiftly depositing them into the trash can. "Maybe there's something wrong with your data set that would explain the jumps in technological advancement without having to rely on information sharing or espionage."

"That's what I'm hoping for," Gada sighed, staring sorrowfully at the wasted potatoes. "Otherwise, it's simply terrifying."

Chapter 6: The Company

The drive to Langley couldn't be described as anything other than stressful. Gada wasn't sure what kind of welcome awaited her, although she suspected that it wouldn't be a warm one after bearing witness to Dubois's call to the head of the CIA's quantum computing department. After passing through a security checkpoint manned by six guards with semi-automatic rifles strapped to them, she serpentined around between the parked cars looking for a vacant spot. She found one and quickly maneuvered into the parking space. It was only after fifteen minutes of frantic searching that she had finally found one. *I hope I'm not stealing someone's assigned parking. I'm going to be late, and it'll be this place's ridiculous parking arrangement's fault*, she thought, unbuckling her seatbelt and grabbing her handbag before dashing toward the building's entrance. Its front door was nestled under a large white metallic arch connecting the building's glass roof to its pale brick exterior.

The lobby area was far quieter than the DIA's entryway usually was, but its front door was also far more heavily guarded. Nearly a dozen officers greeted her at its threshold, each more heavily armed than the next. They put her and her handbag through a metal detector and an x-ray machine, and confiscated her phone to place it in a locked Faraday cage, before admitting her to the building.

"Head to the reception area," the tallest one grunted. "You'll be helped there. Don't stray into any of the hallways without an escort, or you will be detained for trespassing."

"Yes, sir!" she confirmed, awkwardly saluting him as she quickly walked away from the doorway. Gada effortlessly found the reception desk but was shocked to discover there was no one staffing it. She spotted a sophisticated security camera attached to the roof just above the reception area. It had a substantial convex lens with a unique blueish tint. Next to the large lense were smaller flat shiny metallic discs that appeared similar to ultrasonic emitters Gada used previously in her lab research during her academic years. She deduced that it must be a newer model body-scanner that can locate hidden objects under clothing. It appeared to be zooming in on her. *I'm just being paranoid,* she thought. *It's not watching me. Hmmm, I wonder if they can see me naked on their monitors. This place creeps me out.* "Hey there!" she called out while crossing her arms to cover her chest, screaming out in no particular direction. "Is there anyone here that can help me? I'm from the DIA." The security guards stationed at the door looked around at her but didn't deign to heed her cries for help.

"Are you Captain Corey?" someone behind her asked. She spun around and nearly crashed into a well-dressed, tall and handsome, African-American man. He looked just as surprised as she did.

A natural reaction after someone nearly runs you over, Gada admonished herself. "I am," she confirmed, straightening out her jacket in an attempt to reaffirm her professionalism. "I was told Agent Duncan would be down here to meet me this morning, but it doesn't look like anyone's down here...other than you, of course."

"Apologies," he croaked, looking quite guilty. "We don't usually have staff down here. The cameras man the front desk. It's been that way ever since the shooting in 1993. Agent

141

Duncan was supposed to meet you here today, but the plans changed. I'll be helping you get started instead. I'm Captain Tyrone Tupper, but I'd prefer if you just called me 'Tyrone.' I hate official titles."

"I understood that Agent Duncan was your best quantum computing agent, which is why he was assigned to me," Gada started.

Tyrone simply shook his head. "Yeah, I'm sorry about that. We had a little bit of drama, and Agent Duncan refused to come down here. Some people can make it a pretty tough place for people like us. You know, people who look a bit different. Agent Duncan is one of the older agents and apparently isn't ready to accept anyone that isn't a carbon copy of himself. Anyway, I am the second-best person for the job, but I promise what I lack in experience, I make up for in enthusiasm," he smiled, clearly trying to improve the conversation's tone.

"People who look a bit different?" Gada inquired, raising one of her thick eyebrows and leaning against the reception desk as she gazed down at the formal black and white blazer she was wearing. "I think I look quite normal, thank you very much."

"Normal? Maybe. Too dark? Definitely. Plus, you're a woman. In a place like this, that counts against you too. Trust me, I was raised in one of the poorest neighborhoods in Pennsylvania, and I'm the wrong race. There's nothing new you can teach me about systemic discrimination. Like the cliché of this place goes; it lies deep, deep undercover." Tyrone answered sorrowfully. "Outsiders are rarely accommodated here, and like me, you're an outsider in more ways than one. Don't get me wrong, Captain; there are many good people here. However, for the few bad apples, don't you worry, because this bad-ass Philly-boy has your back, Captain."

"I think I understand," Gada nodded sympathetically, instantly wishing she hadn't spoken quite as harshly as she had to her new acquaintance. "Anyway, I'm happy to be working with you. I'm sure we'll have a far better time than I would have had if Agent Duncan had accompanied me instead."

"Definitely," Tyrone chuckled. The sparkle seemed to return to his eyes as he realized that Gada was done berating him about his employer's biases, biases that had unfairly affected him in the past too. "We'd best get going. The day's only so long. I'll show you to the quantum computer immediately. I imagine you're eager to get started."

"I am," Gada agreed as they started making their way toward a large staircase that fully occupied one corner of the room. "No elevator?" she asked as they started ascending it.

"They decommissioned the elevator to encourage us to stay in shape," Tyrone grimaced, climbing two steps at a time like an eager child. "Some of the desk agents complained immediately after it happened, but nothing ever came of it. The field agents are always taken into consideration. Everyone else? Eh, not so much. There's a definite hierarchy of authority in this place, and it's not always based on rank. You'll get used to it eventually."

"I'm sorry to hear that," Gada panted as they reached the top of the staircase. They veered right, sticking to a long narrow hallway that led past several closed office doors. The inside of the CIA's headquarters was as devoid of color as its exterior was: The walls were painted blindingly white, the ivory tiles both reflective and refractive at the same time, and the office doors were made out of wood that could only be described as the lightest shade of beige. "It's really white in here," Gada remarked, grimacing as she drank in the CIA's poor interior decorating choices.

"Oh yeah, in more ways than one," Tyrone chuckled, clearly not done basing jokes off of Agent Duncan's reluctance to meet with Gada yet. Laughter rolled out of his chest like an avalanche rumbling down a mountain, shattering the otherwise dominant silence that seemed to fill the building.

"Shh! You'll get in trouble if they hear that you're onto them," Gada giggled, gawking at the portraits of all of the CIA's departmental heads that lined the chalk-colored walls. "They're trying so hard to hide it," she added, staring into the pale blue eyes of the portrait closer to her.

"What are they going to do if they find out I made fun of them? Treat me like a second-class citizen? It wouldn't be new to me," he chortled, making another sharp turn and quickly striding down a well-concealed hallway to Gada's right. "But we should keep it down. This entire place is bugged, and you never know who's listening."

"Wait up! Really?" Gada gawked, walking a bit faster to catch up with the CIA's second-best quantum computing expert. "You'll have to slow down if you want me to keep up. I don't have my jogging shoes on," she grinned, motioning at the leather stilettos on her feet.

"You know," Tyrone started, suddenly stopping mid-step and turning to face a door for which plaque read "lunchroom." "I can never understand why women choose to hamstring themselves with those silly shoes. My fiancée insists on wearing them to work every day too."

"The lunchroom?" Gada interjected, pointing at the bronze nameplate on the pale wooden door in front of them.

"Don't worry, I haven't gone insane," Tyrone smiled, turning around to wink at Gada, who stood just a few feet behind him. "Watch this," he confidently said, presenting his thumb to a dark square at the bottom of a 3 feet by 3 feet dark marble work of art. It was a replica relief of MichaelAngelo's *Battle of the Centaurs* that hung tastefully next to the door. The door immediately swung open.

"Your lunchroom has biometric security?" Gada scoffed, staring at the terrified expressions of the warring Centaurs depicted in the piece of art Tyrone had used to gain access to the room. "Seems like overkill." As she pointed at the artwork, she asked Tyrone, "What's with the intense artwork here?" Tyrone paused, turned around to face her square, and smirked while looking deep into Gada's eyes as he spoke softly, "You should know that this piece represents the great conflict between order and chaos."

"It's not the lunchroom," Tyrone chuckled, turning around and stepping through the open door. "Follow me," he called once inside.

Gada hesitantly complied, striding over the threshold and finding herself thrust into a room that was illuminated in the strangest light that was only amplified by the overbearing clinical whiteness of its walls and fittings. The only source of light other than the harsh LEDs that had been installed against the walls was the otherworldly green glow being emitted by the computer servers stacked against the room's walls. Tyrone looked almost alien in the strange lighting. He was already standing behind a screen on a table in one corner of the room, typing away on its lime-colored keyboard. A number of technicians, in roles that Gada assumed were similar to those of the roles filled by the supercomputer's technicians, slowly moved around the room. They were all clad in strikingly white

145

scrubs, and for a moment, Gada couldn't help but be amazed by how much they resembled surgeons in a sterile operating room.

"Uhm," Gada made a perplexed face. "You've definitely got some dramatic lighting going on in here, but your technicians admittedly look very cool. It's like Halloween here every day."

"Would you expect anything less spectacular for the country's most powerful computer? Our engineers spent days savoring the installation of those creepy-ass lights in all of the servers. They don't have a purpose other than to make this room look more imposing than it already is. The CIA loves putting on a good show," Tyrone admitted, appearing somewhat ashamed on his employer's behalf. "Anyway, the technicians look like that because they're interacting with elements of the computer like its quantum processor that could easily be destroyed by the smallest fleck of dust."

"Should we even be in here? I'm not prepped for surgery," Gada nervously chuckled.

"No, we shouldn't. We should be in here," Tyrone said, pressing enter behind the computer screen. It prompted a door at the other end of the blindingly white room to slide open. "This way to the user interface," he boasted, confidently striding toward the newly opened door.

"Wait, that wasn't the quantum computer?" Gada gasped, quickly following him.

"Well, the servers form part of the quantum computer, but the screen is just the access point for this room," he announced, walking through the doorway and extending his arms to welcome her into an equally white but much darker room. It was filled with nothing but two chairs and a single unbelievably large screen. "The servers draw from information databases that have been collected by the CIA and the OSS, both overtly and covertly, since 1941."

"1941? Wasn't the OSS established in 1942?", Gada questioned looking quite confused. Tyrone chuckled, "My dear Gada, when you have some time, take a look at file #001 titled *The Kingston Doctrine* dated May 9, 1941, and issued to President Roosevelt." Gada looked confused. She took a deep breath and shook her head, knowing she needed to stay focused.

"I'm not used to all of this showmanship," Gada confessed, nervously stepping into the room too. "The DIA is all about practicality. If something's not practical, it doesn't get done. We don't have all the frills that you seem to have."

"It's probably better that way. Taxpayer money could be put to better use than installing scary lights in a computer room. Okay, so if you're used to using the DIA's supercomputer, the quantum computer should be a breeze. Its software is far more user-friendly. You'll input your search criteria here," he said, motioning toward a complex formula-input system on the large computer's screen mounted against the wall, "and then you'll simply click on 'start.' It'll do the rest for you. Well, it and the technicians will do the rest for you, to be entirely correct."

"Seems simple enough," Gada confidently smiled, trying to hide how intimidated she truly was. "I think I'll be fine. Thank you, Tyrone. You seem to be incredibly knowledgeable on the quantum computer. I really appreciate your help."

"Well, at least that means I didn't waste nearly a decade of my life on getting my PhD in Computer Architecture. I think my degrees from MIT are the only reason they let me within a mile of this machine!" Tyrone quietly laughed and gently patted the side of the large screen. "I'll be in the room next door if you need any help. Just shout if one of these creeps bothers you, and I'll be here in a flash," he chuckled, playfully glaring at the technicians quietly going about their jobs. "On a different note, I hope you don't mind me asking, but what do you think about the deaths down at the South Pole? I knew one of the guys who died there. His office wasn't far from mine. Saw him at the watercooler every now and then."

"I'm not supposed to discuss it," Gada solemnly replied.

"Please? We've got the same security clearance level, and I've been dying of curiosity since the incident happened. Was it the Russians? Or the Chinese?" Tyrone asked, barely whispering.

"Fine, but everything I say stays between us, okay?" Gada frowned, staring at Tyrone's distorted and pleading face. *I hate being manipulated*, she thought. *But he seems nice enough and genuinely interested in the case.*

"I promise I won't tell a soul," Tyrone nodded, offering her his curled pinky finger to seal the vow. She stared at it for a second before hooking her pinky finger into his. "Pinky promise," he said, shaking both of their hands up and down before releasing her finger from his grip.

"Well, I don't think China and Russia are involved. Obviously, it's too early in the investigation to say for sure, but I just feel like there's an unknown force at play here. Perhaps a foreign government that isn't currently on our radar or a corporation that would somehow benefit from stalling research into the origins of Chromosome 2," Gada whispered, lowering her voice to ensure that no one strolling past the room would bear witness to their highly confidential conversation.

"What's Chromosome 2?" Tyrone asked, furrowing his brow and taking a step backward. "I don't mean to be alarmist, but what you're telling me sounds a bit terrifying. An unknown foreign government or corporate espionage that has managed to go undetected? It's like something straight out of a spy movie."

"I don't know much about spies, but I do know this: If we discover what caused the mutation of Chromosome 2 in early humans, we'll figure out how we came to be as a species. Clearly, someone is profiting off of keeping this information from the public. All I have to do is figure out who that is, and I've cracked the case," Gada grinned self-assuredly, gingerly entering some of the criteria she wanted to exclude from her search into the quantum computer.

"You make it sound so simple, Captain Corey," Tyrone chuckled, playfully saluting her. "You know where to find me if you have any questions about the computer. Good luck," he concluded, turning and leaving the room without another word.

Guess it's just me now, Gada thought, staring at the glowing screen in front of her. *Or rather, it's just me and you now, Mr. Quantum Computer.* She spent the rest of the day entering and removing criteria from her list of references, crossing her fingers, and clicking "search." Every time she did, the quantum computer suggested a more ridiculous solution to the murders. "International murder cult," was its first suggestion. *I doubt Heaven's Gate is behind this.* She shook her head, astounded that the country's most sophisticated computer could be spewing such nonsense. The next time she worked up the courage to hit "search," it suggested that a known terrorist named Defaa Al Bachar was behind it. *Al Bachar was killed by a task force last March*, she grimaced. *When last was this darn computer's information updated?* After the computer dared to finish a search by concluding that an ex-President of Japan had single-handedly committed all sixty-three murders, six of which had been committed in the South Pole, Gada jumped up out of her chair and stormed out of the "lunchroom."

"What the hell is wrong with the quantum computer? Is this some kind of stupid CIA prank?" she growled, storming into the room next door to find Tyrone paging through a popular housekeeping magazine. "And what the hell are you reading?"

"Can't a man read pastry recipes in peace anymore?" Tyrone sarcastically lamented, tossing the magazine across the room. It hit the wall on the opposite side with a dull thud. "And what are you on about? Tell me where the big bad quantum computer hurt you?"

"If you leave me alone with it for five more minutes, you'll have to start asking me what I did to hurt it. I swear I'm going to throw it out of a window or something. I've been reworking my equations and criteria for hours, but when I try to make use of your 'wonder computer,' it all goes to crap. Its first suggestion? A cult. Its second? A dead terrorist. Its third? The ex-president of Japan. The ex-president of Japan, Tyrone! I don't know if you had an alcoholic write its code, but its performance is absolutely ridiculous, and I mean that in the most scathing way possible," Gada ranted, angrily pacing up and down the room. She nearly slipped on the magazine that lay crumpled in one corner but managed to regain her composure before Tyrone noticed. "I have to use it to try to explain paradigm shifts in technology, but if it can't even solve a few murders, I'll absolutely fry its harddrive if I try to input that information into it."

"Take a deep breath," Tyrone warmly suggested. "You're going to pass out if you keep hyperventilating like that. Some of the people here would love to see you fail, so don't give them the satisfaction of seeing you struggling. I'll come have a look. Maybe it's a user error."

"Don't try me, Tyrone," Gada grumbled, following him back out of the room. "I'm this close to snapping, and I honestly don't care what anyone here thinks about me. All I want to do is solve my assignments. I'm not interested in the CIA's silly little internal status quo."

"Oh? Well, remind me not to mess with you, Captain Corey. A foe who doesn't care about their reputation is formidable indeed," Tyrone laughed, walking into the eerily lit 'lunchroom' that wasn't a lunchroom at all. However, Gada was starting to think it might have been more useful if it had been utilized as one instead. They marched past the quantum computer's servers and made their way to its user interface. "Let me take a look," he said in a tone that only men who are helping pretty women could summon. He had barely hunched over to get a better view of the screen when all of the lights suddenly went out, including the creepy green ones in the adjacent room and the dim glow of the computer screen.

"Did the power just go out?" Gada gasped, freezing to avoid accidentally wandering into one of the fragile servers that lined the room. "I can't see anything."

"We have generators and backup systems. They should kick in any second now," Tyrone said, staying equally still.

The generators didn't kick in right away. In fact, they didn't kick in at all. "We've been waiting like this for ten minutes now," Gada complained. "I think we need to make peace with the fact that the power isn't coming back any time soon. Is there a way that we can get out of here? Is the door electric?"

"It is," Tyrone confirmed, feeling his way closer to Gada. "But we should be able to open it manually. It has a safety mechanism that allows it to be accessed from the inside regardless of whether it has power or not."

"Thank goodness for little miracles," Gada sighed disheartedly. "I don't think it would work if we called for help. All of the technicians have already left for the day. Our only hope of escape is to open that door ourselves."

"Use the walls to help you find your way out. We'll get to the door if we follow them," Tyrone suggested. Gada could hear him slowly move past her and shuffle along the side of the room.

She quietly followed him, brushing her hands against the wall's rough surface to keep her course. "Tyrone, do you think someone is trying to keep me from conducting this investigation? It feels like I'm being hindered at every possible opportunity. Does that sound paranoid to you?"

"Not at all," Tyrone whispered, although Gada wasn't sure who he was concerned might overhear them in the sealed-off dark cave they now found themselves inside of. "Anyone who can orchestrate more than sixty murders could probably put aside some time to mildly inconvenience you."

"I can't tell if you're being sarcastic or not," Gada growled, nearly bumping into him. "I can't see you, remember?"

"To be completely honest, I'm not sure whether I'm being serious or not either," Tyrone softly admitted. "Hey! Found the door!" he exclaimed. Gada's mood instantly improved as he grabbed hold of a latch and effortlessly swung the heavy door open. Within seconds they had managed to exit the "lunchroom" entirely and found themselves standing in the middle of a sunny patch in the main hallway.

"I've never been this happy to see daylight before," Gada squealed.

"Guess you're going to go home now?" Tyrone said, almost appearing disappointed that his first day with the odd DIA operative had come to an end. "Who knows how long we'll be without power if the generators aren't working. Something must have gone wrong with the wiring somewhere in the building. I can't imagine what else might cause a blackout of this kind."

"I guess so," Gada smiled, feeling more welcome at Langley already. *Made a friend on my first day*, she thought. *This is already going better than kindergarten did.* "Hey, do you think your boss might let me install some software on the quantum computer? I wrote a program for the DIA's supercomputer that would translate well onto the quantum computer too. It would help me to improve the clarity of the search criteria that I'm inputting."

"Probably couldn't hurt to ask," Tyrone shrugged, a shadow falling across his face. "However, I have to warn you that the CIA can be a little... bureaucratic. I don't know how long it'll take for me to get approval for it."

"Do you think I'd get in a lot of trouble if I installed it without Greene's permission?" Gada cheekily suggested, biting at her cheek.

"Definitely. I really wouldn't suggest it. The CIA loves screaming 'treason' when they don't get their way," Tyrone said. Gada could tell that he wasn't kidding around.

"Yikes. Okay, I won't do that then," Gada recoiled, surprised to hear that The Company would be so heavy-handed. "If anything, this whole experience has given me a new appreciation for the DIA and Dubois. Anyway, I'll see you again tomorrow, Tyrone? Same time? Same place?"

"Sure," Tyrone smiled. The suggestion immediately made him seem more cheery. "Don't bother hanging around at the reception desk tomorrow unless you want the guys in the control room perving on you. Come straight up to this room. I'll be in the office next door, as always."

Gada got home just in time to relieve Kevin's babysitter from duty before Mike got home. "Thanks, Annabeth. How was he today?" she asked, helping the college-aged girl to pry her ponytail from the baby's grubby little hands.

"Better than yesterday, Mrs. Corey," she replied, gathering her belongings and roughly shoving them into her modestly sized handbag. "He wasn't as fussy with the bottle, and I don't think he had any reflux. I mean, there was a lot less crying after feedings today."

"That's good news," Gada cooed, scooping Kevin up into her arms and cradling his warm little body against her chest. She sniffed his head. *Why do babies smell so wonderful?* she wondered. *Where do they get their scent? I'd rather not know, I guess*, she concluded. "Thanks for all of your hard work today. Tell your mum I said hello? I haven't heard from her in a while."

"She's just been super-busy with her new boyfriend," Annabeth responded, rolling her eyes as she prepared to rush out of the front door. "Sorry, Mrs. Corey, I've got to go. My ride is waiting outside."

"It better not be a boy waiting out there for you, Annabeth," Gada scolded, suddenly and horrifyingly sounding like her mother. "And if it is, please don't tell your mum I know. She made me promise to keep you away from them."

"That's precious coming from her," the babysitter scoffed, "seeing as she's incapable of staying away from them."

Being a teenager is nightmarish, Gada thought as she watched Annabeth leave the apartment building and get into a red station wagon from her kitchen window. "I promise you'll lead such a spectacular life. There'll be no teen angst for you," she babbled at Kevin, who had fallen asleep on her bosom, already knowing that no amount of sheltering would protect him from it. *The hard part about being a teenager is learning that the adults in your life aren't perfect,* she thought. "I hope you never stop thinking I'm perfect," she softly whispered into the snoring baby's ear.

"Honey, I'm home!" Mike called from the apartment's front door. "I ran into Annabeth on the way up. What are you doing home so early? How'd your first day with the quantum computer go?" he quizzed her as he strutted into the kitchen and demanded a kiss from her before stealing one from Kevin too.

"Careful! You'll wake him!" Gada warned, shoving Mike's face away from their baby. "He just dozed off. If you stir him now, he'll spend the rest of the evening crying."

"Sorry, hun," Mike said remorsefully. "I'm just happy to see you two. It's the best way to end absolutely any day. I'm the luckiest man on Earth with the most magical son and the cleverest wife ever to have existed."

155

"I don't know what has come over you, Mike," Gada teased, feigning disgust. "But you certainly don't have the 'cleverest wife.' Today was a total disaster." She spent most of the dinner recounting all of her misfortunes, ending the tale with the blackout that sent her home. "To top it all off, I asked Tyrone to get me permission to upload my own software onto the quantum computer, but he warned me that he couldn't guarantee he'd be able to fast-track my request. I'm stuck until he gets me that permission, you know, considering the quantum computer doesn't throw up any reliable results with its current programming."

"Bummer," Mike agreed, taking a bite of the sweet peas Gada had made. "So, none of today's results were usable?"

"Not at all," Gada frowned, staring at her unfinished meal. She didn't particularly have an appetite but knew she had to attempt to eat a bit of it to appease Mike. "It was like the quantum computer was actively working against me. I don't know how to make that statement sound any less crazy, but it's true," she lamented, finally forcing herself to take a bite of her mashed potatoes.

"Oh, Gada," Mike sympathized, putting his hand on her knee. "Maybe you're just tired, babe. I'm sure everything will be better in the morning."

***

Everything was not better the following morning, or the morning after that, or the morning after that. In fact, everything was much worse for quite a while after Mike and Gada's conversation. Gada went to Langley every morning only to learn that her request to upload her own software onto the quantum computer was still denied. Greene was reportedly worried that her software was filled to the brim with viruses and possible security risks, and Gada was worried that she'd never get to the bottom of the paradigm shifts in technology or the mysterious deaths of dozens and dozens of scientists.

Then finally, after a month of going to Langley every morning only to spend the day playing Sudoku in the quantum computing room, Gada made a breakthrough. "I've got some good news for you," Tyrone glibly remarked as she walked past his office on her way to the cafeteria.

"It better be very good news," she grinned, stopping mid-stride. "Otherwise, you're currently disturbing a highly critical coffee run for no reason."

"Hmm? Then maybe I should wait until you get back to tell you that your request has been approved," he nonchalantly replied, fiddling with a fountain pen that he'd found on his desk.

"Wait, what! You mean Greene finally agreed to let me use my own software on the quantum computer?" she exclaimed, jumping up and down with excitement. She skipped toward Tyrone's desk before continuing, "Please tell me Greene finally said yes. You have no idea how much I need this."

"Desperate much?" Tyrone teased, playfully swiveling in his chair to turn his back on her. He suddenly froze mid-swivel and sat entirely motionless.

"Tyrone?" Gada squeaked, reaching out to touch his frozen body. He was instantly reanimated.

"Sorry about that," he said, nervously chuckling as he stood up out of his chair. He walked toward the stationery cupboard that stood against one of his office's walls, opened it, and started rummaging around. "I got distracted for a second."

157

"Distracted? You totally dissociated," Gada warned, watching as he continued to dig through a container full of pens. "Are you sure you're okay?"

"Fine, fine," he mumbled, finally stepping back from the cupboard with a new fountain pen in his hand. He hobbled back toward his desk without uttering a single word of explanation. "What were we talking about again?"

"Uhm... The good news?" Gada said anxiously, still unsure what to make of the strange behavior she had just witnessed.

"Of course, of course. The good news. Yes. Agent Greene agreed to allow you to make use of your own software but wanted me to warn you that he'd personally waterboard you if your software damaged the quantum computer in any way," he replied, his voice was strangely monotonous.

"Really?" Gada said, tilting her head to one side. Tyrone's odd tone made it even more difficult than usual to ascertain whether he was joking or not.

"Yes, really," he replied. His face was entirely devoid of any form of expression.

"Oh. Okay," Gada answered, tempted to attempt shaking Tyrone to wake him from whatever form of catatonia had taken hold of him. She decided not to. *They're too fond of hard-handed responses here for me to risk something like that*, she thought. "Thanks, though," she said, smiling at him, hoping that he would smile back at her. He didn't. "I'll get to it then," she whispered sorrowfully, unsure what had caused her friend to entirely withdraw from the conversation.

"Good luck," he added as she turned to leave his office. For a second, she could have sworn he smiled back, but it was gone as fast as it had come.

Maybe he's just having trouble at home, she thought as she made her way back to the quantum computer's 'lunchroom.' It didn't take her more than half an hour to install all of the software onto its hard drive that she was planning to use. *Time for some magic,* she told herself, cracking her knuckles as she prepared to reinsert the equations she had drawn up to narrow down her searches even further. She readied herself to run the scan again, closed her eyes, and clicked on "search." She waited a minute or two before cautiously opening her eyes again.

The words "suggested solution" were sprawled across the top of the computer screen. Just below that, the result was displayed in neon green: "Cult killings."

Not again, Gada gulped, realizing that a month's wait had all been for naught. *If my software can't patch this darn thing's bugs, then the bugs are bigger than any mortal man can squish.* The thought had barely passed through her mind when the room was plunged into total darkness again, just like it had been a month prior. "Another blackout!" she exasperatedly screamed, although nobody heard her.

Chapter 7: Anomalies

"You know how pirates used to believe it was bad luck to have women on board?" Tyrone asked, bouncing a tennis ball against his office's wall. He was back to his cheery self, but Gada was scared to ask what had been affecting him the previous day, and there was little else to celebrate.

"You mean to say men have always been this stupid?" Gada quipped, catching the ball mid-bounce before playfully returning it to him.

"No, I mean that the building's entire electrical grid has gone haywire since you started working here. We never had a single total blackout in the ten years that I worked here before I met you, and now we've had two in just a little over a month. Are you chewing on the building's wiring or something during lunch? Because if that's the case, I'd happily share my sandwich with you, you just have to ask," he teased, accidentally bouncing the tennis ball into Gada's gut.

"Oof!" she grunted, pretending to be far more injured than she really was. "You're just out to get me today, aren't you?"

"Sure am. Hey, maybe I'm the scientist-killer? Ever thought about that? I have enough inside information to pull it off," he suggested. His coal-black eyes twinkled mischievously as he looked up at her, waiting for a response.

"If you're the scientist-killer, my name is Mary-Sue," Gada grumbled sarcastically, stealing a handful of paper clips off of Tyrone's desk. "Mind if I take these?"

"Nah, go ahead. I don't pay for my own stationery, so I don't care," he grinned, pushing another container full of them toward her. "What's on the itinerary for today? he asked, seeming genuinely interested in Gada's plans.

"Except for weeping and an anxiety attack?" Gada joked, stowing her gifted paperclips in her jacket's pocket for safekeeping. "Not much. I realized something halfway through my shower last night," she replied contemplatively, walking over to Tyrone's office window. It was the end of spring, and every patch of grass outside was dotted with a hundred dandelions, as yellow as the morning sun itself. "I've been approaching the whole investigation wrong."

"What do you mean?" Tyrone asked, leaving his chair to join her. They stared out at the parking lot together for a moment, bound by their silence.

"Yeah. I need to break this whole thing down into smaller chunks. I've been throwing complicated questions at the quantum computer, expecting it to solve the whole case. What I should have been doing is giving it smaller questions, broken up into digestible chunks, that I could use to come to a conclusion regarding who the perpetrator of the murders is." Gada leaned over the windowsill to inhale the sweet, warm breeze that flitted through the cloudless blue sky.

"That's pretty clever, actually. I'm impressed, Captain Corey," Tyrone said, stepping away from the window. "I guess that's why they assigned you to the case."

"Thank you, Tyrone." Gada purposefully made her way toward his office door. "I was starting to think there'd be no resolution to these murders. Cross your fingers that my plan works. Otherwise, we'll be back to square one."

"I'll say a little prayer for you," Tyrone said, waving as she threatened to slip out of the door.

161

She only turned around to say, "You don't have to do that. I've found that crossing your fingers is just as effective."

The room that the quantum computer was located in seemed just a little less dark with the sense of renewed hope glowing in Gada's soul; even its eerie green lighting felt less spooky and more welcoming. Gada was confident that things were about to change for the better. She sat down behind the machine's reflective black screen and switched it on. It flickered to life, revealing its usual input options. She uploaded her program and equations. She stared at it for a moment and then typed "significance of Chromosome 2 in the field of theoretical biology" into it. The quantum computer immediately suggested hundreds of thousands of results. She decided to open the document at the top of the list. It read:

"The evolution of Chromosome 2 is a tale of intrigue. Extinct members of the Hominidae family all had twenty-four pairs of chromosomes, but modern humans only have twenty-three. This discrepancy has led researchers to question what evolutionary conditions led to this genetic adaptation. Currently, the leading theory is that Chromosome 2 is a remnant of a prehistoric telomere-telomere fusion that caused two ancestral ape chromosomes to fuse, creating the human Chromosome 2. The question is: What gave rise to this telomere-telomere fusion? What external forces were at play? New research out of the South Pole may be able to answer these questions. Studies done on the effectiveness of gene reparation using biobots have proved that this type of genetic tampering often leads to a similar type of fusion. This conclusion appears to be accurate when one considers all of the evidence in support of it. However, it is unsettling to consider that the part of our genetic code that makes us human seems likely to have been created through some sort of ancient gene splicing."

Ancient gene splicing? Gada wondered. *Am I stuck in a sci-fi movie now, or is this darn computer still bugging out on me?*

She decided to do a quick search on biobots in a desperate attempt to better understand the article that she had found on Chromosome 2's origins. "Biobots are robots that operate at a molecular level, but they're nothing like miniature robotic insects developed by keen computer wizards," she read. "They operate by manipulating a living being's DNA and are often organic themselves. Recent studies have enabled researchers to harness the power of biobots to do everything from possibly curing cancer to treating genetic diseases like Trisomy 2, a disorder that is caused by a split in Chromosome 2."

If anything, I'm more confused about what's going on than I was before I kickstarted my "break everything into smaller chunks" plan, Gada thought, frowning at the screen. *I've got to call in an expert.*

She whipped the landline phone off of the wall next to her and dialed Nori's number. *If anyone knows anything about this, it'll be her*, she argued. The phone rang twice before the receiver was picked up on the other end.

"Nori, good morning!" a cheery voice chimed through the speaker.

"Nori, I'm so happy to hear your voice," Gada blubbered, still shaking from her discoveries, none of which made sense to her.

"What's up, Gada? You sound upset?" Nori asked; the concern in her voice was undeniable.

"I'm doing some research for my new job," Gada explained, trying to steady her breathing. "I know you're more into sociology research than you are into biology—"

"Well, yes. I'm a sociology professor," Nori giggled, causing the phone to vibrate in Gada's hand. "But I did an undergrad degree in biology, so I can probably help if you're not expecting a doctoral-level answer."

"On the contrary, I want you to explain it to me like I'm a child," Gada nervously laughed. "I have two questions: What do you know about biobots, and how could they be linked with rapid technological developments?"

"Woah, Gada. That's a pretty big question," Nori sighed. Gada could almost hear the cogs turning in her brain. "A big question with a complicated answer, I'm afraid, but I'll try to explain it as best I can. Firstly, I need to know, do you know what biobots are?"

"I do. I just finished reading an article about it," Gada admitted. "I wouldn't call myself an expert, but I think I caught the gist of it."

"Great, that means I'll have a little less explaining to do. I suspect our knowledge on the current use of biobots is more or less the same if you've been reading up on it. I know that they're being studied because the scientific community believes that we may be able to use them in the medical field. I also know a little about them and their role in the theoretical development of interstellar civilizations. Do you remember my lectures on Type 0 and Type I civilizations?" Nori probed, breathing heavily on the other end of the line.

"Of course, but I'm more interested in their applications here on Earth," Gada started. She heard Nori loudly sigh.

"I can share some interstellar biobot knowledge, but if you're looking for something else, you might need to phone a biologist instead," Nori grumbled, ostensibly upset that Gada would even dare to suggest that the rant about intergalactic civilizations she was about to go on was any less interesting than earthbound information on the subject.

"Sorry, Nori. I didn't mean to be rude," Gada apologized sincerely. "I'm just under a lot of pressure from my bosses, and I really need to get my head around the subject. I'd be happy to listen to anything you have to say about them."

"Fantastic!" Nori purred. "Well, there's a hypothesis in the study of theoretical interstellar civilizations that says that an M species Type II might use primitive life forms on other planets as biobots to gain access to more resources and materials. Doctors on Earth want to use biobots to attack cancer cells or to rewrite DNA. M species would use them to grow produce, manufacture technology, or mine minerals," Nori patiently but enthusiastically explained.

"The article I read said biobots operate on a molecular level. How would that work if M species are using entire life forms as biobots?" Gada asked, pretending to be interested in Nori's explanation. *Theoretical knowledge of interstellar civilizations that may or may not exist will not help me crack the case,* Gada thought despondently.

"To an M species, we're nothing but molecules. Specks of dust! The biobots that have been studied on Earth are all microscopic. That much is true, but it would be very closed-minded to think that larger organisms couldn't be turned into biobots with the right amount of genetic engineering, too," Nori lectured, giving Gada flashbacks of her time in academia. "Now, you asked me how biobots could be linked to jumps in technological advancement? I assume you'd like an answer relating to Earth, and unfortunately, I don't have one for you. From a galactic point of view, biobots might experience large leaps in technological advancement every time their original creator tampers with their genetic propensity for intelligence or even imparts extraterrestrial information on them. Theoretically, M species might impart knowledge on their biobots to maintain a steady increase in infrastructure development through the successful and efficient extraction of natural resources on the planets under their command. If you don't mind me asking, what kind of work are you doing these days, Gada? Must be something very interesting if you're worried about biobots at 2 pm on a Thursday afternoon."

"Oh, nothing spectacular. I've just been asked to draw up a report on biobots, that's all," Gada quickly lied, unable to conjure up a more believable fib. "My employers aren't really concerned with any theoretical extraterrestrial applications, but I appreciate all of the information nonetheless. At the very least, I feel like I have a better understanding of what biobots are."

"Sorry about that," Nori said softly, sounding a little disappointed to hear that her lecture wouldn't make it into Gada's made-up report. "I wish I had more applicable information to share with you, but I've been out of the loop for so many years. Sociology and the study of theoretical interstellar civilizations have kind of consumed my life. I see everything through that lens and that lens alone. Sometimes I wish that wasn't the case, but what would the world be without us kooky sociology professors?"

"No need to apologize," Gada said warmly. "Like I said, I feel like I understand what biobots are now. As an additional bonus, I got to hear The Amazing Nori's voice again, and that is a treat in and of itself."

"You know I'm not grading you on this, right?" Nori chortled, seemingly in a better mood already. "So there's no need to butter me up."

"I've never been nice to you to 'butter you up,'" Gada replied resolutely. "Not even when I was still a student in one of your classes. I miss it sometimes, you know? I wonder what life would have been like if I'd stayed in academia. I could have become a lecturer, perhaps. We could have had lunch together every day."

"But then you would never have had the amazing life you have now with Mike and Kevin," Nori added. "I would have liked it if you had stayed, but I'm a firm believer that everything always works out the way it does for a reason, and not just coincidences. There's a reason you felt pulled back to the USA. Someday, that reason will become apparent. I'm not sure why you're researching biobots, and I won't press you to be honest with me, but you're clearly already making a difference on that side of the world if you're concerned with such complicated scientific topics."

"You always know what to say to make me feel better," Gada laughed. "I'll phone you again next week? I've missed talking to you. We should make time to do it more often."

"Sounds good to me," Nori agreed. "I've missed you too."

With Nori's words still echoing through the vast expanses of her stretched-to-the-limit mind, Gada decided to dive back into her research on the quantum computer. *But not before a cup of coffee*, she thought. She ran into Tyrone on her way to the kitchen despite doing her best ninja impersonation on her way there.

"How's the quantum computer treating you?" he asked, matching her stride as she marched down the hallway. "Still suggesting a T-rex ate the scientists?"

"It wasn't a T-rex. It was a death cult," she corrected him, staring into the empty depths of her coffee cup as they rounded the corner that signified the home stretch leading toward the second floor's kitchen. "But no, it hasn't offered up anything ridiculous lately. My plan seems to be working. Now I just have to figure out how I'm going to wrap my head around some of the scientific solutions it's giving me."

They made it to the kitchen before Tyrone had an opportunity to reply. Gada immediately busied herself by putting the kettle on. She distractedly scooped large spoonfuls of coffee into her mug, still mulling over her conversation with Nori.

"Don't you have a Ph.D.? Scientific solutions should be easy for you, Mrs. Doctorate of Philosophy," Tyrone finally answered just as Gada paused to decide whether or not she wanted to add sugar to the thick coffee mixture that she was creating. "My fiancée studied English for one whole semester at college, and there's nothing you can tell her about grammar. She's constantly correcting my texts to her. You have, like, a gazillion years of university behind you, so I imagine you're both a gazillion times harder to live with and also a gazillion times less likely to be intimidated by bookish stuff and formulae."

"Formulae? Not formulas? I can tell your fiancée studied languages. I can't remember when I last heard someone say 'formulae.' Actually, I probably last heard it in university," Gada laughed, taking a big sip of the piping hot blackness that now occupied the depths of her coffee mug. She nearly choked as its overpowering taste hit the back of her throat. Its scalding heat caused her tongue to throb. "I'll be fine. I'm not intimidated by the scientific element of it. I just need some time to think about what I've learned. Plus, I have a lot more research to do before I'd say I'm even close to reaching a conclusion. You'll have to excuse me. I'd like to run some more searches and scans before the day ends." Gada scurried out of the room, still clutching her steaming mug in her fists. She could feel Tyrone's eyes following her as she left. *I don't know what to make of him after yesterday's catatonic episode*, she thought, making her way down the hallway as quickly as possible. *I feel like we're back to being strangers.* She could hear his footsteps following her but decided not to turn around. *I don't have time to chat,* she grimaced.

Gada made it back to the quantum computer's 'lunchroom' without having to engage in any further conversations. Tyrone walked past the room just as she entered it. She hastily made her way through the technicians' sterile room, careful not to touch anything, and into the backroom that housed the quantum computer's user interface. *I wonder if he could have been the one following me if he was that far behind me*, Gada thought. *I doubt my hearing would have been good enough to hear his footsteps from that far away.* She decided to put her concerns out of her mind. *You're being paranoid*; she chastised herself. She started up the computer and hurriedly typed her next search phrase into it: "Countries that have experienced leaps in technological development in the past twelve months." *Phew, that's a mouthful*, she thought. *Hopefully, I'm not asking too much of it.*

The computer spent a minute or two calculating its results before opening its "solutions" page. It only had a single output.

"All countries have experienced unprecedented progressions in technological development over the past fiscal year," it read. *All of them?* she wondered. *That can't be right.* She clicked on the hyperlink on the suggestions page. It led her to a list of countries that matched the criteria of her search. *Yup, that's all of them*, she gasped. *From Afghanistan to Zambia.*

***

"Mike, where are you?" Gada called as she strode through their apartment's front door. She dumped her handbag on the coffee table and threw her coat over one of their couches' backrests. The apartment appeared to be empty, but she had run into Annabeth on her way up and consequently knew that both her husband and child had to be somewhere between the entryway and the nursery (that used to be a home office) at the furthest end of the apartment. "Mike! Stop fooling around! Where's Kevin?" she repeated.

"We're in here, honey!" Mike replied, his cheerful voice bounced into the living room from somewhere near the main bedroom.

Gada set out to look for her little family, too tired to continue screaming at Mike to determine what their location was. The main bedroom was empty too, which only left one part of the apartment unexplored: The bathroom. She anxiously approached the closed bathroom door and hesitantly knocked. "Are you guys in there? What are you up to?" she asked while rapping her knuckles against the doorframe.

"Come in, babe! It's nothing you haven't seen before. We're having a little bath," Mike answered, punctuating his sentence with a boyish giggle.

Gada pushed against the door until it slowly opened under her weight, revealing a cloud of bubble bath. Her husband and baby seemed to be prisoners to it. The tub wasn't filled with more than seven inches of water, although it boasted about a foot of foam. Kevin was lying on Mike's lap. Only his head peeped out from the fragrant fluff that floated on the water's surface. "Mike! Careful! You're going to drown him!" Gada exclaimed, rushing to Kevin's rescue. She ripped him off of Mike's lap, prompting him to start bawling. His wailing caused Gada's ears to ring. Mike merely grimaced.

"Baby bathing is tricky," Mike frowned, staring at the squirming baby in his wife's arms. "He had a bit of reflux again and threw up on his onesie. I thought it would be easier to clean him if I got in with him," he explained, blocking his ears with the palms of his hands. "He was perfectly happy until you gave him the fright of his life."

"Sorry," Gada grumbled, gently bouncing Kevin up and down in her arms in an attempt to calm the startled infant. "I just had a long day at work. I should have trusted you. I know you'd never do anything to endanger Kevin. It really does seem like he was enjoying the bubble bath—"

"Of course he was! All Corey men love a good long bubble bath. You know that," Mike laughed, getting out of the bath too. Gada was totally mesmerized by the steam rising off of his broad chest and muscular arms, forgetting to rock Kevin for just long enough that he decided to embark on another screaming session. "What happened at work that you're feeling a bit blue," he asked, wrapping a towel around his waist.

"I found out all of the countries in the world have experienced paradigm shifts in the past year," she sighed, kissing Kevin's fuzzy head.

"All of them?" Mike asked, raising one of his eyebrows as he reached for his deodorant in the medicine cabinet. "How's that possible?"

"I don't know," she sulked, leaning against the bathroom's door frame. "At this point, I'm beginning to suspect divine intervention."

"Divine intervention? It must be a hard case to crack if you've put divine intervention on the table," he chuckled, a sound that could only be described as a chesty rumble.

"It's not really on the table," Gada grinned. A feeling of warm contentment settled over her heart as she realized that Kevin had fallen asleep in her arms. "But I am that desperate," she admitted.

***

Gada woke up the following day with a plan in her mind and a song in her heart. *I think I've found a way to crack the paradigm shift case wide open.* She sped to Langley without giving Annabeth her usual lecture on changing Kevin's diapers in a timely manner or stopping for her normal morning coffee. It was barely 7 am when she passed through the large metal archway that marked Langley's entrance and made her way through the numerous security guards and their checkpoints. *I hope Tyrone's here already,* she thought. *He never told me what time he usually starts working.*

An elderly janitor was busy mopping the stairs, somewhat slowing Gada's ascent to the second floor as she scrambled to maintain her footing on the slippery surface. "Woah there, lass! Careful you don't slip!" the janitor exclaimed as Gada nearly slid back down the staircase. "Nobody is ever here this early. That's why I mop this area first."

"It's okay, Mr. McCreedy," Gada replied, squinting to read his nametag. "I'll forgive you if you can tell me whether Tyrone is here yet."

"Tyrone? Tupper? Of course he's here. That man wouldn't miss the opportunity to tread all over my wet floors if someone offered to pay him for it," he replied. "Mr. Tupper is here at 5 am every morning. He's probably on his fifth cup of coffee already. Goes through coffee mugs faster than anyone else I know. I feel like all I ever do is wash coffee mugs, you know what I mean?"

"I have a husband, so I definitely do," Gada chortled, stepping over another stair-puddle before making it to the second floor. "I'll see you around! Thanks for the chat!"

Mr. McCreedy hadn't been wrong. Gada found Tyrone in his office, gulping away at a large cup of coffee while carefully studying the morning paper. "I think I've found a way to figure out whether there's espionage involved in the paradigm shifts I've identified," she bellowed, storming into the room head first.

"Good morning to you too, Captain Corey," he chuckled, taking one last swig from his cup. "Forgive me if I look surprised. People don't usually storm into my office with world-changing ideas this early in the morning."

"That's because you've never worked with someone like me before," she asserted, strutting up and down along the length of one side of his desk.

"Now you've got me curious," he said, closing the newspaper in front of him before carefully folding it up into a neat rectangle. "Well, go on. I'm waiting."

"Tell me if I'm crazy, but my theory is that if there is espionage involved, I should be able to find out the motive behind the distribution of information between countries by taking a closer look at the global private sector. A tech company somewhere must know something if advanced hyperspeed missile plans are being circulated around by someone," she ranted, still pacing up and down like a caged animal.

"Actually, that's a brilliant idea!" Tyrone enthused, smiling up at Gada. She didn't smile back. Instead, she furrowed her brow as she increased the pace of her fevered march along one side of Tyrone's desk.

"Do you think you can get me clearance to run some data searches on all of the world's private technology companies using the quantum computer?" she finally asked, stopping mid-step to stare at Tyrone. "Do you think you could get it for me today? I know I need to file a Domestic Data Intercept Request. I think it's a D-1703 form or something if I want to bypass some of the privacy agreements that we have with corporations."

"Wow. You're the first agent I've ever met that actually read the quantum computer's policy documents before getting started," Tyrone answered, feigning surprise. "I bet you're the kind of person that reads instruction manuals too."

"I am," she confirmed. "So, how long will it take? I need an idea of the timeframe that we're looking at."

"Usually, about a week," Tyrone replied solemnly.

"A week! I can't wait that long!" Gada exclaimed, anxiously wringing her hands together. The building was starting to fill up with agents as they began to report in for duty for the day. Their noisy bustling and chattering made its way up to the second floor and filled Tyrone's office, only serving to add to Gada's sense of urgency. "Isn't there someone you could call to speed up the process? Perhaps before the day really starts and everyone gets too busy to help us?"

"Hmm. I can't make any promises, but there is something I could try. Just don't get your hopes up," Tyrone gently answered. He watched her continue to pace around in his office as he reached for his camel-colored office phone on one corner of his messy desk. He picked it up off of the receiver, dialed a short number, and held it against his ear. For a moment, he and Gada silently stared at each other, both waiting for someone to pick up the call.

"Hi. Yes, this is Captain Tyrone Tupper speaking. I'd like to lodge an urgent request to access private corporate information using the quantum computer. It's a matter of national security," he stated. Gada couldn't hear the voice on the other side of the line, but Tyrone soon replied, "Yes, really! I'd be willing to stake my career on it." Tyrone winked at Gada. A smile spread across his face as the voice on the other end continued to speak. "Yes. Thank you, sir. I sincerely appreciate it. I won't let you down. I'll be sure to do that, sir," he groveled, doing a little victory dance while seated in the swiveling chair behind his desk. He dramatically slammed the phone back down onto its receiver. "Oooooh, I've got good news for you," he purred, grinning at Gada, who now stood frozen with dread in one corner of the room. "Don't look so scared. I said it's good news!" he playfully scolded her.

"Sorry," she sniffed. "Some of the stuff that has been happening is...well, creepy. I'm a little rattled, to be honest, and would prefer to just have a blunt conversation about whatever the person on the other end of the line just told you. I'm not emotionally up to mind games today."

175

"When have I ever played mind games with you?" he scoffed, getting up out of his chair to join her in the corner where she had positioned herself. "That's a low blow." He placed his hand on her shoulder and calmly said, "I got permission for you to use the quantum computer to spy on tech companies. It's good news. You should be happy!"

"I'm not going to spy on them," she grumbled, brushing his hand off of her shoulder. "It'll be an incredibly professional examination that complies with the CIA's privacy policies."

"I have no doubt that it will," he laughed, making his way back to his seat. "I'd expect nothing less from you, Captain Corey."

Gada wondered who had been on the other end of the line as she made her way to the "lunchroom" next door. *Must have been that asshole, Greene,* she thought. *They must be getting worried if they're actually complying with my wishes now. To think how obstinately they used to oppose me using the quantum computer at all. Makes me sick!* The dark room that housed the quantum computer's user interface had started feeling like home to her. It was a dimly-lit cocoon that she could retreat into when the outside world became too much for her, and it was the room she was planning on cracking the case from. She took a deep breath as she entered it, savoring the musky smell of stagnant air. It wasn't an unpleasant smell, not to her anyway. She cracked her knuckles before plopping down in the chair behind the computer screen. The keyboard felt warm and familiar under her fingertips. She sighed contentedly as she tried to word the perfect search phrase in her head. After a minute or two of planning, while uploading her equations, she extended her sweaty palms and typed "companies that have recently experienced unexplained jumps in technological advancement" into the search criteria selection box. *If I can figure out which companies are experiencing paradigm shifts, I'll be able to surmise which ones are part of this global technology plot,* she told herself. Gada reread all of her input options before finally scraping together all of her courage and pressing 'search.'

The quantum computer returned a result almost immediately. *Oh my.* Gada gasped as she tried to comprehend the information that the machine had availed to her. *It's all of them. All of the tech companies have recently experienced paradigm shifts. So now I know two things, and only two things: All of the countries of the world have been experiencing paradigm shifts and so have all of the world's tech companies. What could this possibly mean?*

She anxiously chewed at her thumb's nail as she tried to make sense of it all. Despite her feverish nail gnawing, she was unable to conjure up a logical solution, so instead opted to go for a stroll across Langley's perfectly manicured lawns. *I just need some fresh air. It'll come to me;* she tried to convince herself. She was still mulling the quantum computer's results over in her mind as she sauntered down the staircase, past Mr. McCreedy, who was now mopping the building's empty reception area, through the metal detector and x-ray machine and out into the open air. The sun felt unpleasantly hot against her skin, and no breeze swept in to offer her any relief. The small footpath leading into the building's gardens soon made an unexpected curve that led to a small gazebo that had been built inside a modest grove of trees. It was filled with a group of people. None of them were talking to each other, although they were each distractedly sucking on their own cigarette. A small cloud of smoke had gathered under the gazebo's roof, giving it a somewhat mystical appearance. *Seems like I've stumbled onto an unsanctioned smoking area,* Gada thought, politely smiling at the small crowd as she strolled past them. *I guess every government agency has their share of Dubois-like characters.* The thought had barely made it from neuron to neuron when an idea finally dawned on Gada. *I could ask Dubois what she thinks of all of the data on paradigm shifts I've collected so far!*

Gada dug through her coat's deep pockets, displacing her house keys and a number of old receipts in the process, until she managed to wrap her fingers around her bulky cellphone's hard plastic cover, suddenly thankful that she'd remembered to retrieve it from its Faraday cage before leaving the building. Dubois was saved as one of her emergency contacts, and she was able to dial her number in a matter of seconds. She continued to stroll deeper into the gardens, walking through a patch of tulips, as she waited for the Lieutenant Colonel to pick up the call. Eventually, she did.

"Lieutenant Colonel Margaret Dubois, how can I help you?" Dubois's raspy voice cracked through the phone's speaker.

"Maggie, it's me. Gada," she replied, finally coming to a stop under a shady oak tree. She reveled in the cool respite of its shadow.

"Oh! Hey you! It's so good to hear from you. We miss having you here every day. How's Langley treating you? Managed to get what you needed from the quantum computer yet? We're looking forward to having you back here again," Dubois gushed, friendlier than Gada was used to experiencing her.

She must really miss me, Gada thought. *I miss her too.* "The investigation is going... well, okay. I wouldn't do it the honor of saying it's going great. The data I've managed to gather on both cases doesn't quite make sense to me yet, but I'm hopeful that I'll be able to piece all of it together soon. That's actually why I'm calling. I'd like your advice."

"Sure, I'd be happy to help, although I'm not sure I'll be able to come up with better solutions than you could," Dubois admitted. Her admission didn't diminish the jolliness of the voice in the slightest.

"I think I just need a different perspective," Gada said, sitting down with her back against the large oak tree's thick trunk. "So, my investigation has revealed that all of the countries have experienced paradigm shifts in the past twelve months. Literally, every country on Planet Earth."

"That's astounding," Dubois gasped, pausing for a second before continuing. "Have you considered some sort of global cooperation?"

"I have, and there's no evidence of it. Most of the lessor developed world countries that have experienced paradigm shifts don't even belong to the same forums that the advanced countries do. They hardly have any interaction outside of humanitarian and basic trade missions. It has to be something else. But that's not even the strangest part," Gada answered somberly.

"Sounds pretty strange to me," Dubois interjected. "I don't think we've ever observed anything like that before."

"I checked; we haven't. But like I said, it's not the strangest part. The strangest part is the fact tech companies, both nationally and internationally, have experienced similar paradigm shifts in the past year, too. This means that the phenomenon hasn't just affected the public sector," Gada argued, picking at a loose piece of bark on the tree's trunk. "Do you have any idea what might be causing all of this? Do you think it could be espionage?"

"What the hell!" Dubois exclaimed. "How's that possible? No, there's no way that espionage could affect the public and private sectors on an international scale. This has to be bigger, much bigger. Honestly, I don't know what to tell you. Do you have any theories?"

"None," Gada confirmed, lowering her head. "But I'm scared, Maggie. I'm petrified, and I need someone to know that I think I've stumbled onto something much more significant than either of us originally realized."

Chapter 8: The Golden Theodolite

10 pm is the new 5 pm, Gada thought as she traversed the empty parking lot. She had let Mike know she'd be home late but doubted he'd still be awake when she got there.

"Meow!" A black cat skid between the cars, hissing as it slinked behind a barren tree a few yards away. Ordinarily, the ruckus might have startled Gada, but nothing seemed to fit into the category of "ordinary" anymore.

Gada's thoughts were elsewhere as she opened the car's door, slid in, and switched on its headlights. In her opinion, there were some places where the veil between the natural and the paranormal was extraordinarily thin. Empty office buildings, hospitals at night, traffic lights flickering away when there was no one on the road, and school playgrounds during the summer holidays. After hours, Langley was one of these places too. Gada imagined that if she was quiet enough, she could hear the cogs of the great machine that the building represented slowly grinding away. She shook her head as she tried to gather her thoughts and turned the key in the car's ignition. Its engine purred to life as she lowered the handbrake and pulled out of the parking lot.

The stars twinkled through the car's sunroof as Gada inched onto the main road and headed toward home. I wonder what goes on up there, she thought, glancing up for a second to appreciate the grand beauty of the celestial bodies sparkling overhead. I wonder if they wonder what goes on down here, whoever "they" are.

Gada had never been overly interested in space, unlike some of the students she'd encountered during her time in university. Sure, she indulged in your average nerdy pop culture offerings (those that contain cliché spaceship battles and attractive aliens), but ultimately she'd never harbored any dreams of ending up at NASA. Mike, on the other hand, had always been fascinated by all things extraterrestrial. A trait that Gada had often found silly and struggled to understand. However, now as she made her way through the dark night, following the black ribbon of tar streaming out in front of her, she wondered whether there were other planets just like Earth filled with people just like her. She wondered whether they were happy, wherever they found themselves.

A flash in her rearview mirror caught her attention, pulling her away from her musings. Gada glanced up and tilted her mirror so that the headlights emanating from the car behind her wouldn't blind her. *I wish this guy would just pass me.* She thought as she slowed the car to give him an opportunity to do so. *The last thing I need now is to be tailgated halfway home.*

Soon, she was traveling a mere ten miles per hour, but the stubborn driver behind her wouldn't budge. In fact, the brightness of his headlights felt like it increased in intensity with every second that he stayed behind her. *Is this guy following me?* She considered the possibility, an icy shiver running down her spine. She could feel the hairs on the back of her neck slowly rising. Her heart raced. Its beat was almost deafening as she struggled to turn the steering wheel with her clammy hands. She tugged the car to the left without bothering to make use of her indicator, hoping that the vehicle that appeared to be following her would continue onward on the main road.

The narrow street she turned into gave way to suburbia. The well-manicured lawns and bohemian dwellings would usually be comforting in their quaintness, but Gada was far too unsettled to allow her surroundings to lull her into a false sense of security.

She was almost ready to celebrate a well-executed maneuver when the car appeared behind her again. *Shit!* she thought. *He is following me!* She was certain her nighttime road companion had something to do with the scientist-killer cases, although she didn't know why, which made the situation all the more terrifying. *Why else would someone be following me? And what happens when he catches up?* She gulped, pressing down on the car's accelerator as she remembered the crime scene photos in the first manila envelope that Dubois had handed her.

The more she sped up, the more the car behind her sped up, always keeping the same distance between them. *I've got to do something. I can't let them follow me home to Mike and Kevin,* she thought, desperately trying to conjure up a plan of action. Then, it dawned on her. Dubois.

She leaned over to access her handbag in the passenger side footwell and started rummaging around in it, finally wrapping her fingers around her cellphone's cool surface. She hastily dialed Dubois's number, careful not to take her eyes off the road entirely, and pressed the phone against her ear. Her hand trembled as she listened to the cellphone's monotonously insistent ringing. Just as Gada was about to give up, the receiver clicked.

"Who's this? Do you know what time it is?" Dubois croaked from the other end of the line.

"It's me, Gada. Are you home? I think I'm in danger," Gada almost whimpered, glancing back in the rearview mirror at the car that was still just behind her.

"Of course, where else would I be this time of the night? What's going on? What danger?" Dubois asked groggily.

"I'm on my way home, but someone's following me. I'm close to your place. Could you come out to meet me? I don't want to risk going home while I'm still being tailed. Do you have a weapon somewhere in the house?" Gada blubbered.

"I always have a gun on me," Dubois replied matter-of-factly. "I'll meet you outside in five minutes. Do you remember where my house is? I'll stand in front of it, don't run me over."

"Yeah, it's the one with the big black gate. Impossible to miss. See you in five," Gada confirmed, falling back on her military training. She decelerated as she turned into Dubois's street. The car behind her turned into it as well, slowing to maintain its distance behind her.

A few yards in, she spotted a figure clad in white standing in the middle of the road. Must be her, she thought. Her suspicions were confirmed as she drew closer. She was straddling the narrow suburban street dressed in a red wine-stained white dressing gown and puffy slippers. A stub-nose automatic assault rifle was slung across one of her shoulders, and her feet were clad in uncharacteristic pink bunny slippers. She motioned for Gada to pull into her driveway by opening her arms like a bird preparing for flight. Gada obliged, readying herself to duck underneath her seat should her pursuer decide to confront Dubois. She had no doubt in her mind that Dubois would engage in a full-blown shootout with whoever had been following her if she deemed it necessary. Seconds passed, and then a minute, but nothing happened.

Knock, knock. Dubois wrapped her knuckles against the passenger side window, startling Gada. "You can get out now!" she laughed. "The bastard sped off when he saw me standing in the road! I think my bunny slippers scared him off."

"Really? Are you sure the slippers made him flee?" Gada hiccuped, throwing her door open and nearly tumbling down onto the gravel below. She scurried around past its hood and flung her arms around Dubois's neck. "Thank you! Thank you!" she blubbered. "To be honest, I wouldn't risk an altercation with a woman in bunny slippers either," she teased, almost overwhelmed by the sense of relief that washed over her.

"Everything okay out here?" Jane asked, peeping her head out from behind the front door. "Can I make you guys some coffee?"

"What did I say about coming outside?" Dubois grumbled, flashing an angry look at her partner. "It's not safe out here!"

"Well, then you shouldn't be out here either, should you?" Jane cheekily asked, punctuating her sentence by sticking her tongue out at Dubois. "Come inside before you both get the flu. It's freezing out here!"

Gada found herself being herded into Dubois's living room. Jane wrapped a fuzzy red blanket around her shoulders and propped a steaming cup of hot chocolate in her hands. Dubois opted for black coffee but chose to keep her rifle with her instead of putting it back in the safe as Jane vehemently suggested she should. Jane, who Gada could only describe as pixie-like in temperament and appearance, was flitting around the kitchen as she wildly attempted to whip up a platter with the week-old leftovers in their fridge. "I'm not hungry. You

185

really don't have to trouble yourself with that," Gada suggested, sipping on her piping hot beverage.

"Oh, don't worry! It's no effort! Maggie and I like having a late-night snack every now and then anyway," Jane insisted, stacking blocks of cheese on a plate.

"Ignore her," Dubois suggested. "It's apparently a cultural thing. I don't try to understand it anymore. Anyway, she won't let you leave unless you eat. That's basically what it boils down to."

"It's called hospitality!" Jane chirped from the kitchen. "An art that seems to be lost to the Western world. My mother would die if she found out that I had guests over and didn't feed them."

"Hmph," Dubois grunted, running her index finger along the length of her rifle's shiny barrel. "Back to the matter at hand, who was following you?"

"It would be a lot less scary if I knew," Gada answered somberly. "I haven't got a clue. It has to be related to the cases I'm currently investigating. Yet, I'm nowhere close to getting any concrete answers. So I can't imagine who would possibly feel threatened enough to follow me home from work."

"You'll have to be more careful. Wherever your investigation's leading you, it's clearly upsetting someone very powerful or very angry, perhaps even both," Dubois suggested just as Jane returned with her plate full of culinary offerings, none of which looked particularly appetizing. "What are the most recent developments in the case? I could try to help you to identify a possible suspect or suspects if I know what you're busy with."

"Don't laugh, but recently I've been doing a lot of research on biobots. The story of how I stumbled onto them is a little convoluted, though. You see, all the scientists that were murdered were looking into Chromosome 2. Chromosome 2 most likely originated because of some form of biobot, either manufactured or naturally-occurring, that changed the structure of our DNA thousands of years ago. If I can just understand why the biobots that played a role in our DNA's evolution were so important to the dead scientists, I'd be that much closer to understanding why they were murdered and perhaps even who did it," Gada passionately explained.

"Biobots?" Dubois asked. "What do some of the agents at Langley think?"

"I don't know," Gada admitted. "My colleague, Tyrone, seems even more confused by it than I am, and I can't blame him. It doesn't really make any sense. I called one of my old professor friends from my time in Britain and explained the situation to her. Still, she wasn't able to give me any information other than stuff that is connected to the weird theoretical extraterrestrial civilizations she studies."

"Your professor friend studies aliens?" Dubois asked skeptically, arching one of her blond eyebrows in response. "Seems like an odd thing to devote one's time to."

"Not E.T. green-martian type aliens," Gada interjected. "It's all just theoretical. It's a way for them to study how civilizations may have developed if they had evolved entirely separate from those on Earth. I don't think the people that study them necessarily even believe that there is other intelligent life out there. It's just an exercise of intellectual rigor that they choose to put themselves through for some reason."

"You've lost me, kid," Dubois huffed, finally putting her rifle down on the coffee table between them. "So, are the biobots the murdered scientists were studying 'extraterrestrial' or not?"

"I don't know. To be honest, I'm not sure it would even matter if they were," Gada admitted, hesitantly picking a piece of ham off of the platter. "At this point, it feels like anything's possible. The cherry on the cake? It appears someone wants to scare me off or even legitimately harm me."

"To be fair, we don't know why they were following you," Dubois added, leaning back on the white leather couch she was seated on opposite Gada.

"Nobody ever stalks someone else this time of the night with good intentions," Gada sighed, putting her cup down next to Dubois's rifle.

"True," Dubois conceded. "At least you have me to protect you."

"And me!" Jane chimed in from the other side of the room, where she'd made herself comfortable on a fur rug in front of the crackling fireplace.

Much to Gada's surprise, Mike was still awake by the time she finally made her way back to the Poto-Pine Apartment Building. It was well past midnight by the time she stumbled through the front door. She tried sneaking across the entryway's carpet, careful not to wake Kevin, who she knew must have been sleeping in the nursery.

"Is this the time to get home?" Mike asked, looking up at her from the couch. He had a thick book cradled on his lap but looked visibly tired. "I hope they're paying you overtime," he added to lighten the tone.

"I struggled to get the quantum computer to cooperate again," Gada lied, making her way over to him. She kissed him on his forehead before flinging herself down on the couch too, sending his book flying across the room. She decided she'd omit the part about being followed and consequently saved by Dubois. *He doesn't need that kind of stress in his life*, she thought.

"Well, I'm glad you're home now," he said, wrapping one of his arms around her shoulders. "Kevin's adorable, but he's a terrible conversationalist."

"Gets it from his father," Gada joked, fishing a hair tie out from underneath one of the couch's cushions before bundling her hair into a tight bun on top of her head with it. "How was your day?"

"Way more interesting than yours," Mike teased; a flash of excitement lit up his eyes. Gada could tell he was preparing to embark on another one of his overly nerdy tales again, the kind that only other engineers truly found interesting. "The most fascinating thing happened at work today. We identified a geologically rich copper deposit at that new site I was telling you about last week."

"Hmm? Copper? Very interesting," Gada playfully yawned, feigning boredom.

"That's not the interesting part," he tut-tutted. "The interesting part happened when we test-drilled at the coordinates the GPS had given us."

"Let me guess; it wasn't copper. It was gold?" Gada said, trying her best to seem supportive.

"Don't be silly," Mike chuckled. "Copper and gold form under completely different conditions. No, the deposit was simply about ten times larger than even our prospectors, and ground radar readings had suggested. I don't want to brag, but it's probably one of the largest copper deposits that have been found in recent history."

"I'm not going to lie, that's pretty impressive," Gada conceded. "I can imagine your boss is pretty pleased with himself."

"Mr. Higginford is elated," Mike confirmed, vigorously nodding his head. "The size of the deposit isn't what makes it interesting either. What makes it interesting is the fact that when we reviewed the map data again, we realized the GPS malfunctioned, and we had actually drilled in the wrong location. Go figure."

"So, there are two large copper deposits on the same site?" Gada asked. "That's quite some luck."

"No, wait. It gets more complicated than that," Mike said, raising one of his palms like a traffic controller trying to halt an unstoppable stream of vehicles. "We went back with a different GPS after the first one malfunctioned, confirmed the real location of the first deposit our radars and prospectors had identified and then drilled there. We drilled and drilled and drilled, but we came up with nothing. Absolutely nothing! When we realized that the first deposit we had identified didn't harbor even the smallest crumb of copper, Mr. Higginford and I looked at each other and knew that if it wasn't for the malfunctioning GPS, we would have aborted the site after drilling through the first area we believed to host a large copper deposit, and we would have never found the immense deposit the first GPS had erroneously and accidentally led us to. We would have lost millions in work effort!"

"That's quite a coincidence," Gada replied, trying to rationalize Mike's tale in her mind. "Statistically, you must be the luckiest engineer in the world."

"That's exactly what Mr. Higginford said," Mike laughed sheepishly. "Mr. Higginford and I knew that it was either an unbelievable streak of luck or some serious divine intervention. He even said that he's planning on gold-plating the malfunctioning GPS and getting its name tattooed across his chest."

"What's its name? I've never heard of a GPS with a name before," Gada giggled, now fully invested in Mike's retelling of his work adventures.

"Well, it wasn't named like you might name a puppy or a baby, but it has a model name: The Autonomous GPS Theodolite."

"You should just call it 'Theo,'" Gada laughed. "He and Sandy at the DIA could be friends."

The last thing that Gada remembered was sipping a cider while listening to Mike go on about his incredibly large copper find, a story that soon felt like it spanned a number of hours. When Gada awoke again, she was tangled in their bed's Egyptian cotton sheets, listening to her morning alarm blaring.

The alarm clock on her bedside table read "07:10 am." Crap, I'm going to be late, she thought, hastily swinging her legs onto the floor. She reached over to touch Mike's empty spot next to her. It's cold already. He must have left a while ago. Annabeth was already cooing over Kevin in the nursery by the time she stormed out of the main bedroom. Her heavy winter jacket flapped behind her like a superhero's cloak as she struggled to get her arm through one of its sleeves. "Thanks for being here so early, Annabeth. Remind me to add ten dollars to your wages at the end of the week," Gada said as she stormed toward the front door, hooking her handbag into the crook of her elbow just as she reached the door's threshold.

"Oh, I won't let you forget," Annabeth assured her, waving at her as she flew out of the apartment.

The drive to Langley was quieter than usual. *Guess everyone that's usually on the road made it to work already,* Gada thought, contemplatively analyzing the remarkable stillness of the streets around her. The parking lot off to one side of the CIA's building seemed even more devoid of life than usual too. Gada saw the feral black cat from the day before chasing flies near a drain close to the sidewalk that connected the parking lot to Langley's entrance, but except for the feline, she was acutely aware of the fact that she was alone. *I just hope whoever was following me yesterday has given up on finding me,* she thought as she rushed toward the small army of security guards stationed at the front door. *At least they'd never be stupid enough to try to follow me inside. They'd have to be absolutely mad or have a death wish to even consider it. I'll be safe once I'm in the quantum computing room,* she tried to convince herself.

The multiple scans that she and her handbag were normally put through before being allowed to enter the building were usually nothing more than an irritation to Gada, but today they offered a weird sense of comfort and familiarity. She spent an extra minute or two conversing with the guards, more thankful than ever that they were stationed where they were. "You haven't seen any odd figures lurking around here lately?" she asked the largest of the armed guards just as she was preparing to depart for the quantum computing room.

"Odd figures?" the guard asked, furrowing his brow. "No, no. Definitely not. Why? Should we be keeping our eyes peeled for 'odd figures?'"

"No, I don't think so. I was just wondering," Gada fibbed. "Thanks so much anyway," she mumbled as she turned and headed up the stairs that would lead her to Tyrone and the "lunchroom" that wasn't a lunchroom at all.

She found Tyrone busy assembling a tiny plastic interlocking brick structure on his desk. "Is this really the most productive way you could spend your morning?" she asked as she strode into his office. "On government time?"

"I worked overtime yesterday. I'm just catching up on my extra-curricular activities," he giggled, putting a final yellow rectangle in place before getting up from behind his desk and stowing his creation away in one of the inbuilt cupboards that lined his office. "Although I didn't work nearly as much overtime as you did. The guards told me you still hadn't left yet when I clocked out at 8 pm last night."

"Yeah, I stayed about two hours later than that," Gada coyly admitted. "There's a lot of research that needs to be done, and the lives of prominent members of the scientific community depend on how fast I'm able to solve this case."

"That's very noble of you," Tyrone asserted, making his way back to the chair behind his desk. "Just be careful not to burn yourself out. I can't afford to lose you. If something happened to you, they'd assign the case to me, and I'm not sure I could achieve a tenth of what you manage to achieve with the quantum computer."

"Thanks, it only took months of practice," Gada laughed, tucking her skirt under her as she lowered herself onto one of the leather seats on the other side of Tyrone's desk.

"What's on the agenda today? Anything I can help with?" Tyrone lifted the coffee cup perched precariously on one corner of his desk to his lips and gulped down its dark contents.

"Guess," Gada replied slyly.

"Biobots?" Tyrone guessed. "It can't still be biobots," he added in recognition of the smile that flashed across her face. "How could there possibly be anything left to learn about them?"

"You clearly still haven't read up on them if you don't get it," Gada cheekily answered. "I'm telling you, Tyrone. I'm this close to understanding where they fit into all of this."

"No need to convince me. I believe you," Tyrone assured her. "But Agent Greene is expecting a report from us on what we're doing that's taking up so much of the quantum computer's bandwidth. Would you be comfortable explaining what's going on in your investigation to him?"

"Of course I would. I'm not doing anything wrong. Since when is he interested in my investigation, anyway? I thought I was just some plague rat to him that needs to be avoided at all costs," Gada grumbled, leaning forward in her seat to fiddle with a miniature globe on Tyrone's desk.

"Ah. Still angry about his refusal to meet with you on your first day here," Tyrone observed. "You can have that globe, by the way, if you'd like. I have a bigger one at home. That one just takes up space."

"Thanks," Gada sniffed, stowing the tiny blue globe in her coat's pocket. "And yeah, I'm still upset. Imagine spending your entire life trying to prove your worth, attending graduate studies for nearly a decade only to have some shriveled up desk jockey tell you you're too leprous to even be met with."

"He wouldn't meet with me on my first day either," Tyrone gently said, offering Gada a sympathetic smile. "Imagine being so insecure that you can't bear sharing your expensive toy with anyone that isn't a stale old white man. If anything, we should be the ones pitying him. His entire concept of self must be incredibly fragile."

"I don't feel pity for bullies," Gada concluded, getting up out of the slick leather seat. "Neither should you."

The short walk to the "lunchroom" was made even more brief by the fact that Tyrone didn't accompany her to it like he usually did. Instead, he stayed behind silently staring out of his office window. Gada hoped he'd take her words to heart, although a part of her knew that he used pitying Greene as a method of self-preservation.

The technicians politely nodded at her as she entered the sterile zone. I wonder if I've ever heard any of their voices, Gada thought. Other than their early-morning nodding and thumbs-up when she was shouting commands at them from the other room, they didn't seem all that interested in interacting with her. You'd think we'd know a bit about each other by now. It's been months, she thought as she made herself comfortable at the modest desk in the backroom behind the technicians' area. The low hum of the quantum computer comforted her, and soon all thoughts of Tyrone's disillusionment and Agent Greene had left her mind.

After hours of research, she stumbled onto an article published by Humnz2AI, a renowned analytical think-tank. It drew comparisons between soldiers and the biobots that were being produced by hopeful medical researchers. She zoomed in to make the scientific journal's text more legible. It read:

"The most striking similarity between the armed forces and what is theoretically achievable with biobot technology is the fact that both soldiers and biobots need to be two things above all else: productive and controllable. Examining a range of nations' offensive tactics over a period of three-hundred years allows the shared characteristics between biobots and soldiers to become even more apparent.

"The first notable armed conflict in American history, the Cherokee War, occurred in 1759. The colonists, searching to expand their control of native resources, clashed with the indigenous people of the land as they traveled inland. This skirmish gave them access to resources that the indigenous people had often declined to harvest themselves, meaning that colonial agriculture and early mining practices were made possible because of the war.

"Just a little more than a hundred years later, the United States found itself embroiled in a Civil War that saw the Union clashing with the Confederacy. With their eye on globalization, the Union's far more organized troops rightly managed to oppress the confederate insurgence, ensuring that the United States would remain a player in the international community. A place in the global economy ensured that the United States would have access to trade deals that it would otherwise have been turned away from.

"Fifty years later, during World War I, the well-being of global cooperative systems was once again tested and eventually defended. This war saw hundreds of thousands of men putting their lives on the line for the betterment of international relations in a conflict that they believed would protect the world from a growing global threat. World War I allowed humanity to catch a glimpse of the type of propaganda that would grow in popularity and prevalence during World War II. The influencing ability of propaganda on the human mind has been studied for decades but is still poorly understood.

"Twenty years later, World War Two saw the Axis Powers trying to break away from the accepted zeitgeist of the time. Through sheer force and determination, the Allied Powers managed to suppress the ideologies that led to some of the reported war crimes of the era by claiming victory over the entire conflict. This victory saw the rise of a number of institutions, such as the United Nations, that strive to ensure international cohesion for the sake of better resource distribution and a healthier global economy. These institutions further led to the creation of a number of international treaties and agreements that regulate the laws pertaining to international trade.

"Just like biobots, the soldiers in this war were 'programmed' [often through the use of propaganda or nationalistic ideologies] to perform a function even if the performance of this function would mean the destruction of the individual or individuals executing it. Recent studies conducted on biobots that could potentially be used for medical purposes show that self-destruction is often the fate suffered by Biobots. Even those that manage to successfully perform their programmed function, proving that military casualties will likely always be in the cards during times of armed conflict.

"Biobots that are not destroyed upon completion of their given task or tasks are often 'reset' to their original state. This behavior has also been observed in soldiers, particularly those that return from the armed conflicts that they were involved in with memory loss associated with emotional or physical trauma or post-traumatic stress disorder that leaves them unable to speak about the things that they experienced during the execution of their duties.

"Biobots, just like soldiers, tend to be used for a range of similar reasons. Biobots could potentially be used to cure cancer, to attack viruses and bacteria in the body, or to influence other cells in the body to perform functions differently than they normally would. Soldiers are often used to defend territories from virus-like invaders and insurgents, fight malevolent threats, and restore order in areas that would otherwise be plunged into chaos.

"Theoretically, biobots could also be used to improve medical technologies that do not necessarily directly utilize them. They could be used to program motherboards, sharpen drills, or fix faulty wiring before a short circuit even occurs. Similarly, soldiers and the wars they belong to often improve the area's non-offensive technologies for the better, too. A study conducted in the latter half of last year found that war often leads to improvements in mining, scanning, drilling, and excavation technologies. However, it wasn't able to explain the reasons behind this occurrence. Medical and biological sciences seem to stall during times of conflict, except when it comes to developing methodologies of helping soldiers to better bear the brunt of war."

That's a lot to take in, Gada thought, leaning back in her chair. *Soldiers? As if biobots weren't confusing enough.* She sighed and slowly got out of the swiveling chair behind the quantum computer's user interface. She reached her arms behind her head and fixed her long curly ponytail before walking out of the backroom and into the blindingly bright white light of the sterile area.

"You shouldn't be researching that," a technician with a thick silver ring through one of her bushy black eyebrows growled, quietly approaching Gada as she made her way across the room. "You shouldn't be researching that," her voice reverberating as she repeated monotonously. Now directly behind Gada. Gada could feel her clammy breath in the nape of her neck.

She spun around to face the technician, unsure of how to react to the intrusion. "What did you say?" Gada asked, trying to sound as polite as possible. "I didn't quite hear you."

"I asked whether you're happy with the current data sample that we're using?" the technician asked, her squeaky voice entirely different than the unsettling tone she'd been speaking in mere moments earlier. "We're struggling to keep the computer's temperature within a safe range, and I was hoping we could find some way to decrease the size of the data sample you're currently running—"

"Can we do this later?" Gada sighed, pinching the bridge of her nose. "I don't have time right now, and stop sneaking up on people. It'll get you knocked out in a place like this."

"Sorry, I didn't mean to scare you," the technician frowned, diverting her doe-like brown eyes downward. "I just want to make sure everything's running optimally."

"Everything's fine. Thanks," Gada huffed, turning on her heel and leaving the "lunchroom" in search of a vending machine. She knew she'd been unjustifiably unkind to the technician who had approached her but couldn't shake the feeling of anger that hung over her. It was an emotion that had no rhyme or reason, but she tried to reconcile herself by telling herself that it was a normal response to being startled. *And I've been getting startled a lot lately*, she thought.

The vending machine was at the end of the hallway. Gada decided to jog past Tyrone's office in hopes that he wouldn't see her passing it. She appreciated Tyrone's friendship but didn't have time for one of his infamous hour-long catch-up sessions. She breathed a sigh of relief as she noticed the "out of office" sign on his door. *Must have decided to go out for lunch,* Gada thought. Odd. His wife usually packs him something to eat. *I've seen some of her sandwiches, better than anything you'd get from Subway.* She decided not to give it too much thought. *You're being paranoid again. People are allowed to go out for lunch without telling you.* As she continued down the hallway, she realized that none of the offices on the second floor had their usual occupants in them. *I wonder where everyone is. Maybe I'm missing some kind of team-building exercise I forgot to diarize?* She wondered. The only sound was that of her footsteps on the hallway's carpeted floor. Gada could swear that she felt the temperature plummet as she drew closer to the end of the hallway. Her skin broke out in goosebumps, and she tugged at her coat's sleeves in an attempt to escape the chill.

The sight of the vending machine propped against the furthest wall returned a sense of normalcy to the empty floor. The luminescent lights that lit up its contents behind the single pane of glass that separated them from the outside world seemed to chase away the dreary feeling that followed Gada down the hallway. *There's nothing in this world a bar of chocolate can't fix,* she thought, smugly inserting a coin in the machine's slot and selecting the snack she'd had her eyes on.

"You shouldn't be researching that."

She spun around. "Who's there?" she yelled, squinting as she tried to spot where the voice had come from. There was no answer. "Come out! This isn't funny!" she angrily hollered, her shaky demands ricocheting down the long hallway.

"Who are you screaming at, lass?"

Gada turned and nearly walked directly into Mr. McCreedy. "Oh, it's you," she sighed, using the back of her hand to nervously wipe at the beads of sweat that had started to form on her forehead. "Were you saying something about my research?"

"Nay, I'm just cleaning," Mr. McCreedy answered gayly, motioning toward a bucket full of suds and a dirty mop. "Did you hear someone say something about research? Because there's no one else on this floor at the moment. They all went out for lunch, I think."

"Yeah, I did... Who told you they all went out for lunch?" Gada pressed him.

"Must be hearing things then, lass," Mr. McCreedy answered, anxiously rubbing at one of his grimy forearms. "No one told me. I just assumed. Where else would they be?"

"Fair point," Gada said, quickly grabbing her bar of chocolate from the vending machine's slot. "I guess I must be imagining things," she conceded, smiling coyly at the jolly janitor. "Apologies, I really must get going."

Mr. McCreedy's expression suddenly changed just as she turned to leave. "Before you go, I don't know if you're the praying type, but if you are, please spare a prayer for my parents' farm back home," Mr. McCreedy started. "My hometown had an outbreak of foot-and-mouth disease, and it looks like their entire herd might have contracted it from the neighbor's sheep. They might have to make all of the affected individuals 'disappear' if they want to keep their export license, if you know what I mean—"

"I'm not sure I do," Gada interrupted as sympathetically as possible, "but I'll spare them a thought. Good-bye, Mr. McCreedy. I'll see you around." She could feel his now teary eyes following her as she made her way back down the hallway. His sudden outburst of emotion made her somewhat uncomfortable. Then again, she thought, I've never been very comfortable with other people's feelings.

Her mind wandered to his parents' cattle, and she wondered what fate awaited the sickly cows. She remembered one of Nori's lectures on Type II civilizations, an entire two hours of education that had been devoted to discussing the types of "natural population control" that Type II civilizations might inflict on their subjugated Type 0 civilizations. Nori always theorized that Type II civilizations would use plagues to control their servant civilizations. Perhaps the cow-overlords are thinning the herd. She giggled to herself, imagining what such a thing might look like. Then it hit her. How many plagues have we had? She wondered, a sudden sense of urgency flooding her mind. She knew it was no small number but now felt that she had to know for sure, although she couldn't quite explain the feeling. Gada rushed back to the tiny backroom that housed the quantum computer's user interface, set her search parameters, and initiated a database scan. She opened the first file on human plagues that popped up.

"The first significant plague was recorded in 165 CE and was called the Antonine Plague. Although the exact virus that caused the more than five million deaths has yet to be agreed upon, scientists are certain that it was either an outbreak of highly-contagious measles or smallpox," the article read.

"Less than 400 years later, the Plague of Justinian claimed between thirty and fifty million lives. Two hundred years later, the Japanese smallpox epidemic claimed one million lives. This trend continued and continues to this day," it read. "In 1347, the Black Death caused by the Yersinia pestis bacteria took over 200 million lives. The most prolific plague in modern history occurred in 1918 and was known as the Spanish Flu. It cost approximately fifty million people their lives."

Gada took a deep breath. *I'm going crazy,* she thought. *Nori's theories on Type II civilizations are starting to hit a little close to home. We're a Type 0 civilization, of that I'm sure, but does that mean we're being subjugated by some unknown Type II civilization? If so, how does nobody know about it?* She pondered it for a moment and soon found herself thinking of the McCreedy family cattle again. *Humans are to livestock what Type II civilizations are to Type 0 civilizations. By that logic, we haven't encountered extraterrestrial civilizations because, like cattle, we're being protected from them. Farmers protect their livestock from predators that might steal them away. A Type II civilization would likely do the same.*

She switched off the quantum computer's user interface and stared at her blank expression in its reflective black screen. *Are we cattle? No, stop being paranoid! Everything's fine. You're fine!* she internally reprimanded herself. She stood up and slowly walked into the sterile area just beyond the backroom. It was empty. *Where are the technicians?*

As far as Gada was concerned, the day had been nothing but a fever-induced dream. She made her way out of the building without saying as much as a word to one of the guards manning Langley's main doorway and quietly made her way back to her car. She pushed all thoughts of the empty floor, the "AWOL" technicians, and Mr. McCreedy's parents' cattle to the back of her mind. The feral black cat that ostensibly lived in the parking lot was seated on her car's hood. "Shoo!" she said, softly nudging it off of its perch. "This car is only for people with knowledge on our Type II overlords, and I doubt you're one of them," she sarcastically tut-tutted at the cat, smiling at her self-deprecating joke. The cat simply blinked in reply. Its green eyes followed Gada as she got into the driver seat and watched her drive off.

Gada pulled her cellphone out of her coat's pocket as she merged onto the main road and dialed Nori's number. "Nori speaking, how can I help you?" her friend and confidante cheerfully answered.

"Nori, I'm so glad to hear your voice. I'm having one heck of a day," Gada started, almost blubbering as she leaned on the steering wheel for support. "My work is taking some scary turns, and my mind has started playing tricks on me. I need you to be the voice of reason for me, okay?"

"Well, that's quite a greeting," Nori giggled. "You really shouldn't let your job stress you out this much. It's not healthy for you. That being said, how can I help? You're the only person who ever phones me for advice," she laughed.

"Tell me more about Type II civilizations," Gada asked. Her knuckles turned white as she pressed the cellphone against her ear. "Tell me everything about them."

"This again?" Nori nervously chortled. "Look, I love the theory behind Type II civilizations, but I can't help but wonder what you're up to."

"I promise I'll tell you someday. I just can't tell you now. Trust me, it's important," Gada insisted. "I need more information on what kind of resources they might want to harvest from a Type 0 civilization and what this might mean for the Type 0 civilization involved."

"Hmm. A fascinating topic," Nori admitted. Gada could hear her fiddling with something, perhaps a piece of paper, in the background. "Well, I could only guess what kind of resources they'd be after on a different planet because there's no way to really be sure what would motivate such a civilization, but if I had to give you my educated opinion, they'd likely be after some kind of fuel sources, either to fuel their home planet or to fuel their vehicles."

"Like, maybe copper?" Gada interjected. "Theoretically speaking, could a civilization like that dominate a society like ours for something like copper?"

"This is all theoretical, right?" Nori asked in a deadpan tone.

"That's what I said, isn't it?" Gada replied impatiently, turning into Twenty-First Street. She could see their apartment building in the distance.

"To be honest, I doubt they'd come to Earth for copper. Copper is abundant throughout the known universe, so there's no reason to come here for it. It could easily be extracted by the civilization in need of it in any number of locations. If Earth were ever put into such a situation, it would likely be over a rare radioactive metal that could be harnessed as an energy source. To answer one of your earlier questions, I believe what

205

would happen to a Type 0 civilization once its ruling Type II civilization had used up all of its resources is similar to what happens to everything that outlives its usefulness. It would be discarded, in one way or another," Nori explained, pausing to let her assertion sink in. "Does that make sense?"

"It's pretty grim, but it makes sense," Gada agreed, pulling into the parking garage a block away from the Poto-Pine Apartment Building that she and Mike preferred making use of.

"Luckily, it's all just theoretical," Nori added. "Keep safe, Gada, and don't let whatever you're working on get to you. I'm sure the answers you're looking for aren't nearly as terrifying as you seem to be worried they are. I mean, what are the chances that ol' Nori dedicated herself to something useful!" She laughed before hanging up the phone.

The walk to the apartment gave Gada more than enough time to mull over Nori's words. *I'm sure she's right. It was ridiculous of me to think that Type II civilizations have absolutely anything to do with all of this. The culprit in both of my cases must be an earthbound person with normal, albeit evil, motivations.* She felt comforted by the thought that the paradigm shifts and scientist killings really might be explainable by pointing a finger at the Russians or the Chinese. *Nori can't be wrong. She's the smartest person I know.*

Once inside the apartment, Gada found Mike half-asleep with a softly snoring Kevin on his chest, both bundled up on the couch in front of the television. A cartoon rerun was monotonously blaring in the background. "Sorry, I hope I didn't wake you," Gada whispered as she made her way into the room. "How long has he been sleeping?"

"Ten minutes or so," Mike quietly replied, sitting up and scooping Kevin into his arms in one smooth motion. Kevin didn't stir.

"You're the baby-whisperer, you know that?" Gada grinned, lovingly staring at the two most important people in her life.

"Oh, I know," Mike smiled, brushing his lips over Kevin's velvety brow before carefully carrying him to his crib in the adjacent room. He returned after a minute or two, still looking somewhat scruffy from his shared nap with the baby.

"Would you be very upset if I picked your brain while I made dinner?" Gada inquired, kicking off her black stilettos and making her way into their open plan kitchen. "I know you hate it when I bring work home..."

"I love it when you pick my brain," Mike added, smirking at her like an obstinate child.

"Very well, but you asked for it," Gada chuckled, reaching into their vegetable holder and wrapping her fingers around a brown onion. She peeled and started chopping it before continuing, "Why were you so excited about finding copper? It's worth so much less than gold. My work has led me to examine how we handle resource extraction, and I'm trying to understand the world of mining a bit better before I continue with my research. I spoke to Nori about it... But you know how it is with her; Everything's theoretical."

"Mining? What a strange tangent for your cases to have embarked on," Mike remarked, handing Gada another onion. "It's a good question, though. Copper's practical uses set it aside as valuable to those who mine it, despite the fact it isn't worth as much in raw financial gain as gold is. Think about it. We need copper to keep the lights on. Gold doesn't do much

207

other than looking pretty and serving as a base point for currencies, but most technologies would be entirely obsolete if copper simply ceased existing."

Gada dropped the onion. It noisily rolled over the floor and came to rest against the refrigerator door. "That's it!" Gada gasped, a smile spreading across her face. "You're a genius, Mike!" she ran toward him and threw her arms around his neck before pugnaciously kissing him on the cheek. "An absolute genius, I'm telling you!"

"Well, I knew that," Mike blushed, wrapping his arms around Gada's narrow waist. "In this case, why exactly am I a genius, and what did that onion do to deserve getting thrown across the room?"

"I've been approaching both of my cases in the wrong way. I've based both of my investigations on the assumption that the perpetrator or perpetrators are doing it for financial gain. However, suppose all resources aren't necessarily worthless just because they're less valuable. In that case, it could mean that I need to turn my approach on its head," Gada excitedly explained, scrambling to pick up the onion that she'd previously dropped. It rolled away from her, prompting her to comically crawl after it across the kitchen's pale tiles.

"You're quite something, Gada Corey. Y'know that?" Mike asked, jovially kicking the fallen onion back in her direction.

That night during dinner, Gada was more confident than ever before that everything would be alright. She lovingly stared at Mike as he enthusiastically shoveled mashed potatoes into his mouth. *Who cares about what's going on in outer space when things are so darn good down here on Earth?* she thought, contentedly taking a bite of her own meal.

The next day, she walked up to the security checkpoint behind Langley's entrance with a new sense of vigor and a strengthened resolve. *Today's the day I crack this case*, she thought as she grinned at the guard checking the contents of her handbag. She all but skipped past Mr. McCreedy and over the wet floors he was mopping. "Sorry, Mr. McCreedy!" she sang in passing, trying her best to step on the driest patches.

"Careful you don't slip, lass!" he screamed at her as she dashed up the staircase.

Gada practically danced into Tyrone's office, somewhat startling him. "Gada! Jeez!" Tyrone exclaimed, nearly dropping his cup of coffee as she leaped toward his desk, a large smile plastered across her face. "What's gotten into you? You're creeping me out."

"I'm just in a good mood," she trilled, gracefully lowering herself onto one of the chairs in front of Tyrone's desk. "Am I not allowed to be in a good mood?"

"I just don't think I've ever seen you in one before. It's unknown territory for me," he joked, leaning back in his chair. "How's that report Agent Greene asked for coming along?"

"That's why I'm in a good mood. I'm going to run a few more searches today, but after that, I fully intend on typing it up for him and handing it in. If I'm right, the search results I'll be able to conjure up today will make an impressive addition to it. Even a sour old man like Greene won't be able to deny the extraordinary nature of my results after seeing it," Gada cheekily grinned, ending her final sentence by winking at Tyrone. The latter still seemed a little unsure of what to make of the situation.

"If you say so," he nervously laughed, fidgeting with a paperclip that he had retrieved from one of his desk's drawers. "Just don't forget to submit your report when you're done. Greene doesn't like being kept waiting."

"Oh, who cares what Greene likes!" Gada chuckled, jumping back out of her seat and making her way across the room. "Gotta go, Tyrone!" she excitedly said. "I'm off to save the world!"

The technicians were all back at their usual posts by the time that she waltzed into the sterile area on her way to the backroom that housed the quantum computer's user interface. "Good morning, team!" she chimed, waving at each of them individually. Only one waved back, the short technician with the eyebrow piercing. Gada consciously decided not to take their reactions to heart. *I guess you have to be a bit of an introvert to sign up to be stuck in the quantum computer's sterile area every day for the rest of your life,* she reasoned.

The backroom's ominous darkness seemed more welcoming than usual. Where it had once felt like a cage, it now felt like a cocoon that held the blossoming possibility of a solution to her cases and justice for the victims that had been affected. She flopped down into the chair behind the quantum computer's user interface and switched it on. The light from its screen cast long shadows across her face, causing her eyes to appear far more sunken than they truly were. She stared at the search input box for a moment, uploaded her equations, and then typed "Rare radioactive metals found nowhere else but Earth," into it. *If Mike and Nori are right, it makes sense that whoever is behind the scientist-killings and the paradigm shifts is after something rare and radioactive but useful. It can't be copper because it's not radioactive and is far too abundant, and it can't be gold because it's both of those things, and additionally, it's not useful enough... It has to be something else,* she thought. She sent the search parameters through to the technicians on the other side of the wall. Upon receiving confirmation of their adjustment, she started running the search. After a minute or two, the quantum computer's database produced hundreds of related articles. Gada opened the journal entry that appeared at the top of the list. It read:

"There are no elements that are believed to be exclusively found on Earth simply because of the vast and unknowable size of the universe. However, there are certainly a handful of elements that are found in larger quantities on Earth than they appear to be found elsewhere in our galaxy and neighboring galaxies. The most notable of these elements is Niobium, which is found in large quantities on Earth but is believed to be incredibly scarce everywhere else.

"Niobium is a grayish transition metal that is known for its incredible strength, ductility, magnetic penetration depth, which is greater than that of any other known element, and its incredible superconductivity. Most Niobium isotopes, with the exception of a single laboratory-manufactured kind, are radioactive. However, their radioactivity is best described as 'low level' and is not significant to pose a risk to human handlers. Niobium's superconductivity is what makes it of such great interest to the scientific community. Some of its less scientific uses include being used as an alloy in the steel manufacturing process and in electroceramics."

Who would want Niobium so badly, and to what end? Gada wondered, completely baffled. She leaned back in her chair and stared up at the room's dark ceiling. *I was so sure today would be the day that everything falls into place,* she thought somberly.

Chapter 9: The Elusive Element

A week had passed since Gada had first learned of Niobium. However, she didn't feel like she was any closer to understanding why the culprit in her cases would be so desperate to get their hands on it. To top it off, the quantum computer was no longer cooperating either. It had started malfunctioning whenever she included Niobium in her search parameters. Its glitches ostensibly worsened each time she ran a search, and now it was at a point where it seemed to crash or reset itself whenever she came near it.

Gada found herself lying in bed, exhausted but unable to drift off to sleep. Her mind raced. Whenever she caught herself, she was thinking of biobots and Niobium.

"Go to sleep, honey," Mike said, rolling over and wrapping one of his muscular arms around her waist. "I can feel you fretting."

"Why do you think Tyrone wants to see me first thing tomorrow morning? Do you think I'm in trouble?" she whimpered. A tear rolled down her cheek and crashed onto her pillow's silky surface. Her lower lip trembled as she tried to stop herself from sobbing.

"Why on Earth would you be in trouble?" Mike sleepily murmured, brushing his lips against the nape of her neck.

"I don't know... Everything just feels like it's going wrong," she sniffed, wriggling deeper into his warm embrace.

"Everything will be okay, I promise," he comfortingly replied, squeezing her. "I'm sure you're worried about nothing."

Gada lay awake listening to Mike's rhythmic snoring for what felt like hours thereafter before drifting off to sleep. She dreamed that she smuggled a baseball bat into Langley and, in a fit of rage, used it to smash the quantum computer to bits. Her dream was interrupted by her alarm clock's loud screeching. *This is torture,* she thought, groggily sitting upright. *I must have gotten no more than fifteen minutes of sleep last night.*

Before she could wipe her eyes out, Gada found herself anxiously climbing the staircase that led to the floor that housed Tyrone's office. The rest of the agents weren't there yet, and the floor was eerily quiet. *I guess all CIA agents are averse to early mornings,* she thought as she looked around while making her way down the hallway. *Dubois should have been recruited here instead. She would have fit right in.*

She found Tyrone sitting hunched over at his desk with his head resting on his hands. He was staring at a piece of paper between his elbows on the mahogany desk. "Hey, Tyrone. I'm here early, like you asked," Gada nervously announced while standing in his office's doorway. "Is everything okay? Can I come in?"

"Oh. Hi, Gada. Thanks for coming," he replied more formally than he typically would. "Please, have a seat."

"Am I in trouble?" she nervously asked as she made her way over to his desk. "You've got me really worried—"

"It's nothing to be worried about, I hope," he reassured her, glancing up from the paper in front of him. "I just wanted to chat to you, friend to friend, before the rest of the agents come in. Is the quantum computer still acting up?"

"Yeah, worse than ever," she said, averting her gaze.

"That's what I feared," Tyrone nodded sympathetically. "Personally, I think it just needs some serious software maintenance, but I've heard some disturbing rumors around the office. Some of the agents believe that you've 'broken' the quantum computer, that you're the one that is causing it to malfunction. I've heard everything from 'She's a Russian spy sent to sabotage the computer' to 'She's bogging down the machine with her software.' If news of this makes its way to Greene, he'll likely retract his permission for you to make use of the quantum computer."

"What? I won't be able to work on my cases without it!" Gada blurted out, more loudly than she had intended to.

"I know. That's why I asked you to meet with me. I want to suggest that you stop making mention of any difficulties that you have with the quantum computer to anybody but me. If other agents ask, tell them that it's working perfectly and that your research is going well. If they ask what happened to the glitches, just tell them that they seem to have resolved themselves. I know it seems like a silly request, Gada, but trust me, it's important. You're this close to losing your access to the quantum computer, and as your friend, I don't want that to happen to you," Tyrone passionately explained, punctuating his last sentence by slamming his fist against the top of his desk.

"I promise I'll keep it to myself from now on," Gada agreed, using her index finger to draw a cross on her chest. "I didn't know the situation was so dire." A part of Gada was relieved that she wasn't in trouble per se, while the remainder of her was terrified to learn that after all of this time, she was still nothing but an unjustified intruder to many at the CIA. *I always knew some people would prefer if I weren't allowed to be here,* she thought. *I just didn't think they were the majority.*

"Thank you, Gada," Tyrone said, warmly smiling at her from across his desk. The dark circles under his eyes betrayed how tired he was. "I wish I could protect you from all of the malevolent undercurrents here, but I can't. The best I can do is warn you against them. I wish I could do more. I consider you to be one of my best friends—"

"Are you going soft on me?" Gada laughed, trying to brighten the serious atmosphere that hung about the room. "You're one of my closest friends too, Tyrone. Thanks for the heads up, but they won't get rid of me that easily. I'm like one of those weeds that pushes its way through the sidewalk. I've got more resilience in me than I know what to do with."

"You describe yourself so flatteringly," Tyrone chuckled, his mood visibly improved. "What are you planning for lunch? Do you want to come sit with me in my office? We can have our sandwiches together, away from the rest of the assholes here?"

"Thanks for the invite, Tyrone. Maybe tomorrow?" she offered, getting out of the seat where she'd positioned herself behind his desk. "I'm meeting Dubois at a coffee shop a few blocks away for lunch. The last time I saw her... Well, it was under less than ideal circumstances. I owe her a slice of cake."

"I understand and admire your commitment to honoring your cake debts," Tyrone chuckled, waving as she walked through his doorway. "See you tomorrow then!" he exclaimed as she disappeared out of sight.

Gada was acutely aware of each pair of eyes that paused to watch her as she made her way to the "lunchroom" where the quantum computer was located. She avoided making eye

215

contact with any of the agents she came across, unsure which of them had been the ones to suggest that the quantum computer's faults were because of her handling of it. Everyone she encountered was a potential enemy and traitor.

The technicians didn't look her way as she entered the quantum computer's blindingly white sterile area, not even the woman with the eyebrow piercing. *Great, there goes my only supporter on the technician team,* she thought as she eyed the short young technician who was trying her best to look as preoccupied as possible. Gada decided not to push the envelope and quietly slunk into the dark room that housed the quantum computer's user interface. It was already switched on. *That's odd. No one else was authorized to use it today... Not as far as I know, anyway,* Gada thought. *I wonder who has been digging around in here. Probably Greene,* she convinced herself, rolling her eyes as she slumped down into the chair behind the large screen that occupied the center of the room. She tapped the screen to stir the device from its "sleep mode."

"You should not be researching that!" flashed across the screen in bold, bright red letters.

Gada blinked. *Did that just happen?* she wondered, staring at the now empty screen. The command had appeared and disappeared so quickly that she felt unsure whether she'd truly seen it or whether it had simply been a hallucination, conjured up by her exhausted and overextended mind. She decided it had to be the latter. *Get yourself together, Captain Corey! You're losing it!* She reprimanded herself, setting the machine's search parameters to include the latest database results on Niobium and the Niobium mining industry. She hesitated for a moment before initiating her search.

Within seconds, hundreds of new entries, posts, and articles filled the screen in front of her. *Weird. Normally it would have malfunctioned and reset itself by now. I guess the technology Gods are on my side today or something,* she thought, quickly scanning some of the results that had appeared. She decided to click on an article that instantly caught her eye. It was titled "Chinese Niobium Discovery Rocks Mining World" and read:

"A mere forty-eight hours ago, the scientific world still theorized that Earth had one of the highest natural concentrations of Niobium in the solar system. Today, we know that Earth's neighbor, Mars, far out does our humble blue planet. Chinese robotic geo-drilling on Mars has unearthed pure Niobium, a discovery that has rocked the scientific community to its core. It also bodes well for the Niobium mining industry that has been struggling to find new mining sites for the past couple of decades. This newly discovered deposit contains sections that are made up of up to 99% Niobium, an unheard-of find."

Gada decided to delve deeper into operational information on the active Niobium mining companies operating on Earth. *I know the answer I'm looking for has something to do with Niobium mining, which means that the Niobium mines are probably involved in some shape or form,* she theorized. She reset the machine's search parameters and prepared to run the search again.

"You should not be researching that!" flashed across the screen in bold, bright red letters. This time, Gada knew for sure what she'd seen.

What the hell is going on? she thought. *Who's been tampering with the quantum computer! This is definitely some kind of*

217

personalized computer virus or trojan software program. I know what type of bugs usually pop up on devices like this, and this definitely doesn't fall into the realm of 'normal.' The thought had barely flashed through Gada's mind when the quantum computer's screen went black. She desperately flicked the user interface's power switch to no avail. *Well, that's new.* Gada sighed, unsure whether she should be frustrated or terrified. *My options are rather limited now that I can't ask anyone but Tyrone for help.*

She defeatedly pushed her chair away from the desk that the large screen was mounted on and got up. She felt five inches shorter, or perhaps the world just suddenly seemed larger. *I'm no closer to understanding how Niobium fits into this, and now I'm no longer sure the quantum computer will help me solve it.* She rubbed at her temples with her index fingers, trying to keep an imminent headache at bay, a battle she knew she'd ultimately lose. The mechanical hum and eerie green glow of the servers in the sterile area informed her that the quantum computer's servers and database were operating normally despite the user interface's odd malfunctioning.

Maybe it'll have fixed itself by the time I get back from lunch, she hoped, glaring at the black screen with glistening eyes as she fought to hold back her tears. She'd never been the crying type, a trait she believed you had to have if you wanted to survive the military as a woman, but her frustration and fear had stirred up emotions that she'd never dwelled on before. She was made somewhat uncomfortable by the thought that the world wasn't what she'd previously thought it was. *Perhaps I'm not who I thought I was either,* she thought, wiping a tear from her cheek with her coat's sleeve. She whipped her handbag's straps over her shoulder and tried to compose herself by straightening her pencil skirt and picking at a piece of lint caught on her stockings. She pushed her shoulders back and plastered a smile on her face as she prepared to cross the threshold into the sterile area on her way out of the building. The technicians didn't acknowledge her as she left the room, but she decided to greet them nonetheless, mostly out of spite but also in an attempt to keep up the ruse that the quantum computer was working perfectly.

The coffee shop where Dubois had agreed to meet her was a quaint French-themed set up just a few blocks away. Gada had often had lunch there with Mike before Kevin was born. In the right lighting, it was quite romantic, but that wasn't its intended purpose today. Gada thanked whatever higher being might be out there for her good fortune as she parallel parked in an open spot just a few steps away from one of the coffee shop's outdoor tables. *Looks like my luck is turning,* she thought sarcastically, if not a bit hopefully, before pulling up the car's handbrake and leaping out of the door.

Dubois had arrived first. She wasn't hard to spot. Her muscular figure sat hunched over a menu at one of the tables in the coffee shop's outdoor smoking area. She was sitting directly in the sun, something that Gada assumed was a conscious choice because three-quarters of the table's surface was drenched in a shadow cast by an old willow tree growing beside it. "Hey there, Maggie! Sorry if I'm late," Gada called as she approached, waving like a nervous child who had just spotted her friend from across the school's playground.

"Better late than never," Dubois chuckled, lighting a cigarette and taking a deep drag of it. She exhaled a voluminous cloud of smoke into the afternoon's honey-like golden sunshine. "Seen that stalker of yours lately?"

"No, I think you scared him off completely," Gada grinned, carefully lowering herself onto one of the steel-framed chairs.

It wobbled on the uneven sidewalk. "Thank you for that night, by the way. I don't know how to repay you, but I hope this lunch will be a start."

"No need to repay me," Dubois scoffed, wagging her cigarette above the dainty glass ashtray at the center of the table. "It's my job to protect my agents, and I'd be pretty upset if something happened to you. Plus, Jane would never forgive me. That woman thinks you're the best thing since sliced bread."

"Well, I'm grateful nonetheless. I haven't experienced the same kind of loyalty at Langley..." she started, staring at a group of school children as they made their way past the coffee shop. They seem so carefree, she thought, thinking back to the days she and Mike did homework together in the afternoons.

"I hope they're treating you kindly, or I swear I'll show up there and beat every one of those CIA wimps to a pulp," Dubois threatened, interrupting Gada's train of thought and symbolically running her thumb across her throat. Gada couldn't deny that Dubois could be quite intimidating when she chose to be.

"I wouldn't say they're treating me kindly, but you really don't have to intervene," Gada backtracked. "I'm handling it. The quantum computer recently started malfunctioning, and some of the agents have convinced themselves I've broken it somehow. I've got a plan, though."

"What might that be?" Dubois inquired, crushing her cigarette butt in the ashtray before calling over the waitress. "Just two long island iced teas, please," she told the young blond server.

"Oh, I'm not supposed to be drinking," Gada said, shaking her head. A large brown curl came loose from her ponytail and dangled across her forehead. She swiped it behind her ear and apologetically smiled at her lunch companion. "It's not that I don't want to—"

"Technically, I'm your boss, and I'm giving you permission to drink." Dubois winked at her before raising a new cigarette to her lips. "We all need our little vices to survive, and I don't want to drink alone. Now tell me, what's your grand plan to fix the quantum computer?"

"Oh, I don't know if I'll be able to fix it. It's more of a 'fake it till you make it' type of plan. I'm just going to pretend the quantum computer is fine until the rumors subside," Gada answered sheepishly.

"Seems like a rather cosmetic solution," Dubois replied almost gruffly. "Are you sure you don't need back-up? I'd love an excuse to waltz into Greene's office and make my voice heard."

"I'm sure," Gada nodded, trying to assume an air of self-confidence. "If you really want to help, you can tell me everything that you know about Niobium."

"Niobium? Don't know a thing about it. I've seen it around on the periodic table before, though. Should I know what it is?" Dubois asked, raising one of her razor-thin bright blond eyebrows.

"I guess not," Gada shrugged. "I suppose I'm a little desperate. I've been asking everyone that question lately."

"Yeah, I'm not the person you should be asking about science stuff. Guns? Yes. This geology or chemistry or whatever it is? No. That being said, I do want to talk about the two cases you're working on. Don't get excited," she said, raising one of her palms. "I don't have solutions for you, but I do have some advice. Brace yourself because it might not be what you want to hear."

"I'm bracing myself," Gada nervously chuckled, smiling up at their waitress as she deposited their cocktails onto the table's glass surface.

"You need to start looking further and thinking bigger. After that night that I chased your stalker off, I started thinking. I've worked on a lot of international espionage cases, and this feels bigger than all of them. If the group who is responsible for all of this just wanted to keep you quiet, they would have assassinated you, but that doesn't seem to be the plan. It's almost like they're guiding you toward reporting your findings as inconclusive or trying to scare you off of investigating further at all. It's all very unusual. I wish I could tell you that I have a hunch about who's responsible, but I don't. However, I do want to warn you to be careful. Whatever's going on, it's bigger than any espionage case I've ever worked on or come across," Dubois said sternly, using her left hand to shield her sky blue eyes from the sun.

Gada took a large sip of her cocktail and stared at the cubes of ice clinking around in her glass as she tried to formulate a reply. "I've suspected for quite some time that whoever is responsible for both of the cases I'm investigating is trying to thwart my investigation because I'm certain the same person or group of people is behind both. I've been seeing things: messages flashing across computer screens, colleagues acting oddly—"

"Seeing things? That's never a good sign. If all of this is getting too much for you, let me know, Gada. I can reassign the case to someone else. Your physical and mental health are equally important," Dubois answered. Her facial expression betrayed the level of concern she felt for Gada.

"I don't think I'm hallucinating," Gada said in a deadpan tone, taking another swig of her drink. "I think someone's trying to convince me that I am, though. It's some kind of psychological offensive. You know, 'Psych-Ops' as the military calls it. They're trying to discredit me at Langley by spreading rumors about my competency to man the quantum computer, and they're trying to make me believe that I'm losing my mind."

"They?" Dubois asked, tilting her head to one side. "Gada, you know that I've got your back. I'm behind you all the way, but I wouldn't be a good friend if I didn't tell you that you do sound like, well, like you're losing it. I don't disagree that whoever is behind all of this is ridiculously powerful and influential, but I don't think they have time to toy with your psyche. If you feel like your grasp on reality is slipping, maybe it is. That's not an insult, by the way. You've been working ridiculously long hours under immense amounts of pressure. It's not uncommon for agents to need a mental health break, especially when they're working on cases that are as unsettling as yours are. If you need some time off, I can take over for a while. I won't make as much headway as you can, but it would give you some time to take a holiday with your family. You can always wrap up your cases when you get back."

"I'm not losing it," Gada huffed, picking at a piece of rust on the underside of the table. "I don't need time off. I just need to solve this thing, but I appreciate the offer, Maggie. I feel like I'm close to making a breakthrough. I'm going to chat to Mike about Niobium tonight. He's been doing a lot of engineering work for several mines. He's rather clued in on it. If all else fails, I might ask you to help me to find some experts to consult on the matter—people who we can trust. I have a strong suspicion that Niobium is the common ingredient in both cases. Langley provided me with the murdered scientists' notebooks about two weeks ago. Despite their research being biological, they had all made notes in their notebooks' margins about Niobium and Niobium mining. It's very odd. Niobium alloys were used to create all of the foreign missiles I'm investigating in my second project, as well. It's all over the place, but no one seems to know anything about it... Except for my extraordinary nerdy husband, of course."

"You're lucky to have Mike," Dubois said warmly, her expression softening. "I've come across a lot of female agents whose male partners aren't nearly as supportive, especially when their cases start taking dark or dangerous turns."

"I haven't told him about some of the more disturbing elements or about that night someone followed me to your house. I don't want him to worry. I am lucky, though. He's an amazing husband and father. I don't think I would have been able to make it through these cases without his support and yours. You've both been instrumental to everything I've achieved so far. I'll remember to thank both of you in my speech when the President awards me with a Presidential Medal of Freedom," Gada chucked, draining the last bit of dark liquid from her glass with a large gulp.

"That's what I've always admired about you, Gada," Dubois smiled, taking a sip of her own cocktail, "Your optimism. I'm sure you'll get that medal, probably with distinction too. Just promise me that you'll be careful? I don't want it to be awarded to you posthumously."

"I promise," Gada said, feigning confidence. She placed her hand on Dubois's tanned forearm in an attempt to reassure her. They stared at each other for a moment. Gada couldn't shake the feeling that Dubois was right and that she was in more danger than she'd originally anticipated, perhaps even in mortal danger.

***

"Mike!" Gada screamed. "Mike! Come here! I need help!"

Mike jumped off of the couch in their living room, where he had been drifting off to sleep behind yesterday's newspaper mere seconds earlier, and sprinted through their apartment toward the bathroom that Gada's voice had originated from. Kevin wailed from his crib. His crying only added to the tangible sense of urgency that filled the air.

"Gada! I'm coming!" Mike hollered in reply, turning the corner. He was met with a closed bathroom door, steam rolled out from underneath it like smoke from a fire. "Can I... Can I come in?"

"Uhm, yeah?" Gada answered, sounding almost impatient.

Mike realized the emergency he had imagined had probably been just that—imagined. He angrily swung the door open and strolled into the bathroom. He was met by the sight of Gada standing under a flow of hot water in the shower. Her long dark hair clung to her neck and back, and she opened the glass door that separated it from the rest of the room and peeked out.

"I forgot I washed the towels. Could you get me one from the closet? I don't want to drip all over the floor," she sheepishly asked, realizing that she'd scared Mike quite a bit rather than just stirring him from his sleep as she had intended

"Really! A towel?" Mike growled, shaking his head. "I thought you were hurt or something!"

225

"I'm sorry," Gada blushed, stepping out of the shower and onto a fluffy blue bathroom mat on the floor. "I'd still really appreciate a towel."

"Hmph," Mike huffed, marching out of the room. She heard him loudly opening and closing the closet. He returned holding her least favorite towel, a raggedy old yellow one that she found far too scratchy, which she'd purchased during her time in England. She decided not to complain. Mike didn't appear to be in a good mood.

"Thanks, Mike," she said, trying to look appreciative as she wrapped it around herself.

"I've got to go calm Kevin down," he replied gruffly, turning and leaving the room.

Who peed in his cereal? Gada wondered, shaking her head as he turned his back on her. She heard him bang into something in the hallway on his way to Kevin's room, a sound that was followed by a stream of obscenities. She quickly dried herself off and slipped into her favorite white silk robe. She kicked on her super-hero themed slippers and quietly slipped out of the bathroom.

Gada found Mike in Kevin's room. He was hovering over the crib, watching Kevin sleep. "Seems like he's calmed down again," Gada whispered, cautiously inching closer. She was careful to avoid stepping on Kevin's favorite blue teddy bear that now found itself lying face down on the floor.

"Yeah," Mike sighed, resting his forearms on the crib's side. "He's a good little guy."

"I'm sorry that I scared you," Gada cooed, wrapping her arms around him from behind. "I promise that I didn't mean to."

"It's okay," Mike said, turning around to reciprocate her hug. He rested his chin on top of her head before kissing her on the cheek and continuing, "I'm sorry too. I shouldn't have overreacted. I'm just a bit on edge these days, and I know you work with some seriously dangerous people... My mind just immediately jumped to the worst-case scenario."

"Oh, you won't get rid of me that easily, Mr. Corey," Gada joked, playfully poking at him. "I'm here to stay."

"You better be," Mike chortled, kissing her again. "I don't know what I'd do without you." He leaned in to kiss her again.

"Is something burning?" Gada asked, interrupting him. She scrunched up her nose and sniffed at the air. "Something's definitely burning."

"Shit! My pasta!" Mike exclaimed, nearly pushing Gada out of the way as he dashed out of Kevin's room. She hastily followed him all the way to the kitchen. A thick cloud of black smoke swirled around the ceiling, dimming the recessed lighting Mike had insisted on installing for "ambiance."

Mike whipped open the half-closed lid on one of the pots on the stove and almost fell to his knees. "No!" he lamented. "It's ruined!"

Gada stepped forward and steered into the pot. *Yup, that's ruined,* she thought as she stared at the charred, almost unrecognizable remains of what used to be Mike's dinner plans. "It doesn't look that bad," she tried to comfort him. "I mean, I wouldn't suggest that we eat it, but we could always make another batch."

"It was the last package of pasta in the house," he sulked, closing the pot's lid again and removing it from the stove. "I'll get some more on my way home tomorrow, but pasta's definitely off of the menu for tonight."

"That's okay, my love," Gada said gently, wrapping one of her arms around Mike's broad shoulders. "I'll order some pizza. We can have pasta tomorrow night. That way, I have something to look forward to."

Mike and Gada huddled around their apartment's stone-clad fireplace, each nursing a glass of red wine, as they waited for the delivery man to make his appearance. The fire crackled away, warming Gada's outstretched hands. "How was work today?" she asked, looking over at Mike.

"I helped that copper mine I told you about to plan the construction of their stepped benches to maximize their exposure to the deposit's veins. They've got some seriously nice veins in their location, and some have up to four percent copper in them. I'm honestly super excited about the whole project," Mike excitedly explained. "Maybe if you have a day off someday, I'll take you to see the mining site. It's a marvel of modern engineering."

"Oooh, Mike has a crush!" Gada teased, leaning into him. "Weird that it's on a copper mine, but whatever. I did some mining-related research today, but now I feel too bad to share it with you because it'll put your four percent copper mine to shame."

"Oh, really?" he asked, turning his head to grin at her. "Now you have to share it with me before I die of curiosity."

"Well, I couldn't let you die. Kevin would be upset," Gada joked, tilting her face upward to kiss him on his jaw. "So, I'm still running a bunch of searches on Niobium every day. Today, I came across something really interesting. Specifically, recent satellite communication intercepts from the Chinese Mars mission. A few days ago, a group of Chinese researchers found a ginormous Niobium deposit on Mars. It's bigger than anything we've ever seen here on Earth, apparently, and it's 99% pure Niobium."

"Ninety-nine percent! That's impossible!" Mike answered, furrowing his brow. "The reason why I'm proud of my 'four percent copper mine' is because four percent is quite a respectable percentage when it comes to just about any kind of mine that's extracting metal. That's simply how natural geological formations work!"

"Oh?" Gada mumbled, fiddling with one of her coat's buttons. "That explains the panic communications going on between Chinese officials."

"How was a small Mars rover able to drill that deep?" Mike asked, visibly awe-struck.

"Well, the intercepted communication report stated that the rover was actually sent down a shallow ramp into a cave-like opening, a geographical structure that didn't look entirely natural from the satellite photos they'd taken of the area, only to stumble onto a cache of pure Niobium ingots," Gada responded, lowering her voice as if to avoid any possible eavesdroppers from overhearing their conversation.

"If that communication intercept is accurate, the Chinese scientific community should be scared out of their boots. After all, how do you justify the appearance of pure metal ingots on a planet that seems entirely devoid of life?" Mike responded, clearly perturbed.

"You've just confirmed that it's even creepier than I originally thought it was," Gada shuddered, running her fingers through

229

her long dark hair. "You know, I've been talking to Nori a lot lately..."

"Nori?" Mike asked, raising one of his eyebrows. "That nutty old professor of yours?"

"Hey! She's my nutty old friend!" Gada chastised him, unable to suppress a giggle as it bubbled up in her throat. "I haven't had professors teaching me in ages. Anyway," she continued, a shadow suddenly falling across her previously jovial face, "We were talking about Type II civilizations yesterday. I brought up a few questions about the possibility of a rare resource that might be valuable enough to a Type II civilization and possibly draw them here. Nori believes that it's possible that the treasured element was completely extracted and processed on Mars and is now in the full production stage on Earth. She said a Type II civilization would likely go about resource extraction using a preset two-stage plan. Maybe Mars was stage one?"

"Or, maybe the Chinese government is just full of it, and this was really an elaborate misinformation campaign and a distraction scam to send its adversaries on a wild goose chase?" Mike said, trying to lighten the mood.

"You know that's not true," Gada warned, wagging her index finger about. "Okay, bear with me. I'm about to share a controversial opinion with you, but you have to promise to take me seriously."

"I promise," Mike said, nodding complacently.

"I'm convinced the Niobium find is connected to the cases I've been working on, and I'm starting to think perhaps a Type II civilization truly is involved. Okay, hear me out for a moment," Gada continued. "What if whoever left those ingots on Mars is also meddling with Earth? The first phase in Nori's theory on the 'two stage' approach would see a Type II civilization exploiting another civilization's natural resources. However, the second stage would see them exploiting this resource to the point where they have to start decreasing the host population's size to adapt to the deteriorating biosphere conditions associated with extracting Niobium, and eventually... Eventually, the planet dies, and so does everything on it," Gada almost whispered. "Then, they move on to the next host planet that has the potential to be turned into a biobot factory and exploited for more free Niobium."

"I think Nori's been telling you her favorite conspiracy theories," Mike sympathetically smiled, ruffling Gada's hair. "It's unnatural, and it's incredibly bizarre. There's likely a less interesting explanation. I wouldn't be surprised if the Russians are storing excess Niobium on Mars."

"It's not a conspiracy theory," Gada huffed, a little upset that she wasn't being taken as seriously as she'd like. "It's a scientific theory."

"Social sciences don't count as a science," Mike joked, cheekily grinning at Gada.

"Hmph," she grunted, glaring at him. "Now you're just trying to work me up."

"I am," Mike conceded, taking her hand in his. "You know, I think all of your ideas are brilliant, even if that one is, well, a little creepy."

"Something doesn't stop being true just because it's scary. You're probably right, though. It's hard not to jump to conclusions when you're working with impossible variables," Gada said. She contemplatively stared off into the distance and then continued, "Where do you think a logical place to store

231

Niobium output would be here on Earth? You know, if you had to store it for a really extended period in time?"

"Well, if I had to guess," Mike answered, clearly still pondering the ingots' origin, "You'd have to build facilities to house it all, and it'd be an expensive exercise. The earthbound Niobium mines would probably prefer to store their Niobium in climate-safe spaces like underground bunkers."

"Hypothetically speaking," Gada started again, her eyes sparkling mischievously, "if Nori's Type II civilization theory is correct and we're the second phase of a two-stage resource extraction plan, where would such a civilization store the Niobium they're extracting from Earth?"

"Hmm. That's a tricky question because it'd depend on how much they needed to store. The problem with underground storage is that it can be incredibly difficult to transport goods to. Sometimes, underground storage areas are entirely inaccessible to large vehicles. A cheaper and more robust solution would be to repurpose an old mine that used a room-and-pillar excavation technique. Due to that, the ideal storage site would probably be located in the Midwest near existing railway lines, exactly where a repurposed and abandoned room-and-pillar mine would be located," Mike passionately explained, sitting bolt upright.

"I think you're right, Mike. Come to think of it; a repurposed mine is the perfect artificial cave, a bit like the one they found on Mars. I know of a large repurposed mine near Kansas City currently being used to store any number of things. A Type II civilization would likely use something similar, especially because of its proximity to a navigable river, train tracks, and a major highway... I read its underground floor space is more than 95,000,000-square-feet. It would be perfect for storing an entire planet's worth of Niobium in. If I was some kind of mysterious civilization and I was looking for an inconspicuous location somewhere on Earth to hide some kind of natively produced resource, that's where I'd do it," Gada said thoughtfully. "It's hidden right in plain sight!" she exclaimed.

"I wonder what we'd find if we went digging around in there," Mike murmured.

A log of wood loudly cracked in the fireplace, startling them both. Mike shifted around uncomfortably, moving further away from the smoldering coals that were slowly heating the living room. "If the Niobium industry seems secretive to you, perhaps it's best that you don't investigate it? The Niobium mine owners are powerful people. I'm not sure how safe it is to be prying around in their business."

"It's my job to pry around in their business," Gada asserted, casually throwing a speck of dirt she'd found on the ground into the fire. "Please tell me everything you know, Mike? If you help me solve this, I promise I'll make dinner for a year."

"I like making dinner, but you can do the laundry for a year? That seems like a fair trade," he nervously laughed. "I'll tell you what I know, but you have to promise that you won't do anything dangerous or get yourself into any kind of trouble with the information that I give you."

Memories of the night that an unknown assailant followed her all the way to Dubois's house flashed through Gada's head. "I promise," she said, "please tell me." She knew it was a lie, she was already in danger, but she justified it to herself. The only way I'll be safe is if I solve these cases, she thought. Mike will be minimizing the danger by telling me more about it. The only way I can defend myself is by knowing what I'm dealing with.

"Fine, but only because you promised," Mike conceded, wrapping a strand of Gada's dark hair around his index finger. "Unlike all the major multinational and publicly traded mining companies, there are only two Niobium mines in the world. The Niobium mining business model is unique by any standard. Private firms control these two companies, and their distribution channels are secretive, which is probably why you've been struggling to find more information on them."

"That's brilliant!" Gada gasped, jumping up from the floor. She happily danced over to the bottle of wine she'd left on the kitchen counter and poured herself another glass. "That means that if there's a human explanation to both of my cases, one of those two companies is likely behind it!"

"Don't get too excited," Mike anxiously chortled from his seat on the ground in front of the fireplace. "It gets even weirder. The mining companies themselves might not be behind your cases. I honestly doubt they are. They're only concerned with their profits. However, whoever is buying up all of the Niobium they produce might be."

"What do you mean?" Gada asked, walking back over to him.

"I recently read a mining journal stating that both firms produce over 80% more Niobium than the global industry is actually consuming. Here's the curveball; no one has a darn clue on where the remainder is going," Mike whispered, almost as if he was afraid that someone would overhear them.

"What? That's ridiculous!" Gada exclaimed, kneeling down in front of Mike, her wine glass tightly clenched in her right hand. "What do you think someone might use all of that extra Niobium for?"

"Like I said, no one knows who's buying up the remaining Niobium, and consequently, nobody knows what's being done with it, including me," Mike said. "I wish I could tell you that I do, but I can only imagine what it's being used for, likely to create weaponry for some kind of shady country that doesn't want the rest of the world to know what they're up to. They're probably even using crypto-currency to hide their financial footprint."

"I have information on all of the countries, and none of it suggests that any of them are buying up large amounts of Niobium," Gada explained, shaking her head. "I've been intercepting a lot of international communications lately, and other than the Chinese losing their minds over the Niobium find, there's been nothing suspicious. No, this has to be some kind of clandestine group that has managed to fly under the DIA and CIA's radars. I swear, we have so little information on what's going on, I'm starting to believe my Type II civilization explanation is the most reasonable one," she said, plastering a smile on her face to sell her last statement as a joke.

"Ding, dong!" The doorbell rang, causing Gada to jump and spill the contents of her glass on her robe.

"Must be the delivery man, finally!" Gada grumbled, staring down at her now stained favorite white robe. "I'll get it," she growled, stomping toward the front door. She grabbed a fistful of dollar bills on the kitchen counter that she'd set aside to pay for their pizza as she made her way past it. Mike stared at her as she left the room. She felt his eyes following her. She unlocked the front door and flung it open without a second thought, startling the pimply blond girl holding a pizza box on the other side of it.

"Uhm, hi," the girl said, visibly trying to steady herself. "You ordered pizza? It's a pepperoni and cheese lovers' special," she gulped. "It'll be $15."

"Here," Gada said abruptly, shoving her handful of money toward the young delivery girl.

"But this is $25? Don't you want change?" the girl hiccuped as she counted the bills.

"No, it's fine. Keep it for your effort," Gada replied almost dismissively. She was far too occupied with thoughts of Niobium and the mystery of who was purchasing 80% of the world's supply to have time to make small talk. *What if it really is a Type II civilization that's using up the majority of our Niobium?* she wondered, staring at the bemused teenager pizza delivery girl's face. *What would that mean for me? And for this girl in front of me? Are we all just pawns in a game?*

"Wow! Thank you so much, ma'am," the delivery girl grinned, pulling Gada back into the moment. The girl's wide smile caused one of the pimples on her cheeks to pop. Gada tried her best not to look at the ball of yellow pus that erupted from it. The girl handed her two boxes and turned to leave. She seemed to hesitate for a moment before slowly rotating her body back again to look at Gada. Her face now seemed distorted. Her eyes and mouth appeared bigger than before. Her once jolly expression was now almost menacing. "You shouldn't be researching that," she growled before turning around again and skipping down the hallway.

Gada was frozen in place. She watched the delivery girl as she got into the elevator and started her descent back to the first floor. *Did that just happen?* she wondered, blinking rapidly as if she could somehow blink away the girl's ominous warning. *Perhaps I'm right. Perhaps the culprits behind both of my cases aren't earthbound. What if I'm right? What if something extraterrestrial really is interfering? Any other answer would have to be supernatural, and I refuse to start believing in ghosts.*

Once she was certain the girl was gone, she retreated back into their apartment, pressing the warm pizza box against her chest. *Best not to tell Mike about stuff like that,* she thought. *He's already hesitant to share information with me for fear that I'll get myself into a predicament that I can't get back out of.*

Mike was still seated in front of the fire when Gada dropped the box containing his meat lovers' pizza onto his lap. "I've got to make a phone call," she mumbled, putting her own pizza box down on the floor next to his thigh. "I'll be right back."

"Everything okay?" Mike shouted at her as she made her way down the hallway that led to their bedroom on the other side of the apartment.

"Yeah!" she bellowed back at him. "I just...uhm... I forgot to do something at work. I just need to call a colleague." She closed the bedroom door behind her and scrambled across their king-size bed. She made her way to the bedside table next to the left side of the bed where she usually slept. Her cell phone lay in the center of it, glistening on its dark wooden surface. She quickly disconnected it from its charger and dialed Nori's number. Gada lay on her back, stretched out horizontally across the bed, as she listened to the phone's rhythmic ringing. After what felt like an eternity, the receiver finally clicked.

"Nori's house!" a friendly voice chimed from the other end of the line.

"Nori? It's me, Gada," Gada hastily explained. "I hope I'm not bothering you. I know it's late."

"You could never bother me!" Nori laughed jovially. "You could phone me at 2 am on Christmas morning, and you wouldn't be bothering me. What's up? I assume it's not a social call if you're phoning this late. Is everything okay?"

"You know me too well," Gada giggled, dangling her head over the bed's edge. *Everything looks so different when it's upside down,* she thought, observing the bedroom. "You're right that this isn't a social call." Her heart raced. "I need help with something. Again. But you're not allowed to think I'm going crazy for what I'm about to ask, okay?"

"I knew you were batty when I first met you in the UK, so I doubt you're any crazier now," Nori teased. Her voice crackled, causing it to sound almost mechanical.

Gada hesitated for a moment. "Is it possible that a Type II species may have interfered with our evolution, specifically human evolution? More specifically, to get their hands on something like Niobium?"

"A good question...but Gada, you know the answer to that question just as well as I do. Is it scientifically possible? Yes, of course! What scientific evidence do we have to the contrary? Something being scientifically possible doesn't necessarily mean very much. The existence of unicorns is scientifically possible, but up until a few decades ago, walking on the Moon was 'just' a scientific possibility too. It's not a good measure to use if you're trying to evaluate probability," Nori started lecturing, speaking in the tone of voice she usually reserved for students on Monday mornings.

"I know, I know," Gada admitted. She had broken out into a cold sweat but was determined not to let Nori know how terrified she truly was. "I just don't have a better system to apply to that question, for now anyway. Thanks, Nori."

"Wait, you don't really think we're slaves to some kind of Type II civilization? Do you?" Nori hastily added, blurting it out before Gada had a chance to end the call. "What kind of work did you say you were doing again?"

"It's all just theoretical. I work for an... uhm... a think tank," Gada lied, trying to cover her tracks. "Don't worry, I don't really think aliens are toying with us. I can't tell you more than that, though. I signed an NDA—"

"As long as you're not in some kind of trouble. If a civilization like that really existed, they probably wouldn't hesitate to exterminate anyone that started asking too many questions," Nori warned. Gada could swear she heard her voice shaking.

"Like I said, it's all theoretical," Gada mumbled. Her hands trembled, and she struggled to maintain her grip on her cell phone. "Keep safe, Nori."

"I feel like I should be the one telling you that," Nori nervously laughed.

Gada ended the call and flung her cell phone onto the bouncy mattress. She sat upright and stared at the bedroom's pale white walls. *If a Type II civilization is behind the occurrences in both of the cases I'm working on, does that make me a biobot?* She wondered. She glanced down at her arms and examined them as if she was looking at them for the first time. *I don't feel like a biobot, but how would a biobot feel?* She clenched her fists. Her long fingernails dug into the palm of her hand. She squeezed harder. *Is our only purpose to extract*

Niobium for whoever is using up most of it? Some kind of Type II civilization that needs it? What happens when the Niobium runs out? Do we end up like Mars?

"Knock, knock!" Mike tapped at the bedroom door. "Gada, are you in there? Is everything okay? Your pizza is getting cold," he hollered, rapping his fist against the wooden door.

"Yeah, I'm in here," Gada defeatedly sighed, getting up off of the bed. She walked over to the door and slowly cracked it open. Mike's concerned face peered through the opening at her. She could see that he was frowning, deepening the lines that had started appearing on his face of late. "I just wrapped up my call. Would you mind microwaving my pizza for me? I'll be right out," she sniffed.

"Sure, anything to help," he sympathetically grinned.

Mike and Gada spent the rest of the night quietly eating their pizza together in front of the fireplace. Neither of them said another word about Niobium or mining. In fact, it was as if they'd come to a silent agreement not to discuss Gada's work at all. Despite not uttering another word about it, Gada couldn't stop thinking about Type II civilizations and what being a biobot would ultimately mean.

The next morning couldn't roll around soon enough. Gada slept even less than she usually did, opting to read far too many chapters of her favorite fantasy novel instead. It was a form of escapism, this much she knew, but the alternative was laying awake all night, and she argued that, at the very least, reading was a more productive way to spend one's time. She listened to the 7 am news on her way to Langley. There had been a gas explosion in Venezuela, the price of oil was set to increase, and they predicted it would be snowing by the weekend. Your run-of-the-mill morning news, but this wasn't a normal morning. Gada wondered how she'd ever be interested in the price of gas again. It seemed so trivial now.

She struggled to get through the security guards that were stationed at Langley's entrance. The metal detector kept beeping when she walked through it. After removing her earrings, watch, bangles, necklace, and belt and passing a manual pat-down, she was allowed into the building. The metal detector screeched as she made her way toward the stairs, but she didn't look back at it or the group of onlookers that had gathered to gawk at the spectacle.

Gada was in no mood to endure one of Tyrone's famous morning chats. She prepared to stealthily slink past his office's door as she approached it, hoping that she wouldn't be spotted. She hunched over in an attempt to make herself smaller and launched herself forward to dash past the doorway.

"Gada? Is that you?" Tyrone's voice echoed out from his office. Gada stopped mid-stride, realizing she'd been caught out. "Come in here for a second! I want to show you my new coffee cup. It's a collectible!"

"Oh! Hi, Tyrone!" Gada backtracked, leaning backward to peep back into Tyrone's office. "Sorry, I didn't see you there," she fibbed in an attempt to spare his feelings. "I've been in a rush all morning. I overslept, and now I'm late—"

"It's 7:30 am, and you only need to be here at 8 am. There's no need to be in a hurry," Tyrone laughed. She watched as he got out of his office chair and wrapped his fingers around a coffee cup with a picture of a cat on it. He made his way toward her, proudly holding it out toward her. "See, it says, 'Today's the purr-fect day for lasagna.' Isn't that adorable? Get it? It's because the cat loves lasagna."

"I get it," Gada said, faking a smile. "It's charming, Tyrone. I wouldn't mind one like that myself. Sorry, but I have to go. I have a lot to do today and not a lot of time to do it in."

"Oh, sounds serious!" Tyrone joked. "You okay? You look a little... Uhm, stressed? More so than usual, anyway," he chuckled, still waving his new coffee cup around.

"I'm fine," Gada replied, trying to sound as confident as possible. "I guess I'm just a little tired, but I'll be okay. No need to worry about me. You know how I am—super resilient."

"Hmm. I don't know. You actually look like you might be ill to me, but if you say you're okay, I won't bug you about it. Just promise me you'll go home if you're not feeling well? I don't want you passing out behind the quantum computer or something. You never know; the technicians might eat you while you're unconscious. They're a creepy bunch," he teased, chortling at his own joke.

"Now that's a sentiment I agree with," Gada nervously chuckled, nodding her head in agreement. "I swear I'll go home if I start feeling ill, but like I said, I'm just a little tired."

The quantum computer's sterile area was already full of technicians busying themselves with their usual tasks by the time that Gada made her way into it. Its eerie green lighting cast odd elongated shadows across their faces. *Hmm. Eyebrow piercing isn't here today.* She noted as she walked through it toward the backroom that housed the user interface.

She was somewhat relieved to find the user interface switched off. Its black screen beckoned her to approach it like an empty mirror. She made herself comfortable in the modest office chair behind it, settling into the room's dark embrace. She switched it on and was momentarily blinded by the beam of light its screen emitted. She waited for the warning text she'd seen flashing across the screen yesterday to appear again. Minutes passed, but nothing happened. *Maybe I imagined it,* she thought, rubbing at her temples. *Dubois is right. I need a break.*

As she sat in the eerie green room, she pondered what she had learned so far. She thought back to the Humnz2AI article she read days earlier, back when things seemed simpler and she believed the world was a safer place. With the knowledge she had since gained, the article suddenly seemed to make much more sense. Without thinking, almost as if mechanically-driven, she typed "NATO military action" into the quantum computer's search parameters and ran the search. She clicked on the first result that popped up, an opinion piece written by someone at The Observer. It read: "Most recently, the NATO has been involved in several military interventions in the Middle East, largely having mastered the offensive techniques and use of military technology needed to ensure their own troops' relative safety while remaining incredibly efficient in organized offensives. Officially, many of these military missions have been for peace-keeping purposes against terrorist organizations. However, dissidents of NATO military action argue that the 'peace-keeping missions' are nothing but a farce in the search for oil."

Gada slowly leaned back in her chair, her palm instinctively covering her mouth and her eyes gradually opening wider with a glaze of morbid fear. She connected the ugly dots of Earth's darkest secrets. *Of course,* she thought to herself. *Why am I surprised? We clandestinely support authoritarian regimes to suppress others to help us secure our critical energy* supply, oil. *Why wouldn't a Type II not covertly oppress the human race to secure Niobium? Logically, the secrets of Type II's oppressive modus operandi should be evident in the similarities between how authoritarian regimes suppress their own people and how a Type II civilization might suppress "lower" life forms like us.* Gada's mind continued piecing the terrifying puzzle together. *We should be very afraid. If we attempt to resist in any form, we could unleash the wrath of the Type II civilization. Who knows what lengths they'd go to to quickly quell any foolish and futile human rebellions! Is it possible that our planet is ruled by onion-style layered authoritarian regimes? All of which are ultimately controlled by our Type II masters for their final objective of securing Niobium? The metaphorical big fish eating the little fish.* Her hands trembled. She closed her eyes as they began to tear. *My head hurts,* she thought, rubbing at her temples. *I've got to pull myself together. I don't have time to fall apart. That's what "they" would want anyway, and there's no way in hell I'm giving them what they want.*

Gada started setting the quantum computer's search parameters again. "The next search is going to be a little different," she told the machine, pretending to pat the corner of the user interface's screen like one might pat an excited puppy. First, she set the search parameters to find the answer to a single question: "What is Niobium mostly used for?"

The computer completed its search and produced hundreds of results from its database within a matter of seconds. Gada downloaded a summary report, a document that contained points from each of the articles and scientific journals produced, and opened it. It read: "In its solid state, Niobium is a super-conducting metal that allows high voltage electrical currents to pass through it practically unrestricted. It also significantly improves the structural properties of other industrial metals. It is also used as an alloy in the manufacturing processes of space re-entry vehicles, nuclear fission reactor cores, and rocket engine nozzles. As little as half a percent of Niobium added to Titanium improves its strength and durability tenfold. Advanced research through the largest particle accelerator in the world, the CERN collider in Switzerland, recently demonstrated that Niobium in its plasma state (the fourth state of matter after solid, liquid, and vapor) is capable of vectoring gravitational fields. The researchers who made the discovery hypothesize that it could be used to advance humanity's ability to travel through space by acting as a potential fuel source. Although our spacecraft's technology is not advanced enough to make use of this kind of fuel source yet, scientists are hopeful that it may be useful to us within the next century."

Gada blinked. The screen's bright light burned her eyes as she tried to digest what she'd just learned. *Niobium plasma can be used to power spacecraft? Perhaps that's why a Type II civilization is after it? What are we to them? Nothing but a Niobium Node? A glorified intergalactic fuel station?* Gada leaned back in her chair and tried to clear her mind. *There's no point in panicking... Not yet, anyway,* she tried to tell herself.

She composed herself and set the search criteria to calculate the possible results of a hypothetical situation, one in which the players were all the countries of the world and an advanced Type II civilization. In this scenario, the Type II civilization would exploit the remaining players to deplete all of Earth's Niobium reserves.

Gada stared at the screen for a moment, rapping her fingernails against the desk that it was mounted on. She wondered what the computer might come up with, then closed her eyes like an anxious child, and initiated the search. *I guess*

245

it would make sense that a Type II civilization would choose us, she thought as she watched the user interface transition onto its loading page. *Earth has Niobium and its own little workforce. What more could any extraterrestrial overlord want? Whatever they use Niobium for, it's clearly vital to their civilization.*

It finally dawned on her that this Type II civilization's plan had likely been put into motion tens of thousands of years ago, back when humankind had been nothing more than apes. *I bet they're responsible for the splicing of Chromosome 2. That's probably why they killed the scientists—they were too close to figuring out that we're manufactured biobots. The paradigm shifts make sense if you factor in our extraterrestrial masters too... They've slowly been improving our technology to increase the efficiency with which we're able to mine Niobium. We're the perfect little slaves: smart enough to think this was all our idea, strong enough to wield tools, and stupid enough to think that our religious and political institutions are more than just another way to control us, to make us obedient.*

Gada started hyperventilating. Every inch of her body told her to run. *Where would I run? I can't run from Earth,* she thought. *Relax, Gada! You have to calm down!* She chastised herself, holding onto her chair's leather armrests as if her life depended on it. She was on the brink of having a full-blown panic attack by the time that the quantum computer finally produced a result.

The first line of the quantum computer's report read, "Earth's life expectancy post complete Niobium extraction: 73 years."

Seventy-three years, Gada gulped. She felt queasy but mustered all of her courage and read on.

"The exhaustion of Niobium reserves on a planet destabilizes its magnetic fields. These magnetic fields are essential for the maintenance of the planet's biospheric habitat. Once a planet's Niobium is depleted, the atmosphere becomes biologically uninhabitable in a matter of centuries. In Earth's case, this time frame is contracted to 73 years because of the extent to which its Niobium reserves have already been depleted," the results page read. "The end phase of a Type II civilization's Niobium extraction on another planet with a biobot population would see the Type II civilization trying to balance the sustainability of the ecosystem until all Niobium reserves are exhausted. Control over the biobot population and their consumption of secondary resources would be essential during the mature production period to allow for optimum workforce and infrastructure sustenance until complete Niobium reserve exhaustion. Control over the biobots' population size would be achievable through transmissible designer viruses and promotion of intra-species conflict. The Type II civilization would likely ensure that viral case fatality rates increase as the end of the Niobium mining period approaches. Virus case fatality rates would likely always remain below 35% to avoid demotivation and productivity collapse among the biobots in question."

I can't read any more of this, Gada thought, quickly switching off the user interface's screen as if it had suddenly started displaying an image that was too grotesque to even glance at. She looked at her reflection on the screen's black surface, examining the lines on her forehead and the dark circles under her eyes. *I guess I shouldn't complain about wrinkles,* she thought. *If the quantum computer is correct, it's a privilege that only those who are currently alive will ever have.*

Gada got up and ran her delicate hand over the top of the user interface's screen. It was icy cold to the touch. *Perhaps I'm wrong,* she thought. *Maybe I've gone off on a tangent. Maybe I've lost the plot. What are the chances that aliens exist?* For a second, she could almost hear Nori's voice saying, "Well, it's definitely a scientific possibility." She shuddered. Deep down, she knew it was more than just a possibility. It was starting to look like a probability. *Hopefully, Dubois is right. Hopefully, I'm just losing my mind.*

She grabbed her car keys off of the desk's mahogany surface and swung her handbag over her shoulder. There were no technicians in the sterile area just outside of the back room that housed the user interface. She breathed a sigh of relief. *Tyrone's right. They are all a little creepy. The scrubs they wear don't really do much for their image either. I wonder if they're having a team meeting somewhere.* She chuckled to herself as she made her way across the room's stark white tiles. She snarkily blew the quantum computer a kiss as she rounded the corner and made her way back into the floor's main hallway. It was empty. Emptier than it should be at 10 am on a weekday.

Where is everybody? She wondered. She didn't have time to mull it over. Instead, one of the hallways' long windows caught her eye. *Is it dark outside?* She gasped, running over to it. She pressed her face against the frosty glass. The stars were twinkling above the fuzzy clouds. They seemed to be hanging lower than usual, brushing against the treetops. *This isn't right,* Gada gulped. She could feel her heart pounding against her ribs like a frightened bird fighting to get out of its cage. *This isn't right at all.*

She backed away from the dark window frame until her back was pressed tightly against the wood-paneled wall on the other side of the hall. Gada kept one eye on the window as if she anticipated something would burst through it at any moment. She frantically dug through her handbag. Her fingers finally managed to wrap themselves around her cell phone's distinctive shape. She shakily withdrew it and stared at its screen. It read: "10:17 am." *Wait, why do I have my cell phone?* She wondered, suddenly realizing that she'd never handed it in at the security checkpoint at the building's entrance. *No wonder the metal detector kept flagging me, but why didn't the security guards realize I hadn't handed it in?*

Gada hastily shoved her phone back into her handbag. *I know I wasn't in there for hours,* she thought, forming a sharp V with her eyebrows as she tried to figure out what was going on. She couldn't come to a reasonable conclusion. *Maybe I'm seeing things, hallucinating. That's it! I must be hallucinating.* She had always been a terrible liar, even when she was lying to herself. Gada hastily made her way down the hallway, careful to keep at least one window within sight at all times.

There were only two security guards staffing Langley's entrance by the time that she made her way down to the first floor. One of them, a lanky man with long blond curls, was propped up in a chair, resting his head against a wall and snoring loudly. The other, a broad-chested brunet, was distractedly paging through a magazine that he quickly stowed away as he noticed Gada approaching. "Hello! Who goes there?" the brunet called. His voice was deeper than most, causing it to echo through the reception area's empty expanse. Its reverberations caused his companion, who had dozed off, to stir from his sleep.

"Gada! I mean, Captain Gada Corey. What time is it? Where is everybody?" she asked as she approached them. *They must think I'm a crazy person.* She thought as she watched their facial expressions change from surprise to concern.

"It's 11 pm, ma'am. Everybody went home about six hours ago. We were under the impression that the building was empty. Where'd you come from? Can we see some identification?" the brunet blubbered, clearly taken aback by Gada's sudden appearance. She could see him trying to maintain a confident demeanor but knew it was nothing more than a thin veneer he'd been taught to put on.

How could that be? How could I possibly have lost thirteen hours of my day without realizing it? Gada wondered. She whipped out her cell phone again, planning on using the time displayed on its screen as an excuse for why she was in the building after hours without specific authorization allowing her to be there. She hoped she wouldn't be chastised for having it with her. Her hands trembled as she turned it over to look at its screen. It read "11:19 pm." "How's that possible?" she asked out loud.

"Excuse me, ma'am? How's what possible?" the brunet inquired, looking down at her.

"Apologies," Gada nervously chuckled. "My cell phone's clock must have lost time somehow. Before I got here, it said it was much earlier than it actually is, which is why I'm still in the building. Kind of seems like it fixed itself on the way here, though. It reads "11:19 pm" now." She knew her explanation frankly sounded like a poorly concocted lie, and she knew it wouldn't be enough to get her off of the hook. She tried to decide what she'd say next as she handed the security guard her staff card.

He examined it like a cashier trying to spot a fake dollar bill, distorting his face as he squinted at the card in an attempt to read the dark text on it. "You sure you're okay, ma'am? We don't usually have ladies working alone here this time of the night, and you look a bit shook up, if you don't mind me saying." There was something comforting about the southern twang in his voice. It reminded Gada of the way her maternal grandmother used to talk.

"I'm sure," Gada answered, flashing him her best fake smile. "You know how we girls are! Always losing track of time!"

"Yeah, my girlfriend says that happens to her when she's shopping for shoes," the brunet chuckled, returning Gada's staff card to her. "Just get authorization next time you're planning on working late, okay? We don't want to get into trouble just because you're lurking around after hours."

"Oh, I promise I will!" Gada vowed, taking her staff card and drawing a cross on the left side of her chest with it. "I'd never forgive myself if I got either of you into trouble."

"That's what we like to hear," the brunet laughed. His blond colleague had already drifted back off to sleep again. Gada waved at him as she slunk through the large glass doors that separated Langley from the outside world.

The air outside was frigid. It burnt Gada's eyes and made the tips of her fingers go numb. *If I knew I'd still be here this time of the night, I would have packed some gloves,* she thought, inattentively rubbing her palms together in an attempt to generate some heat. The feral black cat that had made the parking lot its home was napping on a small patch of grass under a street light. It opened one pale yellow eye to watch Gada as she passed. "Hey, kitty," Gada nervously greeted. *At least the parking lot isn't entirely empty.* She thought, *not as long as that black cat is here.* She knew it was silly, but she felt like the feline was on her side, rooting for her to keep fighting to find the truth. The cat blinked lazily in reply as the thought drifted through Gada's busy mind. *Or maybe not,* she thought as she watched its blank gaze track her movements.

Her car was the only one left in the parking lot. The loud "beep beep" it emitted as she unlocked it was almost deafening in contrast with the all-consuming silence that otherwise smothered the grounds around Langley at that time of the evening. She quickly slid into the driver's seat and locked the doors. *Better check the backseats,* she thought, craning her neck to examine the footwells behind her. *Who knows what lengths a Type II civilization might go to in order to keep me quiet?* She immediately felt a little silly. *Although I doubt there'd be an alien hiding under one of my seats,* she corrected herself, turning back around again. She started the engine, adjusted her rearview mirror, and pulled out into the main road.

Gada compulsively watched the cars behind her as she made her way back to the Poto-Pine Apartment Building, trying to ensure that she wasn't being followed again. *Looks like the coast is clear,* she thought as she watched the third car that she had been convinced was trailing her turn off into a different street. *You're being paranoid, Gada,* she reprimanded herself. *You're letting the investigation get to you.*

Gada parallel parked the car in a vacant spot just a stone's throw away from the apartment building's entrance, killed the engine, crossed her fingers it wouldn't be towed by the time she got to it the next morning and made a mad dash toward the building's front door. Nothing was chasing her other than her own imagination, but she felt that it was imperative to get out of the open as soon as possible anyway. She stumbled over the building's threshold and into its lavishly decorated first floor, hastily making her way to the elevator that would transport her to the third floor.

The creepy statue that usually kept watch over the elevator door was gone, leaving a deep impression on the red carpet where it had once been positioned. Gada paused to stare at the spot where it once stood. *Strange,* she thought. She tried not to make any assumptions about what had happened to it. *The building manager probably just decided to sell it or put it out with the trash this morning. I would have done the same in his position;* she reasoned as she pressed the elevator's glowing button.

The inside of the elevator was lined with mirrors. Gada stared at her reflection as she got in. *I swear I've aged ten years in a matter of days,* she thought, pulling at her face's skin in an attempt to make the wrinkles that were forming on her brow disappear. She didn't have more than a minute or two to lament her tired demeanor before the elevator doors slid open again, revealing the third-floor hallway that led to their apartment. *Mike's going to be upset. He hates it when I don't let him know I'll be home late.*

She opened the apartment's front door as stealthily as she possibly could. The inside was deathly quiet. *Mike and Kevin are probably asleep already,* she thought. She kicked off her stilettos next to the coat rack and tip-toed into the kitchen. Its tiles were slippery as ice under her stockinged feet. She was reaching for a bottle of water in the fridge when a package on the countertop with a large bow fixed to the top of it caught her eye. *What's this?* she wondered, unscrewing the water bottle's lid as she snuck up to the mysterious gift. The bow attached a palm-sized card to the box's surface. *Best to read this before I open it,* she decided. *Make sure it doesn't say 'anthrax delivery' or something.*

She ripped the card off of the box and opened it. It read

"Dearest Gada,

"I'm posting this from my hotel room. I hope it reaches you well. I landed in Washington DC about an hour ago. I took advantage of the long flight and finally finished editing my research paper. I hope you have a chance to look at it before publication. It's on a topic I know you love. 'The Uniqueness of the Chinese Remainder Theorem' and its use in the 'Battle of Yangxia.' I left for the airport early this morning. The concierge said he'd take this package right up to your apartment if I tipped him $17.

"The University sent me to assist a professor here at Burkington University with his research into the early human civilizations that existed around the time that we started experiencing chromosomal changes as a species.

"It's riveting stuff, although I can't say I understand why it's urgent enough that they flew me out here with less than a day's notice.

"Anyway, enough about me. I thought my little visit is the perfect opportunity to see you again! It's not every day I find myself across the pond. I'm staying at The Van Beek Hotel. Let's meet at its restaurant, The Squire and Grill, tomorrow for lunch? You can tell me more about your theoretical research and show me some more pictures of your adorable little lad!

"Hope to see you tomorrow!

"P.S. Enjoy this box of chocolates! I bought it duty-free at the airport.

"All of my love, Nori."

Nori? she wondered. *How unexpected.* She took a sip of her water. It tasted different than it usually did. *Must be an old bottle,* she thought, putting it back down on the counter. She scooped the box of chocolates into her arms and made her way into the television room, planning to devour all of them before retiring for the night.

***

"Gada! There you are! I was starting to think you wouldn't make it!" Nori beamed, enthusiastically waving at Gada as she made her way toward her. Nori was seated at a small round table, occupying one of its two seats.

The Squire and Grill was a high-end restaurant with all of the finest finishes. Its red and beige carpet accentuated the white wood and leather that the seating arrangements were made of, while a larger-than-life crystal chandelier entirely illuminated its interior. Gada couldn't help but feel a little out of place.

"Wouldn't miss it for the world!" Gada grinned, bending down to hug Nori, who had remained seated. She made herself comfortable at the other end of the tiny table and stared at the woman who had once been her professor but who had since become her friend. Nori looked older than Gada remembered. Her scraggly white hair brushed against her bony shoulders and framed her angled face. Her ocean blue eyes, her finest feature, had faded to a light gray color since Gada had last seen her. "It feels like I saw you yesterday! You haven't aged a day!" Gada lied. She considered it a white lie, a harmless little fib. Despite having noticeably aged, Nori still looked far younger than she truly was at 63.

"Oh, I don't know about that!" Nori blushed, hiding her face behind the steaming cup of tea that she held clasped between her hands. "I know I'm an old lady, but you know what? I don't mind it. The older I get, the more I realize that getting old at all is a privilege. Most people never get the chance."

"Strange, I was thinking exactly the same thing a while back," Gada conceded, opening the menu in front of her. A waitress who had been hovering nearby took it as her cue to approach the table.

"Can I get you anything, ma'am?" the red-headed waitress asked, whipping a pen and paper out of her uniform's pockets.

"Just a glass of red wine, please. Nothing fancy, just a middling type of wine, please," Gada explained, grinning up at the friendly server.

"Drinking? On a weekday?" Nori asked, leaning forward to peer at Gada. "Since when do you drink on weekdays?"

"I'm not planning on having the whole bottle," Gada laughed as she watched the young waitress shuffle back to the restaurant's bar. "I won't have more than a glass. Trust me; if you had my job, you'd drink on weekdays too."

"So, are you finally going to tell me a bit about this incredibly mysterious job of yours? You've been asking the strangest questions lately. I can't help but imagine that you're working on something very fascinating. You know, I knew you were destined for great things the moment I laid eyes on your doctoral research," Nori cooed, stirring another spoonful of sugar into her tea.

"I wish I could tell you all about it, Nori. Unfortunately, I've signed some really serious contracts that forbid me from talking about it to anyone," Gada sighed, propping her elbows up on the table and resting her head on her hands.

"You know, I'm starting to think you're a spy. Are you a spy?" Nori probed, smiling mischievously at Gada.

"Eh, something like that," Gada chuckled just as the waitress finally appeared with her glass of wine. "Thank you," Gada smiled at the server as she placed the glass full of purple liquid in front of her before scurrying back to the waitrons' area near the restaurant's entrance. "I was actually hoping you'd be willing to let me pick your brain again," Gada admitted, sheepishly grinning at her companion.

"I didn't think you'd be able to go a whole hour without discussing something scientific, so I can't say that I'm surprised," Nori smirked, momentarily distracted by the tea leaves at the bottom of her cup. "I swear my tea leaves look like a dog today," she added, turning her cup around to show its contents to Gada. "I wonder if that means today's the day someone finally throws me a bone," she giggled.

"Must be good luck," Gada shrugged, taking a sip of her red wine. "Dogs are never a bad thing. They're adorable." She paused for a moment, trying to find the right words to ask Nori the question that she'd been itching to ask. "So, I guess what I want to ask," she hesitated for a moment, "is whether you know if there's any evidence that the Earth's magnetic fields are slowly shifting?"

"What an odd question," Nori laughed, throwing her head back like an amused toddler. "It is a very informed one, though. I assume you've already done a bit of research on the topic, but yes, the Earth's magnetic fields are changing. Some researchers blame global warming for the changes, but in truth, it's happening because of the over-mining of certain key elements that are considered superconducting metals. We've recently discovered a mathematical relationship between the molten core spin and the over-mining of these elements. It seems to be leading to the degradation of the Earth's magnetic sphere. Fortunately, several large private mining companies have recently signed a treaty in which they promise to endeavor to decrease their extraction of these metals until the Earth's magnetic fields have stabilized themselves again. The bigger problem that has been identified is the fact that Earth's shifting magnetic fields negatively affects our already-thin atmosphere."

Gada's heart skipped a beat. *Nori's telling me exactly what the quantum computer told me. That means that the quantum computer was likely right about Earth's 73-year life expectancy too.* A bead of sweat rolled down her forehead. "So, uhm. Do you know which metals they've been over-mining that's causing all of this? Just for interest's sake?"

"Oh, I can't say I really remember. Something with an 'n,' I think," Nori replied dismissively, waving at their waitress who was congregating with her colleagues in one corner of the restaurant.

"Was it 'Niobium?'" Gada gulped, trying her best to hide her anguish by putting on a happy face.

"Yes! That's it! Niobium," Nori grinned, nodding enthusiastically. "How'd you know?"

"Just a hunch," Gada shrugged, attempting to look disinterested rather than shocked. "Say, remember we were talking about Type II civilizations a while back?"

"Do I remember that you frantically called me in the middle of the night to discuss them? Yes. Yes, I do," Nori laughed. "You know, you're the only person who ever wants to discuss Type II civilizations with me. I think that's why I like you so much—"

"Do you mind if I pick your brain about them again? I'm currently working on a project at work that involves them. It's a hypothetical situation that I've been assigned with that involves a Type II civilization exploiting the earth for Niobium. To use the element as a fuel source. So, essentially, in this simulation, Earth is a fuel station for aliens."

"Hilarious! You must have the absolute best job in the universe! I'm jealous!" Nori sang, putting her hand on Gada's forearm. "Tell me more!"

"Well, I was wondering, if they're using us as a fuel station, do you think they'd exploit us in other ways too?" Gada hiccuped, taking another swig of her wine.

"This is all just hypothetical, right?" Nori frowned, tilting her head as she attempted to read Gada's facial expression.

"Yes. Of course," Gada lied. *I wish I could tell Nori the truth,* she thought, *but I can't risk endangering her with it.*

"In that case, I suppose they would eat us too. You know how you'd stop at a fuel station for a Coke and a packet of potato chips on a long road trip? It wouldn't be a stretch to say that a Type II civilization might do the same. However, members of a Type II civilization likely have much higher caloric needs than we do to feed their powerful minds, so normal human food wouldn't suffice, nor would simply eating humans. We aren't all that nutritious in the grand scheme of things. They'd probably have to resort to eating some kind of protein-filled superfood... Like, stem cells perhaps?" Nori said, her eyes glistening with excitement.

I wish I could be excited about any of this, Gada thought. *I envy her a little.* "Stem cells? Like, from babies?"

"Technically, it's easier to harvest stem cells from embryos. Babies only have them in their umbilical cords, and I can't imagine a Type II civilization will be dumpster-diving in a hospitals' trash looking for leftover umbilical cords," Nori laughed, wrinkling up her nose.

"Embryos?" Gada gasped.

The waitress brought them their check as Gada tried to wrap her head around what she'd just learned. How on earth would a Type II civilization go about harvesting embryos? She shuddered.

Chapter 10: Monitor and Control

"Are you sure your calculations are right?" Tyrone asked, squinting at Gada over his morning newspaper. "Seventy-three years? If that's really all we had left, I feel like the USA would be doing everything in its power to elongate that timeline."

"I'm sure," Gada nodded decisively. She was seated in her usual position behind Tyrone's desk, fiddling with a number of things that lay strewn across his desk. *I wonder if his wife knows he's this messy at work,* she thought as she scrunched up a piece of scrap paper she'd found under his stapler. "I ran the simulation twenty times and double-checked the simulation's inputs each time. Unless there's something seriously wrong with the quantum computer, the world won't get to see the year 2100. We'd be lucky if we make it past 2075, to be honest. "

"If you're sure it's not an error, I'll inform Greene about your discovery," Tyrone said solemnly, folding his newspaper up and placing it on one side of his desk. "This isn't something we should keep to ourselves. Hopefully, there's something wrong with the quantum computer. The alternative would break my heart. My little girl, Tanisha, is only two years old. Her kids could be in their early fifties by the time all of the Niobium is depleted."

"My little boy is only a couple of months old," Gada sniffed, biting her lower lip. She quickly wiped a stray tear from her cheek. *This is no place to burst into tears,* she told herself. "I'm just as invested in reporting the facts accurately as anyone else might be," she added. Up until that point, she hadn't considered what Earth's finite life expectancy meant for her. She was in her thirties and was relatively sure she didn't need to worry about anything that might happen in seventy years' time, but she'd never paused to consider what it would mean for Kevin. She realized he'd likely live to see the end of the world and that the children he might have in the future would likely be middle-aged by the time that the Earth literally stopped spinning. She allowed her mind to wander, taking ever darker pathways into her subconsciousness. Before she knew it, she imagined the anguish Kevin would feel once he realized his family would perish in an apocalypse, knowing there'd be nothing he could do to stop it.

"You okay, Gada?" Tyrone asked, pulling her back to reality. "I know it's all very upsetting, but we should try not to get ahead of ourselves until Greene has investigated too. Like I said, it's possible that the quantum computer is simply malfunctioning—

"Tyrone, I'm telling you, it's not a glitch. This is real!" Gada insisted, getting up out of her seat to emphasize her point. She touched her face as she attempted to swipe a loose piece of hair behind one of her ears. It was soaking wet. *So much for not crying,* she thought. "I'm not sure you should trust Greene with this information! There are...uhm...other forces at play. I don't want to go into details, but you have to trust me when I say that we can't trust anyone."

"Nonsense!" Tyrone laughed, slapping his knee. His cheerful demeanor led Gada to believe that he wasn't taking the situation nearly as seriously as she'd hoped he would despite the moment of clarity he'd had surrounding what an apocalypse might mean for Tanisha. "Greene's an asshole, don't get me wrong, but we can trust him. He's been a CIA agent for longer than I've been alive. If anyone knows what to do, it'll be him!"

"Tyrone—" Gada started.

"Don't worry about it," he interjected, flashing a dazzling white smile at her. "I won't mention your name when I tell Greene about it. He wouldn't believe it if it came from you anyway, no offense. Anyway, and diverting from the topic at hand a bit, would you like to join me for lunch later today? My wife made an extra sandwich for you if you'd like it. It's peanut butter and jelly. I remember you saying you liked peanut butter."

"Yeah, I do," Gada conceded, deciding that she wouldn't push the issue with Tyrone. *It's a lot to take in,* she thought. *I'd be in denial too, if our positions were reversed.* "I've... Got a lot of work to do. I'll see you during lunch then," she stuttered, trying to contain the flood of emotions that were ebbing through her veins like the ocean pushing up into a river's mouth during high tide. "I'll be in the quantum computer's back room if you need me," she hiccupped, making her way to Tyrone's office door.

"Gada, don't let this get to you," he said gently. "I know things seem bad right now, but I swear they'll look better again tomorrow."

"I hope you're right," she whispered as she slipped over the door's threshold and into the second floor's hallway. She hastily made her way to the closest window and cautiously peeked through it. *Yup, still daylight out there,* she thought. She still hadn't figured out how she'd managed to lose thirteen hours of the previous day. In fact, she was starting to think she didn't want to know how it had happened. *Nori always said Type II civilizations would maintain control of their biobots through any means necessary. Maybe everything that's happening around me can be considered "any means necessary."* She checked her watch. It read "11:11 am." *I read an article about the significance of 11:11 once,* she bemusedly recalled. *I wish I could remember what it had said.*

Gada's shaky legs carried her all the way out of Langley's main building. She couldn't remember making it through the security checkpoint on her way out. As far as her recollections went, one moment she'd been staring out of the window, and the next, she found herself seated outside with her back against a large oak tree. *I'm losing it,* she thought, looking down at her hands. They seemed almost alien to her. She plucked a flowery weed that had been growing among the blades of emerald green grass and twisted it around between her thumb and index finger. *I'm losing control of everything,* she lamented, watching it break apart in her hand. She remembered her wedding day. *I wonder if things would have been different if I knew then what I know now. Would I still have been happy when I found out I was pregnant with Kevin if I knew what he'd have to endure someday?* She sighed. It was too painful to think about.

Gada hadn't missed a single day of high school during her school career. Her perfect attendance record had been a boasting point during her adolescence. It was a habit she continued to cultivate in adulthood. Other than maternity leave, she hadn't taken a single day off of work since joining the workforce. She had always prided herself on her work ethic, but the dawning realization that humanity was nothing more than a Type II civilization's slave labor had started putting things into perspective. *I'm going home,* she decided, using the oak tree's trunk to help her get up off of the grass. She fished for her car keys and found them in her coat pocket. Her handbag was still at Langley's security checkpoint, along with her cell phone and apartment keys. *I'll get them tomorrow;* she thought as she single-mindedly marched toward the parking lot. *Mike should be home by now to let me in.*

***

"You sure you should go to work today?" Mike asked, pulling a white cotton shirt over his head. He was standing at the foot of their bed, the morning sunlight pleasantly caught in his golden curls. *He needs a haircut again,* Gada thought contentedly, enjoying the sight of him. "I don't think anyone would blame you if you need some time off. Your discovery...Well, it's enough to rock anyone's mental health. I'm sure your supervisor will understand."

A part of Gada regretted telling Mike the whole truth pertaining to what she'd learned. She didn't mean to burden him in the way she'd been burdened, although she had to admit he seemed to be handling it better than she had initially been able to. Even now, she couldn't spend more than a minute or two thinking about it before suffering what could only be described as a mild panic attack. "No, I have to get back to work," she finally replied. "I left without saving a word yesterday. I suspect Tyrone will have an earful to give me this morning. Plus, the report on my research is almost due. Dubois and Greene are waiting for it."

"If you say so," Mike smiled, swaggering toward her. He leaned in to kiss her on the forehead. She was cocooned in their king-size bed's goose feather duvet, a cozy nest she wished she could remain in forever. Mike's cologne stained the air and lingered on everything he touched. Gada took a deep breath, inhaling as much of it as possible. She hoped to carry it around with her all day. "I won't be home late," he said, examining his reflection in the full-length mirror mounted behind their bedroom door. "Promise me you'll come home if you start feeling disorientated again? I don't want you to burn out because of the CIA's unrealistic expectations—"

"It's not their expectations that are getting me down," Gada interrupted. "The alien civilization driving us to extinction is." She pulled the covers back over her head and sulked in the warm darkness beneath them.

"Hey, now," Mike said, gently tugging at the duvet to reveal the top of her head. "Could you try not to think about it? Nothing's different now than it was a month ago. There's no point in worrying about something you can't control. Besides, Tyrone said he'd tell Greene about your findings. Perhaps the CIA will be able to intervene."

"Intervene in an intergalactic crisis? I doubt it," Gada huffed, rolling onto her side. She hugged her own knees and looked up at Mike through a clump of knotted hair that dangled across her face. "Don't worry about me," she tried to reassure him. "Go to work. I'll feel better after a cup of coffee."

She didn't feel better after a cup of coffee. She had her first one of the morning in the car on her way to Langley. It was bitter and awful, so much so that she opted not to finish it. *I guess there are easier ways to break your caffeine addiction,* she thought, *but being scared to death seems to work surprisingly well. I'm jittery enough without hyping myself up on coffee too.*

The road was busier than usual, but she could have sworn the parking lot was emptier than it typically was. She didn't make much of it, other than being thankful that it seemed to be devoid of human life, a fact that meant she didn't have to interact with anyone else just yet. She greeted the feral black cat as it stalked some unseen prey among the parked cars and started the short trek to Langley's entrance. She was surprised to find that it was staffed with fourteen security guards, about eight more than were usually positioned there. She didn't recognize any of them. "Captain Gada Corey," she confidently said as she handed one of them her staff card. He didn't bother to look at her as he took it out of her hands. He hovered a barcode scanner over it for a second before looking up at Gada, a mean grimace plastered across his face.

"System says your access has been revoked," the security guard said gruffly. "Can't let you in."

"What? That's impossible!" Gada replied angrily. "Scan it again!" she demanded, glowering at the uniformed man.

"Fine," he said apathetically, raising the barcode scanner above the card again. "Still says access denied," he sighed, clearly irritated by Gada's insistence that she belonged there. "Who are you here to see? I'll call them down to escort you to their office."

"I'm not here to 'see' anyone. I'm here to work," Gada growled, ripping her staff card out of the man's large grubby hands. "Call Captain Tyrone Tupper. He'll vouch for me and help us to get this mess sorted out. I have urgent business that I need to attend to."

"Fine," the security guard said disinterestedly. He whispered something to one of the other guards, who promptly broke away from the group and made his way over to the empty reception desk. Gada stared at her staff card, wondering what was causing it to malfunction, as she waited for him to return.

"They say no one by that name works here," the young guard reported as he swaggered back from the reception desk. "Greene said he'll come down to hash things out with you. Wait here for him," he said, motioning toward an empty chair behind the metal detector that other employees were streaming in through. Gada disheartenedly took a seat and shoved her staff card back into her purse. *What do they mean "no one by that name works here?"* she wondered, picking at a loose piece of skin on the palm of her hand.

"Ah, Gada! There you are," a bizarrely-tall old man with a well-trimmed gray beard half-sang as he made his way through the crowd. Gada immediately recognized him as Agent Greene, Tyrone's superior and the head of the quantum computing department. She knew better than to let his friendly demeanor fool her.

"Agent Greene," she bluntly greeted as she stretched her neck to look up at him, getting up from the chair and extending her right arm toward him. He took her hand into his and vigorously shook it up and down.

"We haven't had the pleasure of having a proper chat, and now I suspect your time here is up, so perhaps we never will," he smiled menacingly, twirling his mustache between his index finger and thumb. "Your permission to be here has been retracted by the DIA. You'll need to chat with your immediate supervisor to figure out what you have to do to be granted access again. Perhaps they've caught wind of the fact that you still haven't submitted a formal report on either of the cases you're working on?" he cruelly suggested. Gada knew that he was enjoying humiliating her.

"Where's Tyrone? The security guard said he isn't here?" Gada aggressively inquired, scowling at Greene. *I'd love nothing more than to wipe that smug look off of your face, you bastard,* she thought as she watched his smile widen.

"Tyrone? He's a little under the weather," Greene ominously chuckled, straightening the bright red tie that was fastened around his neck. "His wife phoned the office this morning and said we shouldn't expect him back for at least a week. Apparently, he's unable to get out of bed. She did tell me he sends his apologies to you. Sweet that our two black sheep found each other," he grinned, flashing his crooked smile at Gada.

Gada had heard enough. She turned her back on Greene and marched through the crowd of people trying to make their way into the building without so much as glancing back at the head of the quantum computing department. "Get out of my way," she growled, pushing one of the six-foot-tall security guards out of the way like a child might shove a ragdoll to one side of their bed.

The sunlight outside was almost blinding as Gada stumbled out into it. She was happy to leave Greene behind. *A moment longer, and I might have assaulted him,* she thought. She made her way halfway across the building's overly-manicured lawn before deciding that she needed to head to the DIA's offices to get to the bottom of whatever had happened. *I don't believe for even a second that Dubois would have revoked my quantum computer privileges on purpose. Something must have happened,* she realized.

Gada drove to the DIA's offices at a speed that would have made Mike scold her if he'd been there to witness it. The familiarity of the building was oddly comforting. She parked her car in the spot she used to occupy before she started spending most of her time at Langley and nervously made her way down the cobbled path that led to its entrance. The security guards stationed at its entrance welcomed her back. They clearly recognized her, so she felt a little ashamed to admit she didn't remember any of them. Once she was through the security checkpoint, she headed straight toward the reception desk. *Jane will know what's happening,* she thought, *or at the very least, she'll be able to call Dubois down to the first floor for me.*

The reception desk looked just like she remembered it. Its dark wooden surface glistened in the ambient lighting mounted just above it. A pile of old magazines decorated one side of it, while a plastic potted plant was mounted on the other. There was only one thing missing: Jane. A stocky woman with frizzy black hair and freckles stood behind the desk in her place. "Uhm, hi?" Gada hiccuped as she approached. "Is Jane around? Or Colonel Dubois?"

The dark-haired woman spun around, clearly surprised by the disruption. "Oh! Hi! Sorry, I didn't see you there!" she frantically apologized. "I'm Helena, the new receptionist. Of course, I know where Jane is. I'm her replacement!" she giggled. "Jane and her girlfriend were transferred to the bioscience and communication facility in Maryland. Frederick, I think it's called?"

"What? When did that happen? I saw Dubois a few days ago, and she didn't mention anything about a transfer!" Gada gasped, taking a step backward like she was retreating from some kind of mortal threat.

"As far as I know, it was all rather sudden," Helena offered, looking visibly surprised by Gada's reaction to the news. "I was told I was an 'emergency hire.' I don't know why they were transferred on such short notice, though. Perhaps you could ask Campbell? She was hired in Dubois's place," she suggested.

"No, no, no!" Gada repeated, backing away from the counter. Nori's warnings echoed through her head. *Nori was right! It's happening! I'm being targeted by a Type II civilization!*

They're messing up my life to screw with me! She panicked. Her blood ran ice-cold in her veins, and every inch of her being wanted to turn around and run and then keep running.

"Are you okay, ma'am?" Helena asked, her face twisted with concern as Gada continued to rush backward, threatening to fall over at any moment.

"Fine, fine," she mumbled maniacally, rushing back through the security checkpoint. She soon found herself shielding her eyes from the sunlight again, unsure of what to do next. Then it dawned on her: *Nori. She's one of the last people I have left,* Gada thought, pulling her cell phone out of her handbag and dialing her longtime friend and mentor's number. The phone rang, but there was no answer. *I'll try her hotel,* she thought. She hastily dialled The Van Beek Hotel's number, a friendly female voice picked up the call.

"Van Beek Hotel!" the high-pitched voice on the other end of the line sang. "How can we help you today?"

"I'm looking for Professor Natalia Bartoli. She goes by Nori? She was staying in room 1480 the last I heard. Please, it's urgent," Gada half-pleaded, sitting down in the long grass that grew to one side of the DIA's building.

"Hmm. Let me see what I can do," the Van Beek Hotel employee said kindly. "Please hold." Gada could hear her feverishly typing away on a keyboard on the other end of the line. After a minute or two, the clacking keys fell silent again, and Gada anxiously waited for a reply. "Looks like she checked out last night," the voice finally said.

"Can you tell me where she went? Please? I'd do anything to know?" Gada groveled. She held her cell phone with both hands as if steadying her grip on it would somehow alter the end result of the call.

"Sorry, I wish I could," the hotel employee woefully admitted. "Unfortunately, she didn't say where she was going, nor did she ask us to book airplane or train tickets for her. Is she from around here? Perhaps she's staying with a friend?"

"I doubt it. She was raised in the small village of Piazza Dante in Italy and lives in Oxfordshire in England. I hardly think she has shacked up with someone or run off. She's sixty-three years old!" Gada exclaimed. For a moment, she considered launching her cell phone across the lawn but ultimately decided it would be a futile gesture. *You're losing everything. No point in losing your phone, too,* she reprimanded herself.

"I'm sorry," the voice on the other end of the line squeaked. "I wish I could do more."

Gada realized she was all alone, facing an insurmountable otherworldly threat. Her support system had disintegrated, and she couldn't help but wonder whether she was next.

***

A few days passed, and Gada was slowly coming to grips with working under Agent Campbell instead of under Dubois. She still hadn't heard anything from Nori or Tyrone but tried to imagine both of them somewhere happy. At one point, she tried to convince herself that Nori hadn't been taking her calls because she must have gone on an impromptu holiday of some kind to a desolate exotic island in the middle of nowhere. Gada knew she was lying to herself, but it was the best she could do to maintain her sanity.

In the meantime, Campbell had managed to restore Gada's access to the quantum computer at Langley.

Her first day back at the CIA was nothing short of unsettling. She could hear people talking about her in hushed tones as she made her way to the "lunchroom" that housed the machine at the center of her investigations. Fortunately, she found the quantum computer just as she'd left it, or so she initially thought. She switched on the user interface's screen with a renewed sense of purpose. *Maybe if I can find a way to contact the Type II civilization that's controlling us, I can convince them to leave us alone,* she thought. It was nothing more than a pipe dream, Gada was under no illusions about that, but it was all she had left to hold onto.

She was preparing to set the quantum computer's search parameters when she realized that all of her preset calculations had been deleted. She squinted at the screen, unsure what to make of their absence. She opened the file she'd stored her software code in, planning to do some fault finding to get to the bottom of her missing settings, but found that it was empty. *All of my work is gone,* she realized. Her heart sank into her shoes, leaving a burning cavity in her chest in its place. *It'll take months to write all of that code again,* she lamented. *Wait! I have a backup on the DIA's supercomputer!* Gada's hand shot out from underneath the desk and wrapped itself around the landline phone on its mahogany surface. She instinctively dialed Dubois's office, Campbell answered.

"Captain Campbell," her supervisor greeted as she answered the call. "Who's this?"

"Apologies. It's me, Captain Corey," Gada started explaining. "I was hoping you'd be willing to do me a favor. It should only take five minutes."

"I'm swamped," Campbell sighed. "Can it wait?"

"I'm afraid not," Gada replied sheepishly. She knew she was pushing the limits of her relationship with her new supervisor, but she needed answers, and she needed them immediately.

"Fine, what do you need?" Campbell huffed, exhaling so loudly that it caused the phone's speaker to crackle.

"Could you head down to the supercomputer, start it up, and let me know whether you can find a file called 'Gada's backup.' It's a matter of national security. I wouldn't be asking otherwise," Gada half-begged, crossing her fingers that Campbell would be willing to comply.

"Yeah, okay," Campbell grumbled, ostensibly unamused by Gada's request. "Hold on. I'll be right back." Gada sat listening to the annoying "on hold" jingle that streamed from the landline phone's speaker wishing she could travel back in time to when her biggest concern was figuring out what Chromosome 2 was.

The holding tone abruptly ended, putting a stop to Gada's pining for a simpler time. "There are definitely no folders on the supercomputer except for those put there by our software engineers. I asked them to help me search for 'Gada's backup,' but none of us could find it. Sorry," Campbell said bluntly. "I have to go. Dubois left quite a mess for me to work through." The landline's speaker clicked as Gada's supervisor ended the call.

Crap, Gada thought. *I have to be close to the truth if someone's resorting to deleting my software to hinder me.*

***

Gada took a leave of temporary absence upon discovering that someone had sabotaged both the DIA's supercomputer and the CIA's quantum computer. It wasn't a difficult decision to make. Mike had practically insisted on it. She couldn't blame him for being concerned about her, not after Tyrone's mysterious illness and Dubois's sudden transfer to a different facility. Fortunately, Nori made her reappearance a few days after Gada's last day at work. Gada considered it somewhat of a miracle. She'd already assumed that the worst had happened to her mentor. "I just felt like I needed to get out of the USA," Nori had said in her most recent call to Gada. "I wasn't comfortable with the research being done at Burkington University. The project involved evaluating the impact on our civilization with the micro-deletion of the 2q33.5 gene... Never mind, maybe it's best not talk about it." Nori wouldn't elaborate, but Gada sympathized nonetheless. She understood how it felt to realize that your own research was turning on you.

"You okay, honey?" Mike asked, squeezing her hand and pulling her back to reality.

Gada shook her head in an attempt to clear her mind of thoughts of the quantum computer and looked up through the black veil that partially concealed her face. She and Mike were seated hip-to-hip on one of the church's uncomfortable wooden pews. Kevin was fast asleep in Mike's arms, sending a stream of warm baby drool down the back of his black lounge coat.

"It's just a lot to deal with," Gada sniffed, looking up toward the altar at the end of the aisle. The pastor standing behind the pulpit started reading a psalm that Gada half-recognized from her childhood, although she couldn't quite place it. A large picture frame mounted on an easel stood next to him. It proudly displayed a colorful photo of Captain Tyrone Tupper's smiling face. *Must be an old picture,* Gada thought as she made eye contact with it. *The Tyrone I remember looked older than that.*

"What happened to him again?" she heard someone behind her whisper.

"Lung cancer. Came on quick. Nobody knows how he managed to stay asymptomatic for so long. His family didn't know he had it either," a gruff voice replied.

"Did he know he had it?"

"Couldn't say."

Gada tried to block out the conversations taking place around her by flipping up her knee-length coat's collar. It didn't work.

"Tyrone was a fine young man," the pastor finally started concluding his monologue. "He's survived by his beautiful wife, Terra, his daughter, Tanisha, and his son, Thomas. His time here on Earth may have been short, but he touched the hearts of many. The family would like me to invite all of you to tea and coffee on the lawn outside after this service."

"Are we going to stay?" Gada whispered to Mike, leaning into his tall, solid frame. Kevin stirred for a moment. "I mean, would you mind if we stayed a while?"

"Not at all," Mike replied, wrapping his free arm around her waist. "I know you two were close."

"He didn't deserve this," Gada sniffed, using her sleeve to wipe a flood of tears from the corner of her eye. "He was a good guy."

"Nobody deserves cancer," Mike said, trying to sound supportive.

"It wasn't cancer," Gada snapped, whipping her head around to look at him. "You know it wasn't cancer. It was them."

"Shh," Mike hushed her. "We're trying to lay low, remember? We didn't take a sabbatical from work just to be outed by you at a funeral," he joked.

"Hmph," she grunted in agreement, shuffling toward the end of the pew. She appreciated that Mike had been willing to take time off of work to be with her and Kevin, but she'd already grown tired of hearing about it. Mike quietly followed her, still cradling Kevin's sleeping form.

The church's gardens were nothing short of magnificent, although Gada suspected they had been cultivated solely to block the parishioners' view of the cemetery just beyond the hedges. Nevertheless, the rose bushes lining the crumbling stone walls that spanned the church's immediate perimeter's boundary were a sight to behold. Their bright red blossoms looked like blood splatter against the morning's crisp mist-filled air.

"Sorry, I hate to bother you, but are you Gada Corey?" a shaky voice asked from somewhere behind her. Gada slowly turned around, careful not to trip over her black skirt's lengthy fabric.

"Hello there," Gada greeted, feigning the sincerest smile she could muster. "Yes, I'm Gada. This is my husband, Mike, and my son, Kevin," she said, motioning toward her little family.

"It's wonderful to meet you," the petite African-American woman who had greeted her said. Her voice trembled, but Gada thought that she seemed pleasant enough. "I'm Terra, Tyrone's wife. He told me so much about you. He really enjoyed working with you, you know? He always felt like the odd one out at work, which seemed to change when you came around. Thank you for being such a good friend to him. It's a comforting thought to know that his last few months were pleasant," Terra said, wringing her hands together.

"Oh my gosh, I'm so sorry for your loss!" Gada immediately interjected, placing her hand on Terra's upper arm. "My heart shattered into a million pieces when I heard what happened to Tyrone. They never told us how serious it was at work. Otherwise, I would have visited. Greene just told me he was sick, but he made it sound like he had the flu or something. Definitely not cancer."

"We didn't know how serious it was until the end either," Terra admitted, diverting her graze. "We thought he'd developed late-onset asthma. That's what the doctors said. That's what we thought until the night he died..."

"I'm so sorry," Gada whimpered, wrapping her arms around her new friend. "It's not fair. None of this is fair."

Terra shook as Gada held her against her body. She held onto her until the sobbing stopped. Terra broke their embrace first, stepping back immediately. Gada could tell she was embarrassed. After all, Gada was a perfect stranger to her. "How old's your son?" Terra asked, trying to change the topic.

"He's eight months old," Gada proudly announced, squeezing his tiny sneaker-clad feet. Kevin didn't stir. "Takes after his father, already talking too much. He said his first word last week, and of course, it was 'da-da.'"

"Oh, that's unfair!" Terra giggled, a flash of amusement momentarily panning across her face. It didn't last long before it was replaced by her tired sorrowful expression again. "Thomas's first word was 'Ty.' I guess he picked up on my nickname for Tyrone. Kids really are something, aren't they? I just hope they'll grow old in a better world than we get to grow old in."

Gada gulped. She knew the truth. She knew Kevin would have it harder than she ever did, but she didn't dare to tell Terra about that. It's best if she thinks Tyrone died of cancer. *How do you tell someone their spouse was assassinated by our extraterrestrial overlords?* She wondered.

☐

Epilogue: Sabbatical

"Have you heard from your mom yet? I feel bad that she drove so far just to babysit, but I don't trust anyone except our parents to look after Kevin while we're in New York handling my book deal..." Gada started. "I just hope it goes well. I've put thirty-eight months of work into this novel. It's time that could have been spent fighting against you-know-what. If this book doesn't do well, 'they' win," she said anxiously, handing her overnight bag to the bemused-looking porter. The porter, who couldn't have been more than eighteen or nineteen years-old, enthusiastically took it and made space for it on his already full trolley. "Room 201, please," Gada said to him, stuffing a five-dollar bill into one of his hands. "We'll be right up."

"Don't worry about it," Mike answered, pulling her closer to squeeze her against his broad chest. "Everyone's going to love your book. I mean, it'll terrify them, and rightly so, but I think it'll be very popular," he continued. "My mom sent me a message about thirty minutes ago. She says she and Kevin are watching cartoons."

"Cartoons? Again?" Gada asked, raising one of her eyebrows. She took Mike's hand and squeezed it. "I wonder how many times he'll be able to convince her to watch them," she added, feigning genuine concern.

"Hundreds, if I had to guess. He has her wrapped around his little finger," Mike chuckled. They slowly made their way through the polished marble setting and crystal trimmings of the lavish Chrismere Hotel's lobby. Awestruck with the reflective décor and a grand replica painting of Picasso's *Guernica*, they set their sites on the copper-plated elevator doors. Around them, the lobby was filled with people, each going about their business without giving much mind to the others nearby. "You know, I don't think I'll ever grow tired of getting to hold your hand."

"I can't imagine why you'd want to hold it other than to spare my feelings," Gada laughed. Her stilettos clicked loudly against the lobby's glistening off-white floors as she struggled to keep up with Mike's far larger stride. "My fingertips are covered in calluses from using that darn manual typewriter all day every day. It must feel like holding a piece of leather. At least the book's finished now. Hopefully, my hands will go back to normal too."

"I told you to use a laptop instead," Mike chided, rolling his eyes. They got into a waiting elevator and pressed the button for the second floor. "You need fingers of steel to operate that rusty old typewriter."

"You know I couldn't do that," Gada frowned. "We can't risk anyone intercepting it. Using any type of technology that could possibly be hacked just isn't worth it. On a related note, did you remember to take your SIM card out of your phone again after you replied to your mom?"

"Of course," Mike said as the elevator's doors swished open again. "I'm not a complete idiot."

"Of course you're not," Gada laughed, standing on her toes to kiss him on the cheek. His blond stubble tickled her face. "You know I think you're the smartest man in the world."

"Hmm," Mike hummed skeptically. "What do you want? It feels like you're setting me up to ask me for something."

"I want absolutely nothing," Gada grinned as they made their way down the carpeted hallway toward their hotel room. "Unless you're capable of killing the Type II civilization that has enslaved us, saving us from our imminent doom?"

"What if I said that I'd promise that I'd try?" Mike chuckled, unlocking the hotel room's door. Their luggage was already waiting for them inside.

I wish you could, Mike, Gada somberly thought to herself. *I wish either of us could stop the horror that's unfolding, but we can't.* She stepped onto the hotel room's pristine white carpet and dove onto the center of the queen-sized bed. "We're going to need so much more than just the two of us if we want to save the world. You're already a hero to me," Gada finally said, smiling at Mike and patting the empty spot on the bed next to her.

***

"It's the anniversary of Terra's funeral today," Gada said sorrowfully as she and Mike slid into a yellow cab just outside of Times Square. She remembered Terra's tear-stained face on the day of Tyrone's funeral. Her heart ached just thinking about it. "It's been three years since she and the kids died. I don't know where the time went..."

"Did the police ever manage to figure out what caused the crash that killed them?" Mike asked, unscrewing the cap on a water bottle he'd been carrying around with him all day. He gulped down half of it before continuing, "I still can't believe it happened just an hour or two after we saw them at Tyrone's funeral. I really hoped things would get better for them from there. They really seemed like they deserved a happy ending."

"They got a tragedy instead. The police wrote it off as being a nasty accident," Gada replied in a deadpan tone as the cab pulled away and started heading toward Broadway. "Whenever I think about it, all I can see are Terra, Thomas, and Tanisha's screaming faces being consumed by a gas-fueled inferno. It's too horrific to even imagine, and yet I can't help myself."

"It's traumatic. I wouldn't be surprised if you have PTSD or something," Mike said sincerely. "I think it's a relatively normal reaction."

"You'd need to be a maniac to not stress about what our Type II masters are doing to us," she whispered, hiding her mouth behind her cupped hand to stop the cab driver from overhearing her. "Normal reactions don't make you crazy."

"Never said you were crazy," Mike grinned, planting a wet kiss on the center of her forehead. "But crazy and determined can look quite a bit alike."

"A publishing representative wouldn't have asked to see us about my book if I was crazy. Crazy people don't get published," Gada retorted, picking up the manuscript she'd been holding on her lap and waving it about.

"I'd say crazy people are just about the only people that get published. Isn't being crazy a prerequisite?" Mike teased, playfully winking at her.

"Bam!" Gada slapped him across the chest with the thick manuscript she'd been guarding so carefully.

"Be careful. There's more where that came from," she warned him. She fell quiet and allowed her eyes to rest on the manuscript's blank cover. "When I quit my job at the DIA three years ago, I would never have imagined this would be where I'd end up," she sighed, her eyes twinkling.

"You made the right move leaving when you did. Who knows what would have happened if you had dared to return from leave after your software was wiped from the quantum computer? You would have ended up like Tyrone, and Kevin and I might have ended up like Terra and the kids. If you ask me, choosing to walk away was actually pretty heroic," Mike supportively suggested, dangling one of his muscular arms across Gada's shoulders. Mike continued, "Paraphrasing Sun Tzu, a hero walks away from an ill-prepared Battle, rather than risks losing the War."

"It doesn't feel very heroic," Gada started. She didn't have the chance to finish her sentence as the inside of the cab they were traveling in was filled with the irritating buzz of Gada's poorly selected ringtone. "Sorry, I've got to take this," she apologized, sheepishly smiling at Mike before raising her cell phone to her ear. "Gada speaking!" she loudly greeted. "How can I help you?"

"Gada! It's me, Nori!" a voice jovially chimed from the other end of the line.

"Nori! It's so good to hear from you!" Gada laughed, repeatedly pointing at her cell phone with her free hand to show Mike just how excited she was. "It's been months! How are you? Are you still teaching?"

"No, actually. That's why I've been so quiet. I've been settling into the modest little cottage I bought out here in the Scottish highlands. I have a few sheep and two dairy cows to keep me company, plus half a dozen cats and a partially deaf border collie. I'm living the dream!" Nori chuckled, sounding quite pleased with herself. "It's quite a nice set-up. I plan on enjoying the rest of my retirement here. When I die, you can just chuck me into the composter and use this place as a holiday home," she suggested a bit too seriously for Gada's liking.

"Well, you won't be dying anytime soon, although we'd love to visit," Gada suggested, smiling at Mike as she did. She knew he wasn't overly fond of Britain, but she also knew that he wouldn't let her go alone. "I'm enjoying my retirement too, by the way. It looks like we might be getting a book deal. Mike and I are heading to meet the publishers who are interested in my manuscript as we speak."

"Oh, how exciting! Is it about all of that research you were doing into Type II civilizations a few years ago?" Nori asked, sounding genuinely interested.

"Kind of, but not exactly. It's a work of fiction, or at least that's what I'm going to be calling it to keep my former employers from suing the pants off of me," Gada chortled.

"Ingenious!" Nori exclaimed. "I always knew that you'd be destined for great things, Gada. You reminded me of Galileo from the first moment I laid eyes on you in one of our lectures."

"I reminded you of an old white dude?" Gada laughed, unsure of what to make of Nori's comparison. *I'm not even sure it's a compliment,* she thought.

"No," Nori sighed, audibly rolling her eyes. "You reminded me of someone that was willing to face the threat of imprisonment and execution in the pursuit of scientific truth. I don't think you've changed much over the years, but I'm glad to hear you're no longer working on cases where you're tempted to put your life on the line."

"You'd be surprised how dangerous writing a novel can be," Gada half-joked, running her finger across her manuscript's title. It read, The Terrifying Truth of Terra-Farming. The publishers didn't like the title and had already notified her it would need to be reworked. She wondered what they were planning to slot into its place. "Anyway, Nori. I've got to go," Gada finally said. "We're pulling up to the publishers' offices now!"

"Good luck!" Nori practically screeched through Gada's cell phone speaker. "Give Kevin a kiss from me when you get home! I hope he's somewhere safe!"

"Oh, I will! He's with Mike's mom, but I'll tell him his favorite aunt is concerned about his welfare when I see him again," Gada assured her before ending the call.

The yellow cab slowly ground to a halt in front of an imposing gray skyscraper. "This must be it!" Gada told Mike. "Let's get this show on the road!" she enthusiastically screeched as she shoved him toward the cab's door.

"What did Nori say?" Mike asked as he wriggled his way out of the backseat. "Is she doing well?"

"Sounds like she's doing fantastically well," Gada sang as she skipped up the stairs in front of the publishing house. Its thousands of silvery windows glistened cheerfully in the tepid early morning sun. "She said she has retired in Scotland. Actually, it sounds like she might be starting a farm with the number of animal companions she listed. I think she just phoned to tell me that she's doing well and to compare me to Galileo."

"Galileo?" Mike asked confusedly just as they reached the top of the stairs and strolled through the building's entrance.

"What does Galileo, the father of observational sciences, have to do with anything? Although, I suppose you are quite observant…"

"She just said my hunger for the truth reminded her of him. It was pretty weird. I'm not going to lie. She's getting older and seems to get stranger by the day. But, perhaps she does have a point of sorts. Galileo was imprisoned for his writings on heliocentrism. He vehemently believed that the sun revolved around the Earth during a time that saying so was considered heresy. Back then, the church pretty much forced people to accept that the entire universe revolved around the Earth. He was right, of course, but they imprisoned him and put him under house arrest for the rest of his life because of it anyway. Humanity has a long history of imprisoning people for speaking the truth, especially when others aren't ready to accept it yet. Do you think we're doing the right thing, Mike? Are we making the same mistake that Galileo made? Are we making the truth public before the world is ready to hear it?"

"There's only one way to know for sure," Mike said, wrapping one of his muscular arms around her waist as they slowly strolled toward the reception desk, "and that's to publish the book and see what happens. We won't know what people will make of it until we do."

"I guess you're right," Gada sighed, her mind still racing. The busy receptionist had yet to spot them. She was far too preoccupied with a jammed stapler to look up. "Excuse me," Gada hiccuped to get her attention. "We're here to see Miss Gray? We're the Coreys. We're here about the book on Terra-Farming?"

"Oh! Excuse me! Of course," the startled red-headed receptionist replied, pushing her thick-rimmed glasses back up the bridge of her nose. "Miss Gray told me she was expecting you! You can head straight up to her office. It's on the sixth floor. She should already be waiting for you."

"Thanks," Gada grinned, waving at the receptionist as she dragged Mike toward the elevator. *I really hope we're doing the right thing,* she thought. *We might have to disappear for a while after it's published just to be safe.*

The first floor's elevator took them all the way to the sixth floor, where they'd been told they'd find Miss Gray. Her office was the second door on the right. Gada nervously knocked on the door with Mike hovering behind her. She could hear paper rustling inside, which meant they were definitely in the right place. She slowly swung the door open, revealing the hunched-over shape of a middle-aged Asian woman who appeared to be searching for something incredibly important in one of her desk's drawers. "Uhm uhm," Gada cleared her throat, hoping to get Miss Gray's attention.

"Mike Corey? Is that you?" Miss Gray asked, suddenly losing all interest in whatever she'd been searching for mere seconds earlier. "I loved your book, Mike!" she exclaimed. *It worked!* Gada thought, practically ready to do a victory dance. *She believes Mike wrote the book. I'm in the clear!*

"Fantastic to meet you," Mike said, stepping forward to shake the enthusiastic publishing representative's hand. "This is my wife, Gada," he said, motioning toward her. "This book wouldn't have been possible without her. I guess you could say that she was my muse," he added, winking at Gada. "We hope this book isn't too much for you. We know that it's... a little out of the ordinary."

"A little? It's absolutely bizarre! That's what I love about it. You know, at a number of points in the book, I was convinced the story might be real, and we might all really be biobots. It's terrifying! I assume you intended it to be this realistic?" Miss Gray asked, sitting back down in the black leather chair behind her desk. She turned up her hearing aid's volume as she waited for Mike to reply.

"Oh, yes. We want it to be as realistic as possible because it's real," Mike replied seriously, furrowing his brow.

Miss Gray burst into a fit of laughter. "Of course it is!" she roared, slapping her knee. She wiped at a tear that threatened to roll down her cheek before toning her laughter down to a quiet giggle. "I love you writer types, so creative! I believe the readers will find the book just as 'real' as you do," she chuckled, entirely oblivious to the fact that Mike hadn't been joking. "Onto the matter of payment, in your letter to me, you said that you didn't want to receive any payment or royalties for this book. Are you sure about that? It's a very odd request. If the book does well, you stand to make quite a pretty penny."

"I'm sure," Mike nodded somberly. "It's not about the money."

"Of course not! I know you writers do it for the love of writing, but I'm going to have to insist that you take at least $5,000 before I am able to publish the book. I have to be able to prove the publishing house purchased it in case there's ever any contention about who has the publishing rights," Miss Gray said, taking on a more serious demeanor.

"Well, I guess that's okay if you absolutely have to," Mike answered, scanning Gada's face to gauge her reaction. It was expressionless. "Would you mind paying me in cash, though? I prefer not to leave a paper trail. It's an... uhm... superstition, a writer's quirk," he lied.

"Sure, I can do that," Miss Gray grinned. "Before we continue, I'm just curious. You used your wife's real name in the story. Did Gada mind? Did she ever really work for the government? I felt like I was right there with her when the quantum computer started malfunctioning, and during that creepy scene where she realizes that she's lost thirteen hours of her day, it was amazingly immersive!"

"No, I didn't," Gada interjected, walking up to the publishing representative's desk. "It's just a story. Fiction. It's completely made up. My husband is just wonderfully creative. He has such a rich inner world!" Gada didn't usually make a habit of lying, but these days she found herself being forced to do it more and more often. "I teach," she continued. "Not formally, but as a tutor. I love tutoring students and was never a fan of the government or its jobs. However, I like to believe I was a big help to Mike during the writing process. He developed writers' block on occasion, and apparently, I served as some pretty decent inspiration." She looked at Mike and winked, hoping he'd play along. He did.

"Well, we're happy to have your book and excited to distribute it to the world," Miss Gray smiled, getting up to shake their hands again. "By this time next year, every household will have a copy."

I hope so, Gada thought. *The only way that we stand a chance of fighting a Type II civilization off is if we can form a sizable resistance. We're going to need thousands of people who are willing to put their lives on the line for Earth, maybe even hundreds of thousands.* "Thank you, Miss Gray," she said, shaking the elderly woman's hand.

"Yeah, thanks again," Mike grinned, shaking her hand too. "But we're going to hold you to that 'every household in

America' promise. We want every Tom, Dick, and Harry to read this book."

"And so it shall be!" Miss Gray eccentrically announced as they slipped across her office's threshold and made their way back into the hallway. They were a manuscript poorer but far richer in hope for the future.

Mike and Gada soon found themselves stumbling back into the buzzing street in front of the building with $5,000 in cash shoved into their coat pockets. "You know, I still can't shake the feeling that someone's following me... Watching me, constantly," Gada said, a cold shiver running down her spine as she reached down to take Mike's hand.

"Something's watching us. That's a fact," Mike agreed, wrapping his thick fingers around her fist. "Hopefully, there will be a few people who manage to extrapolate the truth from your book. There might still be hope for Earth," he added. "If we can build a resistance, an army, we can fight them. We can take back our planet. No, we will take back our planet!" he corrected himself, puffing out his chest.

"I hope so. For Kevin's sake. For all of our sakes," Gada sighed as they gradually vanished into the crowd of people that filled Manhattan's sidewalks.

Made in the USA
Coppell, TX
16 September 2022

83196748R00173